ASH TO EMBER

ASHES TO ASHES TRILOGY
BOOK TWO

LYRA HAVEN

Content Warning

This book contains descriptions of severe injuries, violence, mentions of suicide, and mental health issues related to trauma and childhood abuse. There is also off-page mental torture and flashbacks/PTSD-like symptoms related to it.

CONTENTS

Author's Note on Language

The written word is a major form of communication throughout this book and the entire series. As such, I've taken some creative liberties and formatted it as standard English grammar.

CHAPTER 1

The wood floors of the cabin were a slab of ice beneath his feet. Near-constant shivering wracked his body, a cold that no amount of sunlight or fire could touch. His mind was muddled and his thoughts came in fits and starts, with no clear beginning or end. Time was a slippery thing, dissolving through his fingers and flitting away when he tried to look closer. He knew he'd lost at least one day, possibly more, after Zex's blood magic had taken him over. How long he'd been here was a mystery he was too exhausted to solve, but he knew it was long enough that his team should have found him by now. They should be here.

Hopelessness was not something Theodric Rhoan was accustomed to. When he'd left the village he'd grown up in, left behind his family, he hadn't given up his hope of someday reconciling with them. Even at his lowest, after the death of his mother, he'd held fast to his dream of a better life for himself and for his brother and sister.

Now, though... now his hope hung by a crystalline thread, gossamer-thin and cut through with tiny faults. He refused to believe Zex's lies, that his team had abandoned him and traveled to Yrasea. Ten years of his life he'd devoted to his queen and country. He had to believe they would never abandon him. And yet...

They should *be* here. Zex left for hours at a time, leaving Theo trapped in this room with wards at the window and door to keep him inside. They were like nothing he'd ever seen, but he knew that James and Kya together could remove them. No matter how strange Zex's magic was, how unnatural, there were few people on the continent who knew more about spells and magic than James. They could free him.

Every time Zex left, hope flared within him. Finally, finally, it would happen. They would come for him today. Every time Zex returned and Theo was still trapped, his faith in his team faltered. He hated himself for it, for doubting them even the slightest. But there were only two options. Either there was something keeping them from him, some trap Zex had set for them, or they weren't there. They'd left him.

"No," he hissed, squeezing his eyes shut. He pressed his bare feet to the cold floor, focusing on the pinpricks of ice stabbing into his exposed skin. The pain centered him, gave his wandering mind something firm to latch onto, something he could control. "No."

"I haven't even made you an offer yet."

Theo pushed himself upright, hunger and fatigue causing him to stumble when he turned to face the door. He kept the wall at his back, a scant bit of protection against the man now standing in his doorway. He hadn't even heard Zex return.

"Doesn't matter," he spat. His voice was rough and raspy, but his glare was white hot. "Whatever you're offering, I refuse."

Zex just smirked and stepped into the room. The tiny warding symbol just above the door frame flared for a moment, recognizing its creator, before going dormant. Theo had seen it happen enough times now to know what it meant. He wasn't stupid enough to run again, though. Bruises still littered his body from his last try.

"There go my hopes of having a quiet evening at home with you, I suppose."

"What do you want? I'm in no mood for your games today." Theo crossed his arms over his chest, refusing to flinch away from him.

"Always so hostile, Theodric," Zex sighed. "I come to you with an opportunity to return to your friends and you won't even consider it? And after all the trouble I went through to keep you alive."

"You left me locked in this room for two days with no food and only one pitcher of water to last the whole time you were gone!"

"Did I?" Zex's tone was mild, almost surprised. "I suppose I forgot how often all of you need to eat."

This man and his cryptic comments were going to drive him mad. "You—no. No, I'm not doing this with you today. Tell me what you meant or get out."

"If you keep using that tone, I'm going to start to believe you don't like me."

Something about the man's tone made Theo pause. The words were right, the usual antagonistic banter he'd come to expect from Zex, but something was missing. It took him a long moment to realize what it was, though.

It was that smirk. The smug, irritating little grin that drove Theo to near violence when he saw it was completely gone. Zex's face was impressively impassive, but there was a grim look about him that didn't bode well.

"What do you want, Zex?" he repeated carefully. Their eyes met and a familiar shiver of fear trickled down his spine at the eerie silver glow. The silence built between them, heavy and dense, but for the first time... Zex broke first. He sighed and rolled his eyes, the picture of indifference, but it didn't change the fact that he had looked away first.

"I've decided I've grown tired of having such a boring hostage," Zex drawled. "I've heard rumors that your little friends reached Yrasea and the hospitality of Prince Kaelas safely."

Theo couldn't stop the full-body flinch at the name. Flashes of memory, razor sharp, slashed through him. Zex standing over him, Theo's blood on his hands. That nauseating pull of blood magic as Zex tried to wrest answers from him. Why was his team going to Yrasea? Why were they meeting with Kaelas? Hours and hours it had gone on, endless questions about a man Theo knew nothing about.

The smirk he so loathed was back when he forced himself to look back to Zex, but it disappeared only seconds later behind that mask of nonchalance. "Is everything alright, Theodric?"

"What's the point?" he snapped. "I already told you I don't know anything about-"

"Yes, yes, you don't know anything about anything. I know. The point is that I know they are in the mountains together, most likely searching for you. Seeing as they've gone to the trouble of coming into my home with something they stole from me, I've reconsidered the idea of a trade."

He had to be talking about Ishaan. If a civilian was with the team, then that proved Zex was lying. If they had truly gone to the capital, Captain Trieste never would have allowed Ishaan to accompany them any further.

That stubborn ember of hope inside him flared up despite his best attempts to keep it in check. It couldn't be this simple. Not with Zex. There would be strings attached to every word he said. Still, anything was better than being trapped in this room any longer.

"Let's go find them, then. I'm sure my captain will be very open to the idea of a trade." His attempt at Zex's bland pleasantries was weak, but it seemed to get the point across. Zex raised an eyebrow and shook his head, giving Theo a tiny surge of satisfaction. Turnabout was fair play, after all.

"Yes, I'm sure it will be a quick and easy transaction," Zex retorted dryly. "Unfortunately for you, I have no interest in dealing with your captain. Prince Kaelas will have the final word, and I can guarantee you he has even less interest in keeping you alive than I do."

"Why would the prince be in the mountains with my team?" If the prince was truly with them, then the team must have gone to the capital, after all, but then why was Ishaan with them? None of this made any sense.

"I have a very good idea, but I find I really don't care. I have bigger issues to deal with than a weak little princeling." The disgust Zex felt for Prince Kaelas was clear, but there was a heaviness to his words, an emotion that Theo couldn't quite grasp. The longer he was free of the blood magic's control, the clearer his mind grew, but there were too many things that still eluded him.

"When are we leaving?" he asked instead, storing those words away to examine later.

The smirk he so despised fell back into place. "We leave now. So get your boots on, soldier. We have a long way to go."

CHAPTER 2

It's been said that there is nothing quite as beautiful as sunrise in the Darsheen Mountains. Poets of old wrote line after line, trying to describe the way the soft golden sunlight spilling over the horizon made the entire world seem new and wondrous. Hundreds of years ago, when traveling the mountain pass that connected Sarkhyr and Nevarre, a merchant had written home to her wife. She'd described the way the light hit the gentle morning fog in such a way that it had moved her to tears. That letter was later copied into a storybook full of fables from around the world, but none of the stories conveyed the same awe that the merchant's had for the beautiful, but deadly, terrain.

As a child, Ishaan Khatre had stolen that book from his brother Doran's room and read it cover to cover, over and over, until it was in tatters. After a lonely childhood spent deep in the forest, he'd longed to see what was beyond the borders of the trees. He ached to see the wild Adelaar Ocean off the western coast of Nevarre and find out what lay beyond that. He'd fallen asleep while reading about the merchant ships that crossed the Barenden Sea east of Gavarria, the vast expanse of water that separated them from the Empire of Caranyvik. The tropical island of Kargha separated the two continents, and he'd devoured stories of the people that ruled the land, turning it from a wild jungle to a way station for ships.

Even the stories of the Canjiri pirates had fascinated him. One book had theorized that the desert island of Canjir had once been as lush and beautiful as Kargha, but over time, had become the barren land it was today. The proud Canjiri had refused to leave their ancestral home, but without the ability to grow their own food supply, they were forced to barter. As prices rose, so did piracy, until it was the most common way of life. The Karjul Straits that swirled between Canjir and the southern coast of Vaetreas protected the pirates and let them escape, as no one else could navigate through the shallow, rocky water like they could.

More than anything, though, Ishaan had always wanted to see the mountains. Growing up as he had, the closest thing he'd seen to one was a steep hill a few hundred feet from the manor. It was almost impossible to imagine anything as tall and imposing as mountains were said to be.

His first view of them had been eclipsed by the pain of his injuries from the fire that had killed his family. His first real experience with the jagged peaks was the days he'd spent with Captain Garrett Trieste's team, traveling as fast as they could to reach Sarkhyr and secure aid in rescuing their missing team member. It had been cold and miserable, but Ishaan hadn't cared about any of it. He'd been numb, weighed down by guilt, and eaten alive by his fear that they would be too late to save Theodric.

Now, though, he'd spent a week riding through the mountains, with nothing to distract him. Ten riders had set out from Yrasea in the dark, cold hours before dawn. The four remaining members of the Nevarrean reconnaissance team accompanied Prince Kaelas, his cousin Alaric, and three of their guards. Ishaan was given a horse despite his unease and had joined Captain Trieste and Prince Kaelas at the head of the line. The tension between the two separate factions was palpable and an uncomfortable silence hung over all of them. Even James was quiet, something that gave Ishaan more than a little concern. The mage, normally so upbeat and cheerful, had withdrawn as the search stretched on.

Guilt still weighed heavily on Ishaan, a throbbing ache in his chest that never went away. The team was incomplete, and he was to blame. He'd tried to push it down, but it kept bubbling back up to the surface. The beauty of the rugged landscape around him couldn't occupy his mind and, as another icy gust of wind cut through his cloak like it wasn't even there, Ishaan came to a firm conclusion.

He hated the mountains.

There were no paths here, no safe places to ride while they searched. The trees that could survive up here were stripped bare, leaving skeletal branches that clawed at his skin if he got too close. Some stubborn brush clung to the bare rock, just enough to tangle around their feet. The ground was treacherous and littered with crevices that could snap a horse's leg if stepped into. With nothing to break it, the wind sliced through him like a knife, battering him almost constantly. Even the tiny flecks of snow that fell were hard and stung his face. Ishaan was cold and sore and miserable, but even if he could have voiced a complaint, he wouldn't have.

It's the least I deserve for what I did. The voice in his head was his own, at least, but it was true. Whatever discomfort he felt was nothing compared to the pain he'd caused the others.

Beside him, Prince Kaelas came to a stop, pulling Ishaan out of his own head. He glanced up at the prince, noticing the others had stopped, as well.

"Is everything alright?" Alaric asked, riding up to join his cousin. Kaelas rubbed his chest, his eyes going distant for a moment, then nodded.

"I thought I felt something," he murmured but offered no other explanation. "We'll need to stop for the night soon. We're losing the light and we won't find them tonight. Do you still feel him?"

Ishaan nodded, resisting the urge to rub his own chest. He could still feel the pull there, tugging him toward something or someone. Kaelas seemed convinced it was a person, someone he knew, but refused to speak of him. All Ishaan cared about was that it was the same pull he'd felt when they'd been tracking Theo before. As long as it got them closer to rescuing him, he didn't care what it was.

"I can scout ahead," Captain Trieste said. It didn't sound like a suggestion. Kaelas looked at him and the tension grew as both men were silent for several seconds, neither one breaking eye contact.

Ishaan's skin was crawling with discomfort when Kaelas finally nodded once. Trieste glanced back at his team, finding Naema last.

"Bhandari, ride point with Prince Kaelas and Ishaan until I get back."

"Yes, sir." Naema nudged her horse around the group and took up position beside Ishaan, with her dog Karsa at her side. "Be safe, captain."

Trieste nodded and rode out ahead of them, disappearing into the darkness.

"Everyone else, keep your eyes open," Alaric called, falling in behind Kaelas when they started moving, rather than taking up the rear as he'd been earlier. Ishaan watched the two men from the corner of his eye, or at least as much as he could while also trying to stay on his horse.

Something was... off about the two of them. He couldn't say what it was, but something about Kaelas and Alaric made him uncomfortable. That little ember of warmth inside him, though, the part that wasn't him, still felt drawn to them. They didn't feel like *home*, not like whatever the pull was, but more like... *family*. That wasn't quite right, either, but Ishaan would be the first one to admit that he didn't know what family felt like. Whatever the feeling was, Kaelas' piercing golden eyes still set him on edge and made him feel like a trapped insect every time they turned his way. While the man focused on Alaric, he tried to edge his horse a little closer to Naema, but the animal responded by blowing out a breath and continuing exactly as he had been.

"Once you get more practice, I'm sure he'll be a little more obedient," Naema offered, and he glanced over to see her biting back a small smile. He lifted his right hand, holding it horizontally with the palm facing him, then circled it once to make the sign for 'maybe', though his expression was doubtful. It seemed to take her a moment to remember what the sign meant, but then she chuckled.

"You'll get there in no time," she assured him. "Whether or not you like it, you're going to get a lot of practice over the next few weeks."

Ishaan gave her an alarmed look. The mountains were vast, true, but he could sense their target and he'd convinced himself that they would find Theo any day now.

"We'll find him," Naema promised. "Once we have him, we'll be heading home and you'll be riding then, as well."

Ishaan looked away and Naema fell silent, the space between them filled with the words she'd left unsaid. Neither wanted to acknowledge that Theo would likely be in no shape to ride when they found him. He also knew that there was a very good chance he wouldn't be leaving these mountains when the team left with Theo.

Prince Kaelas seemed to shift between viewing Ishaan as either an asset or a criminal. Something had shifted inside the man that night back in Yrasea, when Ishaan had told him about that strange artifact his parents had used in their spellwork. The picture Kaelas had shown him looked almost like some kind of egg, covered in scales. He assumed it was some sort of stone, intricately carved, but he couldn't be sure. The fury in those amber eyes was impossible to miss, though. Kaelas wasn't sharing what he knew, but whatever it was, it was big. Big enough that trading Ishaan to a dangerous mage would be worth it to the prince.

The sunlight faded around them and was nearly gone when Captain Trieste rejoined them, informing Kaelas that he'd found a shelter for them for the night. Even with this guidance, it took over half an hour to find it and by then, it was difficult to see anything.

"Mages, some lights, please," Alaric ordered. Ishaan turned back and could just make out James pulling a crystal from his bag. The two Sarkhyrian mages were much faster and had their lights up only a second later. The crystals they used must have been tiny because he couldn't see even a hint of them. Still, they were powerful enough to illuminate the spot Captain Trieste had found.

It was little more than a clear open space, but a heavy stone outcropping hung low over most of the area. The ground was relatively free of brush and the wind didn't seem to be so bad here. It wasn't much, but it would do for the night.

"I will start a fire," one of the Sarkhyrian mages offered, looking to Prince Kaelas for approval. Ishaan hadn't caught his name and none of the Sarkhyrian soldiers with them had offered their own. Their accents were heavier than that of Kaelas and Alaric, and they spoke to each other in their own language.

"Thank you, Chrysaris," the prince nodded. The two other soldiers joined him, leading their horses away from the rest of the group. Irric volunteered to cook for all of them, which left everyone else to ready the camp.

Ishaan winced as he swung his leg over the saddle, sliding to the ground and barely keeping his legs from crumpling beneath him.

"Still getting used to long hours in the saddle?" After a full day of silence, hearing James speak beside him was a surprise. Turning, he looked up at the mage and nodded. One hand clung to the saddle for support until he was sure he could stand. The muscles in his thighs were tight and every part of him ached.

"Remember not to stand still for too long," James advised. "Walking around will help. Why don't you come help me get the horses settled?"

Walking even a few steps sounded like a terrible idea and the look he gave James was skeptical, but Ishaan nodded anyway. It didn't seem like James was lying or trying to trick him, and if it would help ease the throbbing in his muscles, he was willing to try.

Still, he hesitated when he let go of the saddle, keeping his hand close until he was sure he could make it. The first step was agony, but he'd dealt with worse. By the time he and James were across the small camp to the makeshift picket line, he had to admit that perhaps the mage had been right.

"Better?" James glanced over at him as he secured his mount. This was one chore Ishaan was used to doing by now and the only one he felt confident in. He nodded again, then put his right fist on his chest just below his collarbone.

"You're welcome. I remember how long it took me to get used to this. Besides, Theo will kick my ass if he found out I didn't offer to help."

Ishaan's stomach clenched and his breath caught in his throat when the ever-present guilt spiked at the mention of the missing tracker's name. He tried to force a smile, but he couldn't quite manage it.

"Hey. You know we're going to find him, right?" James turned so they were facing each other, his warm green eyes unusually intense. "He's going to be fine." He sounded confident and Ishaan wanted so badly for it to be true, despite his fears whispering to him that they would be too late. Ishaan didn't have the hand signs to say any of that, though, and the leather journal Theo had given him was still buried in his pack, so the only thing he could do was nod yet again.

Frustration ate at him as they finished their chore in silence and walked back to rejoin the group. He'd never truly realized how much he relied on his voice until he'd lost it. He'd learned the value of silence at a very young age, when being quiet and still as a mouse had saved him from a night in the basement laboratory. Those nights were the only time his parents spoke to him, as it was the only time they had a use for him. As for his brother and sister... it was a rare occasion that the twins would speak to him without being utterly horrible. Or at least Dhanara. He could count on one hand the amount of semi-pleasant conversations he'd ever had with her.

Outside the laboratory, away from magic, Doran was the most tolerable of the family.

Unlike the grief and guilt he'd felt for Theo, thinking of the twins and his parents left him feeling nothing. All his life, for as long as he could remember, thinking of his parents filled him with fear and, as they'd grown, that fear had bled over into his relationship with his siblings. He knew they weren't good people, but he didn't feel even the least bit guilty about what he'd done. He wondered if he should. After all, what kind of person didn't feel bad about killing their entire family?

Then again, none of them had ever treated him like part of the family. He still wasn't sure what a family truly felt like, but when James slid over to make room for him to sit, and Naema greeted him with a warm smile... he thought maybe he was beginning to understand.

CHAPTER 3

The nightmares came for him that night, just as they had every night for weeks. Part of him knew he was dreaming, but he couldn't pull himself free from the razor-sharp claws of his mind.

He's back in the basement of the house he grew up in. Thick chains band across his chest and hold him down, their grip so tight he can't draw a full breath. Iron manacles hold his wrists down, pinned to the table. His mother Allesha's voice comes from behind him, speaking a language he's never heard in a soft chant that echoes in the vast room. Through a haze of fear, he can see his father at the table beside him, holding something in his arms. He struggles against his restraints, a desperate fear filling him. He's been here before. He's been the subject of countless experiments, but something feels wrong. More wrong than any of it has before.

"Don't be such a coward," Dhanara snaps and he jerks his head to the side, not realizing until that moment that the twins are here as well.

The fear in his chest turns to ice-cold terror. No good ever comes of anything that involves the twins' magic.

"I'll deal with it. Go help Mother," Doran insists, giving his sister a steady look. He is the calmer of the two, but she's the more dominant twin. Dhanara considers it, then rolls her eyes and walks away, leaving her brothers alone for the moment.

"Doran, what's happening?" Ishaan whispers, his voice breaking. The metal restraints are slicing into his wrists as he struggles, but he barely feels the pain.

"Don't fight. It'll only make it worse," Doran mutters. He is so quiet that Ishaan can barely hear him, which means the others won't hear them, either.

"Just tell me! Please!" It's all he can do not to scream the words, fear choking him until his words are nearly unintelligible. He feels the first tear slip down his face and into his ear, but he can't hold them back. Doran's dark eyes study him. There's no affection in his cool gaze, but there is something like pity there.

"They are going to attempt a power transfer spell," he finally says. "Mother and Father will hold the framework of the ritual. Dhanara and I will do the transfer." A glimmer of excitement replaces the pity in his eyes. "It should work. I've looked it over. Just be still and there's a good chance you'll have some magic ability after it's over."

"What if it doesn't work, though?" The blood from his tattered wrists is starting to pool around his fingertips and the pain is making itself known, but Ishaan can't stop jerking at the cuffs.

"Then it fails," Doran says with a shrug. "I would think you'd be excited by the chance to gain power. I'm sure you're tired of being useless, aren't you?"

The words cut deeper than the iron manacles, even though he'd heard them so many times before he should be immune. 'Useless'. 'Waste of space'. He's heard those words since the moment it became apparent he has none of the magic that the twins have in such abundance, yet they still hold a power over him that he can't protect himself from.

"Doran. Get over here and help us set up the wards," their father, Rasacon, orders and Doran obeys, leaving Ishaan alone.

The nightmare shifts, shimmers, and then all four mages are repeating the soft chant Allesha started earlier. Wards glow in every corner of the room, so bright that even Ishaan can see them. There is a strange glow to his right between the two tables. Something is lying on the other one, but he can't make out what it is. The voices grow louder and the glow intensifies, filling the room with a muddy red light. It throbs in time with the chants and when the chant comes faster, it flares. Dhanara and Doran move as they continue the spell. Dhanara stands at the base of the other table while Doran is at Ishaan's feet.

"Doran, please!" Ishaan screams, but his brother ignores him.

The light pulses again and a dull throb of pain echoes in his chest. With every pulse, the pain increases, building and layering within him until the agony is all he can feel. Beside him, something is happening to the thing on the table. The ugly red light is crawling over it, surrounding it until it splits in two and somehow, the pain gets even worse. He's screaming, begging, until his throat is raw and his voice shatters. He screams until he can't scream any more, until the world goes dark around him.

The cries of fear pull him back from the darkness. Something heavy is resting on his chest for a moment, but before he can look, it's gone and a burning heat pours through his body, enveloping him completely.

"Dhanara!"

The terrified cry is enough to make him open his eyes, and he immediately wishes he hadn't.

Flames surround him. Everything is burning, even things that shouldn't. The stone table beside him is red-hot and molten, sinking into itself as flames shoot up. It takes a moment to realize the shape curled at the foot of the table is his sister. Or it was. The flames devour her in seconds, leaving nothing but charred bones that are overtaken by the molten stone as the table dissolves.

Doran's roar of anguish fills the room as the bond between the twins snaps the moment Dhanara dies. The flames grow and Ishaan closes his eyes. He's exhausted down to the very marrow of his bones, and he only hopes his death will be quick.

No.

The voice startles him, and he jerks at the restraints again.

We are not dying. No!

The restraints turn hot, searing into his skin, scorching his body as they turn as molten as the table. The pain is unimaginable. It's too much. He can't handle it. He can't. It needs to stop. It has to stop. Anything. Anything to make it end. Please, let it-

He's running. The voice inside him is guiding him, urging him, forcing him to keep going as he runs blindly through the trees. The world shifts again and he's mounted, being chased by shadowy figures on black horses. Their faces are blank, but he knows they're coming for him. One pulls ahead and reaches for Ishaan. It catches his cloak, then he's falling, falling, falling from his horse. He lands hard and lays there, too dazed to fight when the figure yanks him to his feet.

Except now, his face isn't blank. Golden skin, soft brown hair, and the bluest eyes Ishaan has ever seen replace the shadowy darkness.

"You killed me," Theo whispers and his voice hits Ishaan like a punch to the gut. "I saved your life and you led me to my death."

"No!" Ishaan tries to protest, but his voice is gone, left shattered and broken in the burnt-out husk of his childhood home.

"It's your fault, Ishaan. It's all your fault."

CHAPTER 4

The nightmare lingered in Ishaan's mind long after he woke up the following morning. Captain Trieste was polite enough not to comment on the tears staining his face when he woke in the tent they shared. Either that or he didn't care enough to ask. Ishaan wasn't sure which he preferred.

It was easy to be quiet during breakfast. The Sarkhyrians kept to themselves, and Trieste's team did the same. They talked in low voices to each other and no one seemed to notice that Ishaan didn't attempt to join the conversation using signs or his journal. The sun was still hours from rising when they set off again, with Ishaan once again at the head of the column with Prince Kaelas and the captain. Exhaustion pulled at him, weighing down his body and filling his mind with fog.

"Is our direction the same?" Kaelas asked once everyone mounted up. Ishaan took a slow breath and focused, searching out the tiny warm ember in his chest. It was still pulling at him, trying to go back home. Usually it was easy to find. It was so distinctly not a part of him that Ishaan couldn't help but feel it. This morning, though, it took a few seconds longer and the pull felt weaker.

It's because I'm so tired, he told himself. All of his thoughts were sluggish, so he shouldn't be surprised that the thing that was *other* inside him was tired, too. Still, he could feel it and it was still trying to pull him in the same direction as they'd been traveling, so he nodded.

"Good. Move out!" Kaelas called, immediately nudging his horse into a fast walk. Ishaan's mount, on loan from the Sarkhyrian stables, followed behind him without any urging, while Trieste kept pace with the prince.

"You still haven't explained why you're so sure that Ishaan can lead us to my missing tracker." The captain's statement was almost identical to what he'd said when they'd set out from Yrasea, though the edge of frustration was sharper now.

"I am aware of that," Prince Kaelas replied simply. When it didn't seem any more answers were forthcoming, Captain Trieste picked up speed until he was even with the other man.

"I've taken your word because Lord Wyrenian trusts you and I trust him, but the life of one of my men is at stake," he ground out, teeth clenched. "I need more to go on than blind trust. At the very least, there should be scouts going out and searching in case this 'mysterious feeling' of his turns out to be wrong."

Ishaan flinched back, trying to draw himself out from the middle of the conflict. His heart beat faster and a sick feeling settled in his stomach. The instinct to run and hide flared up within him, an ingrained response after years of his family's frequent fights. All four of them had been stubborn and arrogant in their own ways and no matter who was fighting and who won, Ishaan always ended up being the one to suffer the consequences.

"Your scorn is noted, captain, but don't mock what you do not understand. It isn't as simple as you make it seem. It's magic you could never begin to comprehend, and I have absolute faith that it will lead us to our target."

Trieste's eyes narrowed. "You're right. I don't understand why someone who is not a mage would have a connection to another non-mage. A connection forged by magic, apparently. But since you don't seem inclined to answer, I am going to question your choice of words, your Highness. 'Our target'? I'm beginning to wonder if our targets are indeed the same."

"I vowed I would help you find your missing soldier, did I not?" Kaelas' voice was cool, his words clipped and sharp. "When I make a promise, I keep it. So when I tell you that what this man is feeling will lead us to your soldier, I mean it."

Ishaan managed to slow his horse as the two men argued, which removed him from the center of it but put him right beside Alaric. He was watching his cousin and Captain Trieste with an inscrutable look on his face. It was only because Ishaan was trying so hard to avoid drawing the attention of the two leaders that he saw the look of alarm flash across Alaric's face at Kaelas' promise. It was brief, but Ishaan was sure he'd seen it. He bit back a frown as Alaric's expression smoothed, though he held himself stiffly and his eyes were hard as he studied his cousin.

"We should pick up speed," Alaric cut in when it looked as if Trieste was going to snap out a reply. "The weather in the mountains is unpredictable. It would be wise to find the soldier and return home as quickly as possible."

Kaelas shot a glare at his cousin but nodded. "Mages, keep the lights going. Ishaan, you will tell us if anything changes."

Ishaan smothered the urge to give the man a dirty look and simply nodded instead, but Kaelas had already turned away. A surge of resentment welled up inside him, threatening to bubble to the surface despite his efforts to hold it back. It ate at him, how easy it was for the others to silence him simply by turning away. He knew it was stupid to be angry in the face of their mission. Finding Theo was his first and only concern. He knew his feelings weren't important in the grand scheme of things, but he couldn't force them away.

What he could do was bury them, though. That anger and resentment were forcibly bundled up and shoved to the back of his mind, alongside the fear and the pain that made up so much of his life. It was something he was used to, but it was more difficult now. Perhaps because, for once, he'd started to believe that what he felt was just as valid and important as anyone else. That was yet another mistake in the long list of mistakes he'd made.

The only good thing about riding in near-darkness was that it required all of Ishaan's attention. Clinging to the saddle was difficult enough on its own without even taking into account how dangerous the terrain was. No one spoke, instead keeping their focus on the rocky ground in front of them. The silence lingered even when the sun finally rose, chasing away the shadows but doing little to combat the chill in the air. He'd cobbled together his gear from both Nevarrean and Sarkhyrian pieces, collecting whatever would fit him and could be found in a hurry. However, he'd refused to part with the cloak Theo had given him. It was too long for him, the bottom hem nearly to the ground when he stood, but it was thick and warm. Most importantly, though, it was something of Theo's that he could keep close to him.

Hours passed, broken only by quick, infrequent breaks to eat a few bites of food before they were mounting up again. Quiet conversations brushed past him, but the only person who actually spoke to him was Prince Kaelas, to check their direction. Captain Trieste had fallen back at some point in the afternoon to confer with his team, leaving Ishaan alone with the Sarkhyrians. The soldiers still made no attempt to speak to any of them and the two cousins spent the afternoon in whispered, but fervent, conversation in their own language.

Somehow, Ishaan found himself surrounded by people and yet he was utterly, completely alone.

By sunset, he was exhausted, staying upright only through stubborn pride. He'd draped his reins across the saddle, dropping them there when he'd accepted that his mount was going to go where it pleased no matter what he did. He sat curled in on himself, with Theo's cloak pulled tight around his body, his mind drifting in a haze of weariness. His body felt weighted and heavy, his head stuffed full of cotton. His thoughts came slowly and were a messy jumble of words and emotions, but not all of them were his own.

Ishaan blinked slowly, feeling something shift inside him. Cold and tired, it took his mind several long seconds to realize that the warmth in his chest, the part of him that was *other*, had changed. It was growing hotter, lighter, and an emotion not his own was flooding through him. Excitement, but something more? Almost like anticipation. That overwhelming feeling of *home,* so strong it overtook everything else, pulled at him, growing and growing with every passing second.

He tried to make a sound, to call out, but all he managed was a gasp that was immediately snatched away by the wind. The captain was still behind him, along with James, Naema, and Irric. None of them were paying him much mind. Prince Kaelas and Alaric were still deep in conversation, also ignoring him. None of them so much as glanced his way when he tried again to get their attention.

Tugging on the horse's reins just got him an annoyed huff from the animal before it went on exactly as it had all day. Jumping off the saddle would likely end with him getting hurt and still, no one was even looking at him.

The anger he'd repressed all day surged to the forefront and tangled with the strange, warm anticipation that wasn't his. The two battled inside him, a confusing mess of feelings that he didn't have time to focus on. Searching around for any other option, he spotted his water canteen hanging off the saddle horn. Without allowing himself a moment to change his mind, he picked it up and threw it, hitting Kaelas directly in the back of the head.

It was as if time had stopped. There was complete silence, broken only by the quiet *'thud'* of his canteen hitting the ground. For the briefest moment, no one moved at all. Even the wind abated, the world around them becoming silent and still.

Before the strap on the canteen hit the ground, the three Sarkhyrian guards burst into movement and suddenly, Ishaan found himself at the center of *everyone's* attention and on the wrong end of the guards' blades. The woman was barking orders at him, but nothing in a language he could understand. He could see Captain Trieste hurrying up the column to intercede with the others close behind, but he couldn't focus on them or even the angry guards. He glared at Prince Kaelas as the man slowly turned his horse in a circle to face him.

"Halbrig, stand down," the prince ordered, staring down the woman until she relented and lowered her blade. The two men followed suit, but none of them sheathed their weapons. Behind Ishaan, the Nevarrean team flanked him, with Trieste and James on either side of him. Kaelas kept his focus on Ishaan, though. "I'm going to assume you have an excellent reason for assaulting me? You should know that my guards take their job seriously."

As if he couldn't see that for himself. Burning resentment joined the war of emotions within him, and Ishaan clenched his teeth to hold it all back. He wanted to just open his mouth and explain, but the words remained stubbornly locked behind his ruined throat. The resentment flared again, a burning coal within him that threatened to burst into a flame of impotent rage.

Theo. Stay focused so you can help him.

He took a breath and repeated the words to himself until the anger settled back enough for him to meet Kaelas' eyes. He touched his chest, then pointed out towards the mountains in front of them. The pull was shifting, more to the east now than it had been just a few minutes ago, and it was getting stronger. When Kaelas frowned, a look of impatience flickering across his face, Ishaan made the gesture again, sharper now.

"Did it change?" James asked suddenly. Relief flooded through Ishaan that *someone* understood and he nodded quickly, pointing again.

The prince's eerie gold eyes darted over to James for a moment, then focused back on Ishaan. "He's moving?" He straightened in his saddle and beside him, Alaric did the same. Unlike his cousin, though, Alaric was looking around as if he expected whatever was on the other end of the tether to suddenly appear out of nowhere. He even glanced up toward the darkening sky, which made no sense at all.

"How long ago did the direction change?" Kaelas barked. Ishaan couldn't hold back the nasty glare he gave the man when he immediately looked away to search their surroundings, though by the time Kaelas realized Ishaan hadn't replied and turned back to him, he'd smoothed it out. Mostly.

"I'm sure he let us know as soon as it happened," Captain Trieste said, cutting the prince off when he opened his mouth. "My apologies, Ishaan. We should have been paying attention."

The apology surprised him so much that Ishaan didn't know how to react. No one apologized to him. Not for anything. Especially not people more powerful than him. Admitting to being wrong was a sign of weakness, according to Rasacon Khatre.

"We can sort everything out after we determine where he's going," Kaelas cut in. The captain's eye twitched and his jaw tightened, but no one else seemed to notice.

"Ishaan, do you have your journal?" James asked from his other side and Ishaan shifted in his saddle to face the mage. Of course he had it. He never let it get too far away. Nodding, he dug into the pouch at his waist and pulled it out. The leather cover opened easily for him and he jotted out a response, leaving a few inches between it and his half of a conversation he'd had with Naema yesterday.

"It feels like it's shifted east. It's getting stronger, too. Maybe we're close?"

A bout of spite had Ishaan handing the journal to Captain Trieste to read first. Prince Kaelas didn't miss the intentional move, if the barely banked anger in his golden eyes said anything. Part of him was terrified, already calculating the best way to appease the other man and avoid whatever punishment was coming his way. Fear slid down his spine, a fear born of instincts that had kept him alive for twenty-two years. The feeling was nothing new to him. Ishaan and fear were old friends.

What did shock him was the sliver of defiance that warred with the fear. It wasn't quite confidence, not yet, but maybe it could be someday. Maybe it was enough to know that, for the first time in his life, he wasn't alone. He may not fully trust the Nevarreans, but he did trust that they wanted him alive and safe, if only to help them get Theo back. If it came down to it, they would protect him. Ishaan couldn't remember a time at any point in his life when anyone had stood up for him. Even Doran's attempts were half-hearted at best and easily brushed aside by Dhanara or their parents.

Knowing that the others were on his side gave him just enough confidence to straighten his spine and sit up straight. He couldn't quite bring himself to meet Kaelas' eyes, but he wouldn't cower from the other man.

Captain Trieste read the words on the page out loud, rather than pass the journal to Kaelas, which Ishaan appreciated. The moment the captain gave it back to him, he closed it and held it against his chest, just in case the prince or anyone else tried to take it again.

"We keep riding," Kaelas ordered, his voice tight. "If Ishaan is telling the truth and he can feel it this strongly, we're close. Be prepared."

"Prepared for what? You still haven't given us any idea who we may find at the other end of this," James pointed out. He stayed close to Ishaan, as did the others.

Instead of the reprimand Ishaan was halfway expecting, Trieste actually nodded in agreement and gave Kaelas a hard glare. "Since you still refuse to share any pertinent information with us, I'd at least like to know if we should expect a fight."

Alaric murmured something to the prince, causing Kaelas to let out an annoyed huff. It was rapidly becoming clear to Ishaan that Alaric was the more reasonable of the two men. He may be just as reticent as Kaelas, but he didn't seem as openly hostile as his cousin. When Kaelas looked as if he planned to ignore Alaric, the younger man said something in Sarkhyrian, his tone sharp.

"Fine," Kaelas growled, then turned his attention back to Captain Trieste. "I believe I know who took your soldier. He's a traitor, convicted years ago for a long list of crimes against our kingdom, not the least of which was practicing forbidden magic. He fled before he could face justice. From what I've learned from Ishaan, I believe he was involved in the spell that injured him and it created a bond between the two of them, somehow. That is what Ishaan is sensing, and that is what will lead us to your soldier."

He's lying.

Ishaan narrowed his eyes, locking his focus on Kaelas. He'd spent his entire life navigating among liars and manipulators. He'd learned at a very young age how to look past the words someone was saying. Words were lies, but the truth could be found in body language and tone if one knew how to look. Parts of what Kaelas said were true, or at least the truth as he believed it, but some if it was lies.

He waved his hand until Trieste noticed and glanced over at him. As soon as he had the man's attention, he held his open hand vertically and rocked it back and forth twice, making the sign for 'wait'. While the captain translated to Kaelas, Ishaan opened the journal again and quickly wrote out a note before passing it to Trieste.

"No stranger was there. Just my parents, brother, and sister. No one else was involved. That doesn't make sense."

Trieste skimmed the words, then nodded toward James. Ishaan took the hint and passed the journal to the mage to read as well. Once James had read it, he looked up at his captain. Something unspoken passed between them, a silent conversation that Ishaan had no hope of understanding. James handed him the journal before sitting up straighter in the saddle.

Usually, it was difficult for Ishaan to remember that James was anything but the excitable, somewhat silly mage he was around them. Now, with his regal bearing pulled around him like a cloak and the last light of day giving his auburn hair an almost fiery glow, there was no denying that James was a royal prince of the Delphine line.

"There was no one else there the night of the fire, your Highness. How would your traitor be involved in a spell if he wasn't even there?" James' voice commanded attention, and Ishaan sat up straighter in response. It seemed he wasn't the only one, as even the Sarkhyrian guards reacted to the man's tone before they could stop themselves. Only Kaelas and Alaric seemed immune. If anything, Alaric looked almost bored.

The sound Kaelas made, however, could only be described as a snarl. His amber eyes flared, a trick of the fading light lending them a burning golden glow that sent a fresh shiver of fear crawling across Ishaan's skin. He would wager money he didn't have that Kaelas had only a passing familiarity with the word 'no'.

"We do not have time for this," he spat. "Every moment that passes is another moment that your soldier is in danger. You do not know what Zex is capable of."

"Kas!" Alaric grabbed his cousin's arm, seemingly to stop him, but it was too late for that.

"Zex? That's the name of this traitor who attacked my soldiers?" Trieste asked. Ishaan caught the tiniest flinch from Kaelas when the captain said the name, barely perceptible, but there. Whoever this man really was, there was a history between him and Kaelas.

The Sarkhyrians were still, none of them moving. Even Alaric was quiet, waiting on Kaelas to speak.

"Yes," he finally said, his voice oddly rough and his words stilted. "He is dangerous, far more so than he will appear, and if we are getting close to him, then yes, your people should prepare for a fight. Now, we need to stop wasting time and get moving before it is too dark to continue."

It wasn't much to go on and it didn't look like it appeased Captain Trieste, but the Sarkhyrians were already moving out. Ishaan's horse tried to follow, but the captain grabbed the reins, holding it back.

"I really do not like that man," James muttered darkly once they were out of earshot.

"We don't have to like him, but if he can lead us to Theo, we can tolerate him a while longer." Trieste shifted in his saddle, looking at the four of them. "Stay alert. We don't know what we're facing. If any of you get hurt because you're not paying attention, you're cleaning the barracks for a month. That includes you, Ishaan. Am I clear?"

"Yes, sir." James spoke first, echoed by Irric and Naema. Ishaan nodded his agreement, trying to smother the little flare of pleasure that filled him. He really shouldn't be happy about being threatened with a month of cleaning, but the way he had been so casually included in the warning...

Ahead of them, Ishaan could see Alaric looking back over his shoulder at them. Their eyes met for a moment, Alaric's gaze sharpening a moment before he finally looked away.

"Alright, team. Move out." Trieste's order got them all moving again, but the captain kept hold of Ishaan's reins, forcing the horse to stay with their group. For the moment, at least, Ishaan finally felt like part of the team.

\#

CHAPTER 5

"Kas, it's time to stop for the night." Alaric kept his voice low, despite the distance between the two of them and his cousin's guards. The Nevarreans were too far away to hear anything, so he paid them little mind.

"We're close. We're not stopping now," Kaelas growled, but Alaric was far too used to his moods to be intimidated.

"Don't be a fool," he snapped back. "It's past midnight and everyone is exhausted. If we found him tonight, he would have the advantage and you know it. It would be best to begin again in the daylight, when we can actually see what's coming for us."

He could see the barely tempered fury in Kaelas' molten-gold eyes. The faint glow was more obvious now in the dark, making him momentarily grateful that the Nevarrean soldiers took such effort to remain apart from his party. Patience was the key to handling his tempestuous cousin, so he waited in silence until Kaelas finally came to the same conclusion.

"We're stopping here for the night," Kas finally called back down the line. "We will continue the hunt at first light, so I expect everyone to be awake and ready before then."

The order would no doubt grate at Captain Trieste, given what Alaric knew about the man, but there was nothing to be done for it. He had his hands full dealing with one ego; he had no time to handle another.

"We're exposed here, your Highness," Ereyan said, pulling his horse alongside them. "There's no cover."

"We'll set a watch. Given that Ishaan and I can sense our target, we'll take turns," Kaelas decided, raising his voice so the other half of the party could hear him.

"Not alone," the prince, James, declared. "I'll sit watch with Ishaan." He glanced to the side, likely seeking permission from his captain, which was granted with a brief nod.

"And I will do the same for Prince Kaelas," Alaric responded smoothly. "It's settled, then. We'll take the first watch. Everyone else should sleep. Chrysaris, would you mind getting a fire going for us?"

While everyone was busy settling the horses and setting up camp for the night, Kaelas pulled Alaric back into a scraggly stand of trees away from the group.

"What is it now? I'd like to get some food before we spend the next several hours sitting on cold rock."

"What are you doing, Alaric? I'm not a child that needs to be handled. Do you think I'm going to go off after him if you're not there to watch me?" Kas' voice was hot with anger, but his grip was loose enough that Alaric could have easily broken away if he wanted to.

"You still can barely bring yourself to say his name, even after all this time." Alaric tilted his head, looking up at his cousin. "You know what that tells me?"

"No, but I'm sure you're going to tell me in excruciating detail."

He fought the childish urge to roll his eyes. "It tells me you're still letting your emotions lead you where Zex is concerned." He didn't miss the way Kas flinched at the name. "Do I believe that you'll go after him? Not right now, no. But after you've been sitting on your own for hours thinking about him? Perhaps. That's not a chance I'm willing to take. We can't lose you, too."

Kaelas looked away and Alaric heard him take a slow, steady breath, centering himself as he'd been taught. He waited in silence, letting him focus.

"I suppose I can't fault you for taking precautions. I asked you to come to Yrasea to be my adviser," Kas finally conceded. "Very well. We'll keep watch together. If I feel him getting too close, though, I can't make any promises about what will happen."

"I don't expect you to. I just need to be sure you're safe." He reached up, resting his hand lightly along the side of Kas' neck, a gesture of peace and comfort. It took a moment, but some of the tension eventually drained from the other man.

"I will do my best." Kaelas returned the gesture, both of them silent for a moment until the growling of his stomach broke the tension. "Let's get you fed before you waste away, brat."

It wasn't much, barely a hint of the Kaelas he'd once known, but it was enough to bring a fleeting smile to his lips as they rejoined the rest of the group. He only hoped the sense of peace would be enough to help rein in his cousin's emotions when they finally found Zex. If Kaelas couldn't control himself, they were all going to be in serious trouble. But that, he decided as he sat down to eat, was a problem for tomorrow. Tonight, he just had to concentrate on keeping the situation under control. After all, it was the reason he was here.

"What are we going to do with him?"

They had spent the first few hours of their watch mostly in silence, but the question was gnawing at Alaric and he couldn't seem to let it go. He looked over at his cousin, barely visible in the moonlight.

"What do you mean? You know what his fate will be."

Alaric scoffed. "Don't act foolish. You know I'm not talking about Zex. What are we going to do about him?" He nodded back towards the camp, where everyone else had settled down to snatch a few hours of sleep. Ereyan, Chrysaris, and Halbrig had settled on one side of the fire, with the Nevarreans on the other. He didn't miss the way the four soldiers had situated themselves around Ishaan. Even the dog was laying curled up against his side, another layer of protection.

"I suppose that truly depends on what happens when we find our target," Kas finally replied. "If he really did this, if he tried to force it... there's no way to undo it. We may have to finish what was started."

He'd been hoping not to hear that answer. "Even if it kills Ishaan? The odds of him surviving aren't good."

"The odds of him surviving if we don't try are even worse," Kaelas reminded him. "The power is already affecting him. I've seen it. I know that he's likely an innocent bystander in this, but what else can we do? That power can't remain in flux like this forever. Something has to be done. I won't risk what remains of our people over the life of one person. I won't be like him."

"I wouldn't let you become like him. That's why I'm here, isn't it?" Even miles away in Althaea, he'd heard the rumors of the so-called "dark prince" who had murdered his bodyguard. Everyone said he was the one who had discovered Zex using illegal blood magic. The other, darker rumors, the ones whispered behind closed doors, said Zex had released the plague that had decimated Sarkhyr to cover his use of that magic.

"You're here to be an adviser. If I were to do what he did, you wouldn't be able to stop me."

"What did he do? The rumors say so many different things. The only thing anyone seems to agree on is that he killed his bodyguard. No one in Yrasea will talk about it, even after six years."

The silence grew between them until Alaric was certain Kaelas wasn't going to respond. He was turning away to resume his watch when his cousin finally spoke.

"That much is true. Eamon, his personal bodyguard, fell ill with the disease. Zex..." He sighed, as if needing a moment to collect himself, before he continued. "He insisted he could cure the illness with blood magic. Eamon begged him not to, but when he fell unconscious and couldn't be woken, Zex ignored his wishes and tried anyway. He failed. Instead of curing him, he killed him."

His voice wavered, barely perceptible, but Alaric knew his cousin better than anyone did. He leaned forward, trying to get a better look at Kaelas, but it was impossible in the darkness.

"That's not the story I was told," he whispered. "If he was only trying to help, why was he arrested?"

That got a reaction. Kaelas growled, an utterly inhuman sound. "He broke the law, no matter what his intentions were. When the royal guard tried to arrest him, he killed four of them before he could be subdued. When I begged him to repent, he laughed in my face."

"Kas-"

"You can't imagine what it was like in the city during that time. Everyone was scared. They wanted someone to blame for their suffering and he made himself a target by killing Eamon. The chancellors wanted him executed for his crimes. He's lucky I convinced them to agree to life in prison. The moment he ran, his life became forfeit. There's nothing I can do for him anymore."

A frisson of foreboding shivered through him at the venom in Kaelas' voice. More alarming, though, was the golden glow in his eyes.

"Kaelas! Calm down. You can not lose control of yourself right now."

"I am in full control of myself. And last I checked, I ruled in Sarkhyr, not you."

"And you specifically brought me to Yrasea to keep you in check, which is what I'm trying to do. You need to pull back, unless you want to have a very long conversation with the Nevarreans?"

The silence around them was broken only by the sound of Kaelas' ragged breaths as he fought back the fury within him. It took longer than it should have, which did nothing to ease Alaric's concerns. Finally, though, Kaelas spoke.

"Fine. We have more important matters to focus on at the moment."

"You're right. At least our watch is nearly ended. Can you still feel him? Is he closer?"

"I believe so. He has to know we're coming for him. It goes both ways. Or it did once." He shook his head. "This would be so much easier if I were alone. I could go to him right now and finish this."

"He has a hostage, in case you'd forgotten. You're a prince. You don't get to act without thought. If anything happens to the Nevarrean soldier, it could cause an incident between our countries that even I may not be able to smooth over."

Kaelas sighed, harsh and heavy. "I'm aware of that." He scrubbed his hands over his face, then finally shifted to face him. "I'm not trying to be difficult. I just..."

"I know." He reached over, resting his hand on his cousin's wrist. "I don't envy you having to do this. No one would want to face this, prince or not. But you're not alone this time. I will be right here with you."

"Thank you, Alaric." The smile Kaelas dredged up was weak and tired, but it was enough to calm some of his worries. Alaric gave his cousin's wrist a gentle squeeze and let the quiet surround them once more as they finished their watch. He had a feeling it was going to be the last moment of peace any of them got for a very long time.

CHAPTER 6

"What is this place?"

James' question echoed Ishaan's thoughts as they stood at the edge of a massive clearing. After rising hours before dawn, their party set out again in silence, each of them caught up in their own worry. Ishaan knew he wasn't the only one anxious to end their hunt. They were close.

We're going to find Theo today, alive and healthy.

That thought spun in an endless loop inside Ishaan's mind. He clung to it with everything he had. Nothing else was an option. He couldn't allow himself to think that Theo wouldn't be there. If he allowed that idea to creep in, the darkness would swallow him whole. He was barely holding on as it was. The frozen wasteland inside him, that protected him, also held the power to destroy him completely if he allowed it to take hold of him.

Already he could feel it grasping at him, trying to pull him down. A heavy exhaustion settled over him like a wet blanket, sucking away his energy almost as soon as he regained it. While the rest of him weakened, though, the warm ember in his chest continued to grow. Every step closer to their quarry seemed to breathe life into it until it threatened to burst into flame. Ishaan was stuck, trapped between fire and ice.

"Our people have tales about fields like this," Alaric offered. He was still riding beside the prince, but they had stopped, as well. "In the old stories, this would have been where a dragon could land safely, avoiding the trees."

James didn't quite roll his eyes, but it seemed like a struggle to manage that feat. "You all take your obsession with mythical creatures pretty seriously, don't you?"

Though Alaric's face remained passive, it was clear to Ishaan that he was offended. "Who are you to say they weren't real? Dragons are creatures of the magic that you wield so freely, after all."

"Who are you to say they *are* real?" James countered.

"This is neither the time nor the place for this," Captain Trieste cut in. "Focus. Rhoan is our mission."

James immediately backed down and fell silent. Alaric tilted his chin up ever-so-slightly, but he, too, quieted, turning his attention to Kaelas.

"He's here." The prince's voice was low and guttural, edged with a barely restrained fury. His words sent a surge of heat through Ishaan, the thing that was *'other'* inside him reacting with a soul-deep yearning that stole his breath. The pull came again, so sharp it hurt.

"Ishaan?"

He pressed a hand to his chest, trying to soothe the growing ache within him. He waved his other in a feeble attempt to assure the captain that he was alright. Prince Kaelas was right: they had found their target. The pull grew and grew within him, the heat almost too much to bear. He felt stretched tight and something would have to give before he snapped completely.

"There!"

Irric's warning was almost drowned out a moment later by a harsh, inhuman roar. Ishaan's ears buzzed and his vision wavered as a visceral *need* surged within him in response. The thing inside him was clawing at his mind, ripping him to shreds as it fought for control.

"Yes. Home. Safe. Yes yes yes! He is here! We have to go to him! He is here!"

The voice in his mind, the one he'd started to believe really was gone, was echoing in his ears now. He was distantly aware of another roar, followed by a loud cry, but he saw nothing but flames.

"Stop fighting! He is here and I will go to him. You can't keep him from me!"

"Ishaan!"

Someone was calling for him. A voice he knew, somehow. He tried to grasp it, to anchor himself, but the thing inside him was desperate. It tore through his thoughts as easily as one would swipe away a cobweb. Like a cornered animal, it was fighting for its life, fighting to get to the person who was *home*.

And it was winning.

Theo. Think of Theo.

For a moment, he could see the soldier's face. Clear blue eyes and the soft smile he always seemed to reserve just for Ishaan. Theo was safety. He was protection against a world that never stopped disappointing him. Ishaan held onto that image, that feeling, for as long as he could, but it was ripped away only seconds later. The embers within him were burning him up from the inside out, phantom flames licking along the scars left behind by the fire that had killed his family.

"Ishaan! He's here. Theo is here. Whatever is going on, you need to pull yourself together. Now!"

He's here. The fiery beast inside him still fought, still flayed his mind wide open, but those words gave Ishaan something to hold on to. Something real. Theo was here. He was alive. His other thoughts scattered, ashes in the inferno, but he held fast to his bedrock, to the truth that Theo was alive and he was here.

"He is here. I want to go home..."

The fire within him raged, but no fire could burn forever. Not even this one. Slowly, so slowly, the flames inside him burned themselves out, their fury spent, until all that remained was the flickering coal in his chest where the thing hid.

When it finally surrendered, he was shaking, a fine sheen of sweat coating him. It took him agonizing seconds to pull his thoughts back together enough to realize he was flat on his back in the grass, an endless blue sky above him. Everything felt muted and hazy as he struggled to find himself again. He was aware of a buzzing sound near his head, but it wasn't enough to penetrate the fog of confusion.

The sound came again, only this time, a sharp pain that radiated from his cheek followed it. He blinked in confusion and in that moment, the haze shattered and everything came rushing in. His ears popped and his world filled with a devastatingly inhuman growl. James' face appeared above him, his green eyes wide and stark.

"Thank fuck," he snapped. "Get up! Now! We have to go!"

Questions tried to escape, but the sounds remained as elusive as ever. The confusion must have been clear, though, because James continued speaking as he gripped Ishaan's arm, yanking him to his feet.

"Theo is across the clearing. The others are already trying to get to him, but first, we have to deal with *that*." He pointed behind him with his free hand, but he didn't need the direction.

Ishaan knew that sometimes he could be oblivious. He wasn't a skilled tracker like the soldiers, nor did he have the sort of information-gathering skills they possessed. He wasn't special. He was just Ishaan. But even had he been as untried as a child, an oblivious fool, he couldn't have missed seeing the two massive dragons that stood in the field.

Chapter 7

"I'm sure I don't have to remind you to behave when we meet Prince Kaelas? He is a royal prince, you know. You'll need to be on your best behavior."

The magic holding Theo bound tightened, a silent warning that he didn't need. The chilly whisper of Zex's magic was supporting him almost as much as it was restraining him, the unseen bonds holding him upright in his saddle. A full day of relentless travel had rapidly stolen what little energy he'd regained. He'd eaten this morning, at least, which was an improvement over most days he'd spent under the man's half-hearted care.

He didn't respond, which was usually the best course of action when conversing with Zex.

"Theodric. I'm warning you. You would do well to remember that you and nearly all of your team are expendable to me. I really don't care what happens to them, so long as I get what I came for."

"If you touch a single one of them, I swear to you I won't stop until I make you pay for it." He leveled a glare at the man, letting all the fiery hate he felt show in his eyes. Until he'd met Zex, he hadn't been sure he *could* ever truly hate another person.

"Doesn't it ever get exhausting to be so full of hostility all the time?"

"Not when it comes to you."

Zex smirked, but like before, something was missing. In the days he'd spent with him, Theo had seen glimpses of who Zex really was beneath all the banter and sarcasm. He'd caught flashes of a deep cynicism and hints of a bone-deep weariness that he was all too familiar with. But now, he was certain he saw something almost like fear in his eerie silver eyes. He hoped it was fear of Prince Kaelas. He knew nothing about the ruler of Sarkhyr except what he'd gleaned from Zex, but he knew his fate hinged on this meeting.

"Ah. They're here already." Zex's voice hitched, barely noticeable, just the smallest stumble over his words, but Theo caught it. He didn't have time to linger on it, though, as the two of them rode out of the tree line and stopped at the edge of a massive open field. He pulled his leg back as much as the magic would allow out of instinct, narrowly avoiding the horse's teeth when it turned to bite him.

"Stop it," he hissed at the beast, but he didn't spare it another thought because there, on the far side of the field, stood his team. Or some of them, anyway. They were too far away to make out details, but he saw Captain Trieste and James at the head of the group, with Ishaan planted firmly between them. Naema and Irric protected their backs, but Vesa, Kya, and Kellan were missing.

The blond man on the captain's other side had to be Prince Kaelas. Even this far away, he could almost feel the animosity pouring off him as he faced Zex across the field. Beside him, a low growl rumbled through the air, a deep sound that no human should be able to make. The air felt heavy, pressing at him, an oppressive weight that bore down on him relentlessly.

"Ishaan!"

James' startled cry drew everyone's attention and suddenly, several things happened all at once.

He could only watch as Ishaan curled in on himself, then slid sideways from his saddle. It looked like James caught him, but barely, the mage throwing out some kind of spell to slow his fall. Naema sprang into action a moment later, dismounting to help lower Ishaan to the ground.

At the same time, Prince Kaelas jumped from his own saddle and came right for Zex at a dead run. He felt the magic holding him slip as Zex's full focus went to the man. Zex dismounted and stepped away from his mount, but held his ground, waiting.

The morning sun caught Kaelas, casting him in an otherworldly golden glow that seemed to expand as he charged the field. It took several seconds for Theo to realize that it wasn't the glow that was expanding. It was Kaelas.

Golden mist covered the prince in a haze, his figure seeming to blur and somehow *shift*. The glow intensified until it was like trying to stare into the sun, finally growing so bright it forced Theo to look away. When he looked back, his breath caught in his throat, stealing away any words he may have tried to say.

But what could one truly say when, between one blink and the next, a prince disappeared and in his place, there was a massive golden dragon? Theo was numb with shock, his mind struggling to comprehend with what he was seeing.

The beast was enormous, with spikes along its neck and horns that curled back from its face. Dangerously sharp spikes ran down its spine, ending in a cluster at the tip of its tail.

Silence filled the clearing, but only for a moment. The dragon *roared*, and Theo was ashamed to admit that if he hadn't been bound, his instincts would have driven him to run. As it was, the horse was dancing nervously beneath him, edging back toward the tree line.

"Kaelas!" Another blond man, so similar in appearance to the prince that they must be related, ran onto the field, but the golden dragon ignored him. The beast only had eyes for Zex, who, far from being intimidated, was facing down the approaching creature with that infuriating smirk.

A moment later, a silver glow began to emanate from him, but where the golden light had been a heavy haze, this was as diaphanous and fleeting as moonlight. The change that overtook him wasn't smooth and seamless, instead coming in fits and starts. It was as though the change was a struggle for him. Still, by the time the golden dragon closed the distance, a silver dragon was there to meet him.

It was slightly smaller, sleeker, with two delicate horns that rose upwards in a graceful swoop. Instead of jagged edges, delicate ridges ran down its spine, its tail tipped in gleaming silver spikes similar to that of the golden dragon.

He barely had a moment to grasp what he was seeing before the two creatures collided with a force that sent the silver one stumbling backwards. Sent *Zex* backward, because somehow, the prince of Sarkhyr and the traitor were both *dragons*.

Facing down two massive beasts finally broke his horse's nerve and it bolted, nearly unseating Theo. It wasn't until he was scrambling to grab the reins that he realized the magic holding him had fully fallen away the moment the two dragons met. He was still weak, his thoughts buried beneath a layer of fog, but for the first time in countless days, he was in full control and he didn't waste the moment.

He fought the reins until the horse was under control, using that momentum to make a run for his team. He saw movement ahead and realized they were already coming for him, Captain Trieste in the lead, with Naema and Irric behind him. They met him halfway across the field, wheeling around to run beside him back the way they'd come.

They didn't stop until they were out of the clearing and into the scant safety of the trees, where he had to pull the horse to a walk. Both of them were panting heavily, a combination of fear and exertion, when they finally stopped. He immediately looked around, searching for the other two.

"Theo! I'm so glad you're okay." Naema was right beside him, her voice thick with relief.

"What the fuck is going on?" he asked instead of replying. His thoughts still felt scattered, but he wasn't so confused that he'd somehow hallucinated dragons. That he knew for sure.

"I wish I could say I had the answer," Trieste said grimly. "All I care about is that we have you back. We're leaving. This is beyond even our capabilities."

Under any other circumstance he may have protested, drawn by the sight of two creatures that were supposed to be only myth. Now, though, Theo wanted nothing more than to get away from this entire damn country. "Where are the others? Where's Ishaan?"

"He's with James," Naema assured him. "They're..." She looked around, turning her horse back the way they'd come. Through the gaps in the trees, it was possible to see the immense field. In the short time it had taken him to reach his team, the silver dragon had regained his footing. He looked to be losing ground quickly, though, overpowered by the bigger gold dragon that was Kaelas. Dark crimson blood soaked silver scales, wounds opened by talons as long as Theo's arm. Zex was already staggering from a huge gash across his front left leg, every movement sending a fresh scattering of blood across the field. He did something, some kind of magic, that hit Kaelas hard enough to push him back, putting space between the two.

As impressively gruesome as the sight was, though, the fear that washed over him had nothing to do with the dragons.

No, he reserved all of his mounting horror for the tiny figure that was running across the field towards them. Even from this distance, there was no mistaking who it was.

"No..." He kicked the Sarkhyrian horse into a run, a desperate attempt to stop what was coming even though he knew he'd never get there in time.

He could only watch in sheer terror as Ishaan ran onto the field to stand directly between the two dragons, right as Kaelas charged for Zex.

CHAPTER 8

I'm going to die.

That was the only thought in Ishaan's head as he stood between two dragons, facing down the huge golden creature that was going to be the death of him. He only vaguely remembered moving. The moment he'd laid eyes on the silver dragon, the thing inside of him had resurfaced. This time, there was no fighting it. It took over before Ishaan even realized there was a need to fight.

"Home safe yes it's him yes finally!" Whatever it was, its thoughts were a chaotic jumble of fear and relief and that aching yearning that had filled him earlier. It took him over and the next thing Ishaan knew, he was staring down a wildly different Kaelas than the prince he'd known.

Those golden eyes didn't even spare him a moment's glance. Kaelas was blind to everything but Zex, focused solely on the silver dragon at Ishaan's back. He couldn't even run, fear locking him in place.

"Ishaan!"

He knew that voice. Theo. He was safe, then.

A strange, calm acceptance settled over him. He may have failed at everything else in his life, but he'd done this one thing right, at least. Theo was alive, and he was safe. Whatever happened next didn't matter.

His vision blurred with unshed tears, so Ishaan closed his eyes, waiting for the feel of teeth and claws on his skin.

Instead, he suddenly found himself wrapped in a wall of warmth. Something closed around him, protecting him, as the gold dragon slammed into Zex. Ishaan felt his feet leave the ground, his bones jarring from the force of the collision. The world spun around him and his body jolted, but whatever was protecting him kept it from hurting. A few seconds later, the tumbling stopped. He was fairly certain he was facing the ground, but it was impossible to tell. All he could see was darkness.

He could hear, though. Someone screamed and he heard words being shouted, both in Nevarrean and Sarkhyrian, but he couldn't make out what was being said. Everything was strangely muffled, he assumed by whatever magic was wrapped around him. It had to have been James. He was fairly sure the mage had been close behind him when he'd lost control and run onto the field.

Another shout rang out, louder, the words in Sarkhyrian but undeniably an order. A moment later, he had the sensation of being lowered. The world tilted until he was upright and the moment his feet touched the grass, the wall of protection fell away. Off-balance, Ishaan stumbled forward, blinking in the bright sunlight.

He turned, expecting to see James at his side. Instead, he came face to face with a dragon. He froze, fear and yearning warring within him. The massive silver eyes staring him down were hauntingly familiar. They were the same eyes he saw every time he looked in a mirror now. The look in the creature's eyes wasn't the anger or hatred he'd expected, though. Instead, there was a moment of recognition. The thing inside him surged to the front of his mind and the dragon's silver eyes took on an eerie glow.

The odd moment was over almost before it began. Ishaan was still struggling to make sense of what was happening when the gold dragon pounced. He landed directly on top of the smaller silver beast, pinning it to the ground. Kaelas' jaws closed around Zex's throat and in that moment, the fight was over.

"Do not kill him! We have to take him back." Alaric rushed forward, seemingly oblivious to the danger of the two dragons. The silver one twitched and focused his gaze on the new man, but Alaric was watching Prince Kaelas.

The golden dragon growled, sending tremors of ice through Ishaan's body. It took another vicious warning before the silver dragon responded, though. A soft silver haze covered him and his body began to shrink. Kaelas only released his hold when soft human flesh replaced hardened dragon scales. His change was faster, smoother. Zex was still shifting in the time it took the other dragon to finish.

The thing inside of him seemed almost to whimper when the dragon disappeared, leaving a very human-looking Zex behind. It still clawed at him, fighting, trying to get to him for some twisted reason.

Ishaan felt a hand on his arm and glanced to the side, relieved to see James beside him. Seeing a familiar face helped to ground him, giving him something to hold on to. The mage looked dumbfounded, staring at the two men, but his other hand was at his belt, touching one of the tiny bags of burning powder he'd used near Esterdon.

"Ishaan..."

That voice, right behind him, nearly sent him to his knees. The relief that poured through him nearly overwhelmed him, but he forced himself to steel his spine. Drawing a breath, he turned.

Only a few minutes ago, Ishaan had been sure he was going to die. He'd held back the tears, held back the show of weakness. Now, seeing Theo's face, the dam finally broke.

The man had suffered. That much was painfully obvious. A deep gash ran across his forehead, the wound barely beginning to heal. Old bruises spattered in blues and purples across his skin and he looked thinner. It was the haunted look in his clear blue eyes that broke him, though.

"It's good to see you," Theo breathed. His hands were shaking when he laid a gentle touch on Ishaan's cheek. His skin was clammy and rough, but nothing had ever felt as good as that simple touch did. He felt Theo's thumb brushed away a tear from his cheek, and he had to fight back a sob.

Theo.

Ishaan's whole body was trembling, but he brought his hand up to cover Theo's. The other man smiled and for a moment, he looked like himself, bruises and all. He had so much he wanted to say, so many things he needed to tell Theo, but he couldn't. Instead, he squeezed his hand as tightly as he dared and nodded, a tremulous smile breaking free.

"No wonder you were so keen to get back to your team, Theodric. Or just one person in particular?"

Theo's smile dropped and he tugged Ishaan closer, stepping back so they were both facing the rest of the party.

Zex was on his knees on the ground, his hands bound with manacles made of a strange black metal, but the look on his face wasn't the look of a defeated man.

No, there was no defeat in Zex's eyes when he looked at Ishaan. There was only fury and a deep hatred that burned into the very core of Ishaan. He didn't know what he'd done to earn that hate, but he knew without a doubt that Zex would kill him if ever he got the chance.

"You just lost the fight you came here looking for in under a minute. I would think you'd be using that smart mouth of yours to avoid execution."

Theo's words were harsh, cutting in a way Ishaan hadn't ever heard from the man before. He held himself upright, still holding Ishaan's hand, but his tight grip told an entirely different story. A very faint tremor wracked Theo's body almost constantly and, with every passing second, he was leaning slightly more weight onto Ishaan. Whatever had happened to him, it seemed to have pushed him to the very edge of his endurance.

"I suppose this hostility means you're not going to come visit me in prison?" Zex's voice was mocking. Still, it had an effect on Theo. His grip on Ishaan's hand tightened almost to the point of pain and his weight shifted as if he'd meant to take a step back, but stopped himself just in time.

A fierce protectiveness surged up inside him, strong enough to fight back the thing inside him that was still reaching for Zex. He was still scared and so very confused, but this was something he could do. Theo needed him.

James was still standing beside him, so he reached out to the mage, tugging his sleeve to get his attention. Their eyes met and Ishaan darted a quick glance over at Theo, trying to convey his concern. Thankfully, the mage understood and edged around to stand beside Theo, keeping the tracker between them.

"There is nothing more you need to say to him," James spat at the bound man. "Captain?"

Captain Trieste, Irric, and Naema immediately closed ranks around Theo, with the captain putting himself between Theo and Zex. The Sarkhyrians ranged out behind Zex, with Prince Kaelas and Alaric standing directly behind him. They were the ones that ended up on the receiving end of Captain Trieste's fierce scowl.

"Prince Kaelas, I believe it's long past time for an explanation. What the fuck is going on here?"

CHAPTER 9

Captain Trieste's question hung in the air, the silence growing and thickening with every passing second. Kaelas was at least paying attention to him, but Alaric kept his eyes on Zex. Even bound in manacles of iron and black tourmaline, he exuded an aura of power. He'd heard the stories, but had never gotten the chance to meet him.

He seemed completely at ease, resting comfortably on his knees as the tension built between the two parties. From the tiny smirk on his face, he seemed to even be enjoying it a bit. The Nevarrean captain was growing more upset while Kaelas stayed stubbornly silent, like this whole mess wasn't his fault. If he'd just stopped to think for one moment instead of charging the field...

But he hadn't, and it was growing increasingly obvious that he wasn't going to deal with the situation. Which meant that *it* was now Alaric's problem. Again.

Stifling a sigh, Alaric straightened to his full height and stepped forward. The movement seemed to catch Zex's attention. His cool silver gaze shifted to him, but Alaric didn't have time to deal with him at the moment.

"Captain Trieste, I understand that you're upset and have a lot of questions," he began. Years of working side by side with Kaelas and his temper had taught him to modulate and control his own voice and emotions in response. It was a skill he had to call on increasingly often these days.

"Your prince and the traitor we were chasing both just turned into dragons. So yes, Lord Alaric, I have a few questions," Trieste snapped, voice taut.

"Traitor? Is that the story you're telling these days, Kaelas?" Zex glanced up over his shoulder at Kaelas. His cousin's jaw clenched tight, a sure sign that his anger was getting the best of him.

"It's nothing but the truth. You know what you did. You broke-"

"I did what I had to do!" Zex was on his feet before Alaric even realized he was moving. He made it a step closer to Kaelas before Ereyan and Halbrig took him back to the ground. He didn't fight them, but he didn't go down easily, either.

Through the drama, the Nevarrean team was silent, their eyes darting back and forth between Kaelas and Zex, with two noticeable exceptions. Theodric, the soldier they rescued, was keeping his focus on Ishaan. To Alaric, it was clear the man was deliberately avoiding looking at Zex.

Ishaan, meanwhile... Ishaan hadn't taken his eyes *off* Zex. Not since Kaelas had defeated him and shackled him with manacles designed specifically to block his ability to shift forms. Given what he knew of Ishaan and what had happened, Alaric couldn't say he was surprised.

A deep, vicious growl pulled Alaric's attention back to the two men at the center of this whole mess. The sound had come from his cousin, so he hurriedly took a step forward, putting himself between Kaelas and Captain Trieste.

"Kaelas. Control it," he ordered, careful to keep his voice low and speak Sarkhyrian. No need to give the Nevarrean soldiers more information than strictly necessary.

"Yes, Kaelas, control it," Zex mocked, which just pissed Kaelas off even further, his eyes molten with fury.

"No one asked for your input. Keep your mouth closed or I will have the guards gag you." He didn't look away from Kaelas, didn't break eye contact. Doing so was almost guaranteed to draw out the dragon lurking just beneath the surface.

"You have spirit. Interesting."

Zex fell silent, thankfully, allowing him to focus on Kaelas. "Kaelas, you need to calm down. It's going to be difficult enough to smooth this over without you losing control again."

"I'm trying." He hissed the words through clenched teeth, barely audible. "It's more difficult when he's here."

"I understand that. If you need to walk away, do it. I can deal with the Nevarreans. Take a minute to calm down. Take an hour and go fly off some of your anger. I don't care what you choose, but if you can't contain it, you need to leave."

Kaelas was silent, visibly struggling. Alaric kept eye contact with him to keep Kas' focus on him, not on the prisoner. The man's eyes were burning gold, a clear sign the dragon was very near to breaking free again. The struggle was painfully obvious. As the prince, Kaelas wanted to stay and deal with the situation as he'd been trained to. As the dragon, he wanted nothing more than to finish the fight and rip Zex limb from limb. At the moment, the dragon appeared to be winning.

With a low growl, Kaelas turned on his heel and stormed away, heading into the trees and disappearing from sight.

"Even more interesting yet," Zex murmured behind him. Alaric turned to face him head on now, glaring. Dragon or not, he wasn't scared of Zex.

"I don't make idle threats. Stay quiet or I will have you gagged."

"I wasn't aware our relationship had progressed so quickly. I don't even know your name. Then again, sometimes that's half the fun."

His tone, dripping with mockery and disdain, infuriated Alaric. The intensity of his anger shocked him. It was rare that anyone could get under his skin, but Zex had slipped in effortlessly, cutting through his usual defenses like a razor-sharp blade.

"Halbrig." He forced himself to look away from the arrogant man, catching the eye of the tall guard who'd accompanied them. "Do it, please."

"With pleasure, sir." She dug into a pouch at her waist and withdrew a strip of cloth. Zex didn't struggle or attempt to fight it when she came over. He simply opened his mouth and let her gag him. He caught Alaric's eyes and the two of them stared each other down in silence until Halbrig stepped back.

Shaking his head to clear it, Alaric hurriedly looked away, finally turning his attention back to the foreign soldiers. It put Zex at his back, which wasn't a comfortable feeling, but he needed to gain control of this situation before it got completely out of hand. The captain's dark skin was flushed with anger and, honestly, Alaric couldn't blame him. This whole situation was a nightmare.

"My apologies, Captain." He dipped his head just the right degree to convey sincerity without appearing obsequious.

"I'll take that explanation now," Trieste bit out. He crossed his arms over his chest, his dark eyes hard. It was no wonder he was in charge of a squad like this. If Alaric didn't spend his days keeping rein on a dragon, this man would intimidate him. As it was, he couldn't help but respect him. He was a good man caught up in something that he was in no way prepared for, but he still put his soldiers first. That said a lot about the kind of person he was.

"Of course. I'll try to explain to the best of my ability," he promised. Casting about for where to start, he remembered his conversation with Kaelas when they'd shared the watch. "Around seven years ago, a plague swept through Sarkhyr. Some of the coastal towns were able to protect themselves, but nowhere was truly safe. Yrasea, being the capital, got the brunt of it, though."

"I'm sorry, but what does this have to do with what just happened?" the captain interrupted.

Alaric bit back a flare of annoyance. "You need to know what happened to understand why we are in this situation now. May I continue?"

"Keep it brief, if you don't mind. We're losing travel time."

"Well then, we could always continue this conversation when we return to Yrasea?" Alaric offered. Even to himself, his voice sounded sharper than he'd intended. He thought he heard a snort of laughter from behind him, but he couldn't focus on Zex and his questionable intentions right now.

"No. I want to know what happened," Theodric cut in before his captain could argue further. "I want to know why he did… why he did what he did to me."

Judging by the haunted look in the man's eyes, it wasn't difficult to guess that Zex had used blood magic on him. For how long and to what extent, he wasn't sure, but it wouldn't have been a pleasant experience for the man.

Focusing on the captain again, he continued the story. "As I was saying, Yrasea had the most people struck down. All accounts say it was a horrific disease. Once the fever took hold, almost no one survived. Our healers had never seen anything like it before. No one knew how to treat it or even how to ease the pain. Our people were terrified and looked to their leaders for answers, but there were none. All we could do was isolate ourselves and try to wait it out. After a year with no end in sight, that's when Zex came forward and claimed he could cure the disease with blood magic."

Behind him came a muffled grunt, as though Zex were trying to speak. He glanced back at him and their eyes locked for a moment. The eerie silver sheen, so unlike the warm gold of Kaelas' eyes, made him shiver. Zex tilted his head, as if he could sense Alaric's unease. Instead of backing down, Alaric straightened and held his gaze. He refused to be intimidated by a backstabbing traitor.

"Are you going to finish, or are you going to continue your pissing contest with a prisoner?" James' voice cut through the tension and gave Alaric an excuse to look away. He turned his back to the man and gave the Nevarrean prince a curt nod.

"My apologies. Anyway, Prince Kaelas and the council of chancellors refused to allow him to try it, as blood magic is, of course, illegal in every country. Rather than accept their ruling, however, he tried it anyway when his personal bodyguard fell ill. The process failed, and the man died. Zex was found quite literally coated in the man's blood, but when guards attempted to arrest him, he used his magic to kill four of them before he could be subdued. Our people were horrified, and the chancellors demanded Zex's execution, but Prince Kaelas stepped in and ordered him imprisoned instead."

"Why?"

Confused, Alaric turned to the man who had spoken. He was at the rear of the Nevarrean group, the quiet one. It took him a moment to remember the man's name, though. "Irric, was it? I don't understand the question, I'm afraid."

"Why did Prince Kaelas intervene? Did they know each other previously? If this man killed five people, why would he spare him?"

Well... that was something he had hoped they wouldn't pick up on. He kept his face carefully expressionless, rapidly running through his options in his mind.

In the end, though, he never got to decide on an answer, because that damned Nevarrean prince spoke first.

"Oh fuck," the man breathed. His eyes darted to Zex, then to the woods where Kaelas had disappeared. "It makes sense now."

"What? What does?" Theodric asked. The rest of their team just looked confused, though Captain Trieste was staring intently at Zex now. Alaric would almost see him putting the pieces together.

"One thing that's been bothering me since the moment we set foot in that castle was the imagery," James explained. He, too, was now focused on Zex. "I wondered why there were so many dragons everywhere, but that makes sense now. Everywhere I looked, I saw two dragons. A gold and a silver."

"Oh shit..."

He could barely hear the captain's quiet curse as it all came together in his mind. It was all he could do not to curse, himself.

Kaelas was going to kill him.

"The double throne makes sense now, too," James went on, oblivious to Alaric's growing panic. "Sarkhyr doesn't have one prince. It has two."

CHAPTER 10

Stunned silence hung in the air. Ishaan gripped Theo's hand harder, his mind racing as all the clues and signs fell into place. The tapestries with the two dragons. The double throne that had so confused him. The unnatural, inhuman eyes the two men shared.

The unnatural, inhuman eyes that he shared, as well. Fear snaked down his spine as the night of the fire flashed through his mind. The strange artifact his parents had somehow gotten, the one that had been on the table beside him. The one that had looked like a large *egg*.

"No."

Theo's voice was still rough and raspy from his ordeal, but there was no hint of weakness when he spoke. He stood tall next to Ishaan, though he was leaning more and more weight on him, his hold on Ishaan's hand bordering on painful as he fought to stay steady. He hid it well, showing no outward sign of the effort it took to stand. Still, there was concern in Captain Trieste's eyes when he looked away from Zex to take in his soldier.

"Rhoan, perhaps-"

"No!" Theo cut him off, a blatant show of rebellion that Ishaan would have never thought him possible of before now. The captain hadn't thought so either, apparently, because he actually paused as though shocked. Theo didn't waste anymore words on him. He turned back to

Alaric and the burning fury in his eyes made Ishaan's breath catch, instinctive fear gripping him tight.

"You're telling me that your *prince* is the man who did this to me? That he was free to do so because your *other* prince was too spineless to deal with the problem?"

Alaric glared at Theo, his expression hard and unforgiving. "You would do well to watch yourself, soldier," he warned. "You are still a guest in our country and it is only due to us that you are safe enough to stand there spitting insults and spewing accusations about a situation you could never understand!"

It was the most he had ever heard Alaric speak at one time, and certainly more emotion than the man had ever shown. The fear within Ishaan was growing, his stomach churning as tempers clashed. The Sarkhyrian guards were moving to circle Alaric, their hands drifting dangerously close to their weapons. A rustle of leather and the scrape of metal behind him told him the Nevarreans were doing the same.

Theo, though, ignored all of it. His sole focus was Alaric. He was visibly shaking now and Ishaan wasn't sure he could have pried his hand free of Theo's if he'd wanted to. The only thing keeping him standing now was Ishaan's support and pure stubbornness. His skin was ashen, save for two spots of color high on his cheeks as his anger rushed through him.

"Oh, I understand well enough. A guest in your country? I'm here because your weak excuse for a prince didn't want to do what needed to be done!"

Alaric opened his mouth, probably to argue, but Theo didn't give him a chance. He took a step toward him, leaving Ishaan to stumble along beside him to keep him from falling. One of Alaric's guards drew their sword, but no one else moved. Everyone's attention was on Theo. When he spoke again, the pain in his voice was one Ishaan was all too familiar with.

"Do you know what it's like to have blood magic used on you? Do you? To have someone crawling around inside your mind, digging through everything that makes you a person, twisting it and pulling out information until you don't even know for sure if your memories are real anymore? Because I do! I know what that feels like now because Kaelas turned his problem into *everyone's* problem. Every single day since we came north has been cursed, and it is entirely the fault of your fucking prince. So you don't get to stand there and defend him against something that *you* don't understand!"

He could have heard a mouse sneeze in the silence that fell over the clearing. Alaric's face was back to his usual blank mask, but something was swirling behind his stormy blue eyes as he studied Theo. Behind him, Zex settled on the ground, the very picture of nonchalance even with a kerchief tied around his mouth as a makeshift gag.

"Theo..." Unsurprisingly, Naema was the first one to break the silence. She took a step towards them, but he stepped away. It was a tiny move, barely even a few inches, but it stopped her in her tracks, her eyes widening.

"Help me?" Theo whispered in his ear and Ishaan looked up at him. "I need to not be here but I don't think I can make it."

As if there were anything Theo could ask of him that Ishaan would ever refuse. He nodded and moved so he was against Theo's side, allowing him to rest his arm on Ishaan's shoulders for support. To the others, he held up his hand and rocked it back and forth twice, the sign for 'wait'. It was the only one he knew that would hopefully keep them from following.

The silence was deafening as the two of them walked away. Theo didn't offer any direction, so he picked the way that would take them into the trees and out of sight the quickest. He could feel their eyes on him, like tiny daggers of hurt and suspicion. He couldn't blame them, really.

He was practically carrying Theo by the time they were out of sight. The other man wasn't especially broad, but he was solid, his years as a soldier leaving him leanly muscled. The first large tree they came across, Ishaan stopped, helping Theo lower himself down until he was sitting on the grass.

Of course, he hadn't thought to bring his pack or even a water canteen. Everything he had that might offer Theo some relief was nestled in his saddlebag, right next to the journal that would allow them to speak.

Typical of you, Ishaan.

"Thank you." Theo's voice plucked him out of his rapidly darkening thoughts as easily as ever. Shaking his head, he sat down across from him, their knees touching. He brought his fist to his chin, holding it there for a moment.

It was a sign Theo had come up with, but it seemed to take him a moment to understand. "You have nothing to apologize for, Ishaan. If anything, I should be the one going back there to fix things, but I just..." He trailed off. His head fell back to rest against the tree trunk as he sighed. "I'm just so tired."

Ishaan's chest squeezed, his heart aching as he watched Theo. He was too familiar with that tone, with the way his shoulders slumped. Even if he could speak, he didn't have the words to describe the soul-deep weariness that had dragged him down into darkness after hours in the basement laboratory. The exhaustion that made even breathing a chore that almost wasn't worth accomplishing. He didn't have the words, but he knew what it felt like to be pushed to the very edge, to be standing on that cliff and wondering if that final step would make everything okay again.

He knew it, and he saw it in the way Theo's shoulders were hunched, curling in on himself in an unconscious attempt to protect himself from the world. He felt it in the faint tremors that wracked Theo's body. He heard it in the shuddering breath the other man drew, the same one he'd drawn hundreds of times in a vain attempt to hold back the tide of his emotions.

Ishaan knew all the signs, all the tells, but he didn't know what to *do* to fix it. What could he do when the only person who had ever made him feel safe was the man slowly falling apart in front of him?

CHAPTER 11

They were close enough to the group still that Theo could hear when the arguing started, but far enough away that he couldn't make out any words. He preferred it that way. Just making it this far had drained every bit of energy he'd mustered, even though Ishaan had supported him the entire way.

He *hurt*. It wasn't even the pain from what Zex had done to him. Physical pain was just another part of life for a soldier. No amount of training could have prepared him for the emotions that were crushing him, the anxiety and fear and betrayal ripping him apart. He curled in on himself, trying to hold it all back, but it was a battle he was quickly losing. Now that he was safe and he could finally lower his guard, everything he'd held back since the fight outside Esterdon was flooding in.

A gentle touch on his knee caught his attention, pulling him back into the moment. He forced himself to open his eyes. He couldn't manage even a fake smile for Ishaan, but he could at least look at him.

The man sitting in front of him looked far different than he had just a few days ago. Or had it been weeks? A shudder crawled across Theo's skin when he realized he couldn't be entirely sure how long he had been held in that tiny cabin. Time slipped and slithered through his mind, some moments flashing by in an instant, while others lingered.

"You healed." His voice was rough, his throat dry after his rant. He coughed once to clear his throat, for all the good that did.

Ishaan nodded, one hand coming up to touch the mostly healed welt across his throat. Even the horrific burns on his wrists looked better, though his skin still looked raw, and the scars were still obvious.

"I'm sorry. I shouldn't have lost my temper like that," he whispered. It had felt justified at the moment, but now all he felt was mortified that he'd shown his weakness so easily.

Ishaan's grip tightened for a moment and he shook his head. The smile he gave Theo looked sad, and guilt gripped him for adding to Ishaan's pain. He forced himself to lift his head up enough to meet his eyes.

Silver.

Pain.

Fear.

He had to get away.

The panic took him before he even realized it was happening. He scrambled back, pressing against the tree. Distance. He needed *distance.* His chest was tight, his breaths labored, clawing at his throat. Those silver eyes came closer and he froze, waiting for the pain to start.

Nothing happened.

The touch on his knee was gone, and there was no pain. Still, he stayed where he was, his body tense and waiting for what he knew was coming. What always came whenever those silver eyes got too close to him.

Theo waited and he waited, but still nothing happened. The longer the moment stretched, the more the panic receded. His breathing settled and finally, the fear that had overwhelmed him dissipated. In its wake, though, the realization of the situation set in.

He'd pressed back against what felt like a tree with his knees tucked against his chest, making himself less of a target. He knew he was trembling, something he couldn't stop no matter how hard he tried. All he wanted to do was stay like this, to pretend everything was normal and he wasn't losing his mind.

Unfortunately, a hitched breath reminded him he wasn't alone. He reluctantly opened his eyes, looking around to assess the mess he'd made.

Ishaan was on his feet but as far away as he could get without completely losing himself in the trees. His lips were pressed together into a tight line, the only outward sign of distress. As muddled as his thoughts were, Theo remembered how good Ishaan was at hiding his emotions, and he knew he'd hurt him.

"I'm-" His words stuck in his raw throat and he coughed, tasting bile. "Ishaan, I'm sorry," he managed. "I'm okay."

The other man took a step closer, but stopped there, shaking his head again. He brought his fist up until his index finger touched his chin, and it took Theo almost too long to realize that somewhere along the way, Ishaan had found new hand signs. As absurd as it was, given everything going on, a brief pang of bitterness shot through him. What else had he missed while he was being held hostage by a madman?

"I don't know what that means," he confessed quietly. "Sorry."

Ishaan's hand fell and Theo felt like an absolute ass for hurting him, even though he couldn't help the situation. Ishaan seemed to consider for a moment, then pointed first to himself, then to the ground near Theo's feet.

"If you're asking if it's alright to come closer, it is."

He must have guessed right, because Ishaan slowly made his way back over and lowered himself to sit on the ground in front of him. He didn't miss how Ishaan kept his head down, hiding his eyes. Humiliation chewed through him.

"I'm alright. Really." Maybe if he repeated the lie enough, it would become truth. "I didn't mean to upset you. I just... it was just my mind playing tricks on me."

Ishaan quickly looked up, but only for a moment. He pointed to himself and shook his head, then pointed to Theo. With what he knew of Ishaan, he could make an educated guess.

"I assume you want me to worry about myself?" he asked, and Ishaan nodded. "I'd rather not think about anything that just happened, to be honest. Or *anything* that's happened since we left Osirith."

Ishaan nodded again, but from his tiny scowl, Theo guessed the limitation frustrated him.

"Do you have the journal still?"

Ishaan sighed heavily and nodded, but then pointed back toward the group they'd left behind. Which made sense, he supposed, but it didn't make the current situation any easier.

The panic had fully faded by now and he was no longer shaking, but the embarrassment wouldn't fade. For the first time since their paths had collided, the silence that surrounded Theo and Ishaan was awkward and tense. Ishaan wouldn't look at him, and Theo didn't know what to say to fix it. He couldn't even calm his own mind, let alone someone else's, but he couldn't leave things as they were. The quiet was already affecting him, making him anxious in ways it never had before.

"Thank you again for helping me," he blurted into the silence and Ishaan jerked a bit. "I didn't mean to say any of that. I just couldn't seem to stop myself once I started."

He glanced up and caught Ishaan watching him, but the other man looked away before their eyes met again. Theo was pathetically grateful for that small mercy. He felt more stable now, but even the idea of another bout of panic exhausted him down to his bones. He sighed quietly and let his head fall back to rest against the tree trunk, looking up at the canopy of green overhead. Autumn had settled in and splashes of gold and red and orange danced across the green leaves of summer. The chill wind set them moving and that motion, so familiar after all these years, did more to soothe him than anything else could have in that moment.

He didn't mean to keep talking, but before he knew it, the words were escaping. "He told me that all of you were tracking me. I don't remember how long or when he said it, everything is still a mess, but I remember the day he said you turned west and went to the capital instead. Since you arrived with the prince, I'm guessing that's true?"

From the corner of his eye, he saw Ishaan nod. Betrayal twisted through his heart, sharp and hot. He didn't miss the way Ishaan's fists clenched as though frustrated and he huffed sharply, but whatever he wanted to say was trapped in his throat.

"I didn't want to believe him, you know," Theo whispered. "I told myself that the captain was setting up an ambush of some sort or that Zex had left traps or guards that were keeping him away. Deep down, I think I knew he was telling the truth, but I didn't want to believe it. I think if I'd let myself accept that I'd been left behind, he would have succeeded in breaking me."

A hand hovered in his periphery, reaching for his arm, but stopped just short of touching him. A tiny part of Theo, the bitter, angry part that had grown since he'd been with Zex, wanted to lean away, to make him hurt like Theo was hurting. When he looked over at Ishaan, though, he couldn't bring himself to do it. The look in his eyes made it clear that Ishaan was already hurting, and out of everyone involved in this mess, Ishaan had been given the fewest choices. If the captain had ordered them all to abandon the trail, Ishaan couldn't have changed it or come after him on his own.

He *knew* that, but the cruel little voice in his head wouldn't go away. All he could do was try to bury it.

"I won't panic again. You can touch me," he assured him and he hated how his voice wavered as he spoke. It was apparently enough for Ishaan, though, because he brought his hand down to rest on Theo's forearm, squeezing gently. He shook his head, lips moving in the shape of the words he couldn't speak, over and over until Theo could make sense of them.

I didn't want to. Over and over he mouthed it, the desperation clear in the lines of tension running through him.

"I know. You didn't have a choice."

Ishaan slumped and nodded, his hand lingering on Theo's arm.

"I'm not upset with you. Captain Trieste's word is law when we're in the field." That didn't stop a small part of him from being furious that the rest of his team, the ones trained in tracking and stealth, hadn't disobeyed orders and come looking for him. He was a soldier, too; he knew what it was like in the field on a mission, when lives depended on following orders. But *his* life had depended on them. The only reason he was here now, alive, was because Zex had wanted Ishaan more than he'd wanted to kill Theo.

Silence fell between them again, but the tension between them was already fading. He could still hear raised voices from the clearing, but he couldn't bring himself to feel anything anymore. He didn't want to deal with anything else. He couldn't.

"Ishaan?" he murmured, and the other man looked up at him. "Will you stay here with me a little longer? I don't want to go back yet." He shifted over, making space for Ishaan to sit beside him against the massive tree trunk.

The smile that he got in response was tiny and tired, but so genuine it made his heart ache. They shifted around, getting as comfortable as possible on the hard ground. Ishaan ended up tucked against his side and, without thinking, he put his arm around his shoulders. It felt so natural, like they'd done this hundreds of times, but the way Ishaan's shoulders tensed just a little reminded him that wasn't true.

"Is this alright?" He was already lifting his arm to pull away when he felt Ishaan's hand come up to his wrist. They both went still for a moment,

Theo waiting to see what Ishaan was going to do. He wouldn't push him into something he didn't feel comfortable with.

The seconds passed like hours as they stayed frozen like that, but finally, he felt Ishaan release his hold. A moment later, their palms touched, then Ishaan was gently twining their fingers together and tugging Theo's arm back down to rest on his shoulders again. A spark of warmth kindled within him and he managed a tired smile when Ishaan tucked himself against his side, all but cuddled against him. They sat in comfortable silence until a thought came to him and he looked down at Ishaan.

"So... dragons."

It was an inane comment, a gross misrepresentation of the shock and fear and awe and horror all roiling around inside him. Ishaan looked up at him with those wide silver eyes and this time, Theo didn't feel any fear. He cracked a tiny smile and Ishaan responded with a grin that spread slowly, as though it wasn't an expression he was used to making.

Warmth filled his chest and he hugged Ishaan closer. He was still hurting, physically and mentally, and he was more exhausted than he'd ever believed was possible. Still, despite everything that had happened, sitting here with Ishaan was the most at peace he'd felt in a very long time.

CHAPTER 12

The shouting was starting to give him a headache.

After Kaelas had stormed off and Theodric had done the same, Alaric now stood alone in the middle of two groups of people who had every reason to dislike each other and were very loud in their opinions of what should happen now. The Nevarreans were supporting their soldier, while his cousin's bodyguards were defending their prince.

Just to add to his problems, he also had the *other* prince beside him, resting comfortably on his knees and watching the arguments with something like delight in his silver eyes. The gag in his mouth didn't hide the tiny smirk as the group threatened to rip itself to pieces.

"I'm going to kill him," he muttered under his breath. At the moment, the sentiment applied to both Kaelas and Zex.

The accusations weren't slowing down and more than one soldier had their hand on a weapon. He needed to step in before the situation got entirely out of hand.

"That's enough!"

He knew his voice carried well. He was one of the most powerful people in all of Sarkhyr and he'd spent several years perfecting the aura of poised control that he was so well-known for. He wasn't broad and bulky, lacking the build of a soldier, and he looked younger than his years, but even the chancellors, the group of counselors second only to Kaelas himself, knew to tread lightly on the rare occasion that Alaric raised his voice.

So to have seven soldiers completely ignore him to continue their childish argument was a very unwelcome development.

Behind him, Zex's laughter was clear even through the gag. The sound had him bristling with barely contained anger. He was not accustomed to being ignored, and he refused to tolerate it from these childish idiots.

Alaric drew himself up to his full height and did something he hadn't done in a long time: he reached for the magic that rippled within him and *pushed*.

"Enough!"

This time, his voice echoed through the clearing with enough volume to set even his own ears ringing. A flash of light, tinted the palest blue, exploded between the two groups, forcing them all to step back from each other. They all fell silent, and a few clapped their hands over their ears to block out the lingering echoes of his voice.

Even Zex had gone quiet behind him. It shouldn't have given him as much pleasure as it did to shock the arrogant prince, though he'd never admit it to anyone.

Once the last echo had faded, he stepped forward, putting himself between the two feuding groups. "Your childish arguing is accomplishing nothing. I mean all of you," he added when Ereyan, the youngest of the Sarkhyrian guards, shot a smirk at the Nevarreans. "There is nothing to be done until Prince Kaelas returns, so I suggest all of you take this time to eat and rest your horses. We will be traveling quickly once we set out for Yrasea."

"How did you do that?" James, the Nevarrean prince, asked instead of backing down. It was all Alaric could do to keep his expression free of annoyance.

"You are a mage, are you not? Surely you know how to amplify your voice."

James scowled at him. "Of course. I learned that as a child, when my teachers gave me my first piece of quartz to use as an amplifier. I was watching you, though. You never used any sort of crystal or reagent. So how did you do it?"

"After what you just saw, you have to ask?" Alaric tried to keep the scorn from his voice. Judging by the look on the mage's face, he'd failed. "Dragons are the embodiment of magic. We are the people of the dragon. We have never needed the aids the rest of you rely so heavily on."

Not yet, anyway, but he kept that thought to himself. James seemed unconvinced, though he at least stopped asking questions. Alaric stayed between the soldiers until they scattered, each group going a different direction to do as he'd so strongly suggested. Only once they were settling down did he let himself relax. It was an effort to hold back a sigh when he turned and found himself alone with their captive.

Zex was watching him intently and Alaric had a feeling the man was reassessing him. Most likely he, like many others, had assumed Alaric held his position as adviser to the ruler of Sarkhyr simply because they were cousins. It had never crossed the man's mind that Alaric could be powerful in his own right.

"My advice applies to you, as well," he said, his voice cold as winter snow. "Those manacles are more than strong enough to keep you in your human form and block you from your magic. If I were you, I would take this time to rest and savor your last days of freedom."

Unsurprisingly, Zex rolled his eyes at the suggestion. He shifted, but only to settle cross-legged on the ground and rest his elbows on his knees, his bound hands brushing the grass. Seeing as the three soldiers had wisely decided to give him space, Alaric found himself in the unfortunate position of being the only one left to guard the renegade prince. While the man was bound, there was nothing stopping him from trying to flee on foot. Setting any sort of ward seemed pointless when Kaelas could return any moment.

Resigning himself to keeping watch, Alaric lowered himself down to sit across from Zex. Given that he'd ordered the soldiers away, he had no one to blame but himself. Still, he certainly wasn't enjoying it. He kept an eye on the two groups of soldiers, as well, making sure their temporary ceasefire continued.

Alaric couldn't help but be impressed when Zex stayed silent for nearly five minutes before he started making muffled noises of protest. He ignored him at first, only relenting when he'd made it clear that he didn't answer to Zex.

"I assume you want me to remove your gag?" he asked dryly. "Why would I, when the silence has proven so peaceful?"

Zex scoffed and pointed to the Sarkhyrian soldiers, who were making a quick, hot meal while they had the chance. His meaning was fairly clear.

"We will not be starving you. I'll remove the gag when it is time to eat."

That earned him a scowl, and he tried to smother the tingle of satisfaction it gave him to needle the man. Alaric knew that his patience was his best virtue, and it served him daily when dealing with finicky chancellors and his cousin's temper. He had to be careful of every word he said, mind every flicker of expression that crossed his face. In the tense political landscape in Yrasea, it was impossible to simply say what was on his mind. Here in the wilderness, though, with only Zex to hear him, he didn't have to watch every word so carefully. It was strangely liberating.

The peace only lasted until Chrysaris brought over a bowl of thick, spicy stew for him. The guard was mindful to keep his distance from Zex, even though the man was still lounging in the grass at his ease.

"Thank you. If there is any left, could I trouble you for another bowl?" He kept his tone light but firm, walking the line between a request and an order.

"For him?" Chrysaris asked, jerking his head toward Zex but refusing to look at him. "He thinks he can get whatever he wants since he used to be a prince?"

Alaric straightened, narrowing his eyes at the guard. "He is under our care until we return to Yrasea and he is handed over to the courts. We do not abuse prisoners, as you well know. I don't want to order you to do as your training dictates, but I will if necessary."

Chrysaris at least had the decency to look abashed. "I'll send Ereyan over with more," he muttered as he walked away. He didn't meet Alaric's eyes as he went.

Propriety dictated he make sure a guest was fed before he ate his own food. It was a rule he followed strictly when he was dealing with those who lived and worked in the castle at Yrasea. Zex, however, was not a guest, which meant Alaric wasn't bound by the rules of polite society.

Still... he could almost feel the man's eyes on him as he stirred the stew. He had no cause to treat him with anything but scorn after everything he'd done. Unfortunately, he couldn't very well chide the guards on how to treat a prisoner, then refuse to do the same.

Sighing, he put his bowl down and rose to his knees, putting him closer to Zex.

"Watch your tongue, or this will go back on and you can spend the day's ride without food," he warned, leaning over and untying the gag. He wanted to toss it on the ground, but settled for draping the damp cloth across Zex's knee instead. The other man worked his jaw open and shut as though it ached, which was complete nonsense.

"I'd look rather foolish if I tried to watch my own tongue."

"Of course the first words out of your mouth would be sarcasm," Alaric muttered. Only an hour in Zex's company and he already knew everything he needed to about what kind of man he was. Suffice it to say, he wasn't impressed.

"Would you prefer flirting to sarcasm?" Zex was smirking again and something about it made Alaric want to slap him.

He shuddered. "Absolutely not. Try that and I'll make sure this gag is permanent until we return to Yrasea. Now be quiet and eat." He all but shoved the bowl into Zex's bound hands, distracting him from whatever biting comment he wanted to make.

"It's going to be difficult to manage a spoon with my hands like this, you know."

"I know," Alaric assured him. "I just don't care. Drink it like soup, if you must. I'm not unbinding you for any reason."

"What if we were being attacked and you and I were the only ones left? You wouldn't unbind me to protect you?"

"If we were being attacked and I released you, you'd be long gone before the dust settled," he scoffed, voice heavy with disdain. "Besides, I wouldn't need you. I can protect myself just fine."

"You certainly can, can't you?" Zex hummed, his eyes assessing as he studied Alaric. "That was quite an impressive display of magic for one so young."

"I didn't remove that gag so we could sit here and gossip. Eat while you can, or it goes back on." He bristled at the mention of his age.

"I would think someone with so much latent power lurking inside them would want to brag about it. It's rare to see such control from an inexperienced mage."

"I'm not a child!" Alaric snapped, the words breaking free before he could control them. He immediately pressed his lips together, forcing himself to count out a slow breath to rein in the flare of anger. The way Zex's smirk grew said the man had gotten the reaction he'd been seeking, though, which did nothing to quell his frustration.

"I never said you were," was all Zex said before taking a slow sip of the stew. He never broke eye contact, and Alaric refused to be the first to look away, leaving them stuck in a stalemate while the unease grew between them.

In the end, Ereyan saved him from further embarrassment. The young soldier came over with a bowl in hand, but he kept a wary eye on Zex and gave him a wide berth as he approached.

"Chrysaris said I should bring this over?"

Alaric looked away, ignoring the satisfied little laugh from Zex. "Yes, thank you, Ereyan," he said warmly, taking the bowl and giving him a faint, reassuring smile. Ereyan was the youngest of Kaelas' guards, still barely out of training, but his magic was strong enough that they'd chosen him to come along. His inexperience was showing now, though, in the wide-eyed way he was watching Zex. It was clear the fallen prince made him nervous.

"How is your uncle?" he asked, waiting in silence until Ereyan tore his eyes away from Zex and focused on him before continuing. "He is recovering from his injuries?"

"Uncle Grayan? He's healing, yes." Ereyan chuckled. "I think being stuck guarding the doors and unable to train is pushing him to recover faster. He hates being stuck in one place."

"I'm sure he'll be back to fighting form in no time," Alaric assured him, giving him another gentle smile. "I won't keep you from your own meal. Thank you for bringing this."

"O-of course. It was my pleasure," the young soldier stammered, his cheeks flushing, making his freckles stand out. He started to bow, as one would for Prince Kaelas or a chancellor, realized what he was doing and caught himself before finishing the move, then finally just spun on his heel and hurried back to join Halbrig and Chrysaris.

"Quite the reaction." Zex's voice cut through the silence Ereyan had left in his wake. Alaric took a slow breath to fortify himself before turning his attention back to him.

"I don't know what you're talking about. Be quiet and eat."

His order had no effect on Zex, not that he was particularly surprised. "Really? I'd say it's quite obvious that your little friend is smitten with you. It's quite adorable, really."

Alaric poured every bit of derision that statement deserved into the look he leveled at the other man. "If you are going to waste time with such ridiculous comments, then I assume that means you are finished eating and I can replace the gag?"

"You're almost as prickly as my friend Theodric," Zex sighed, but a smirk quickly replaced the false melancholy. "Speaking of..."

He trailed off and Alaric turned, following Zex's gaze to see Ishaan leading Theodric out of the trees and back to the Nevarrean group. Neither of them spared even a glance toward Zex, though it was obvious from the tension in their bodies that they were very aware of him. He didn't know Ishaan very well and Theodric not at all, but he could easily imagine what could have happened to the soldier while they'd been searching for him.

"If you attempt to speak to either of them on the return trip, or even go near them, I will personally ensure that you are kept silent and immobile until the moment you are finally thrown into a prison cell."

"But-"

"No." Alaric cut him off before he could make another droll comment. "This isn't a warning or a threat. This is a promise. If you cross me, I will make you regret it. Stay away from them."

Zex was silent for several seconds, his cool silver eyes assessing as he studied Alaric. When he spoke again, the sarcastic drawl was gone and there was a weight to his words that hadn't been present before. "I think I'm not the only one who underestimated you. Kaelas has no idea who he has on his side, does he?"

It was an effort to keep his surprise off his face at Zex's words. In part, he hadn't been expecting anything but more sarcasm and innuendo from him. However, a large part of his surprise was that this man, this traitor prince, was perhaps the first person to not only admit he'd underestimated Alaric, but to acknowledge that there was so much more to him than the front he put on.

It was disconcerting and the very last thing he needed in his life. Zex may be oddly observant, but he'd still kidnapped and tortured a man. People were dead because of him. He would not let a few words cloud his judgment of him.

"I assume you're finished, then." His voice was cold and free of emotion when he reached to take Zex's bowl from him. The man scowled and pulled it back out of Alaric's reach, the heavy manacles rattling together.

"Why is everyone I meet so hostile?" he muttered. He finally fell silent after that, at least, which gave Alaric the time he needed to clear his head and focus on the task at hand. He still needed to calm his cousin down once he returned and ensure that the entire group made it down out of the mountains in one piece, including the injured Nevarrean soldier and their prisoner. Given that there was a very clear divide between his people and the soldiers, it would be easier said than done. The only uniting factor at the moment seemed to be a mutual hatred of Zex.

This was going to be a very long ride.

CHAPTER 13

The following five days were some of the most miserable of Ishaan's life. Nothing could compare to the hours on horseback when he'd still been recovering from his burns, but at least that had been something tangible he could blame his discomfort on. Now, he couldn't put his finger on exactly what it was, but everything felt *wrong*.

Once Prince Kaelas had returned after storming off, they had set out immediately for the return trip to Yrasea. They'd found the horses Zex and Theo had been traveling on and put Zex on one of them, but Theo had steadfastly refused to ride the other. Captain Trieste had thankfully had the forethought to bring a mount from the stables at Sarkhyr for the tracker, though Ishaan secretly wouldn't have minded sharing a saddle with Theo again.

It wasn't just... whatever was happening between the two of them. His emotions were a tangled mess when it came to Theodric Rhoan, and he didn't have the time to sort through them. He had bigger worries at the moment and no idea how to remedy either of the major issues plaguing him, the first of which was the voice inside his head.

Ever since the moment in the clearing when the princes had disappeared and two dragons had taken their place, the thing that was *other* inside him refused to be locked away again. He could feel it inside him, could feel the way it reached for them. It hadn't taken long to realize that, while the pull towards both of them was strong, it was noticeably stronger whenever Zex came into view. He didn't know what to do with that knowledge and he hadn't told a single soul, not even Theo.

Not that he would have even if he'd wanted to, though. Even more than the foreign presence within him, his biggest concern was Theo. He'd been worryingly quiet since they'd rejoined the team. He'd avoided questions from the others and claimed he was too tired for conversation. Captain Trieste had stopped short of ordering Theo to tell him what was wrong, but Ishaan was beginning to think that's what it would take. He was the only one Theo spoke to at any length, and even that was minimal. The man had withdrawn into himself, riding his horse beside Ishaan and keeping a slight distance between himself and his team.

The effect on them was palpable. Trieste couldn't hide his concern. Naema was visibly tense and worried, while Irric silently watched over all of them. The worst was James, though. The mage wrapped his hurt around him like a blanket, visible to anyone who looked at him. Theo rebuffed every attempt at conversation, or kept it so short that he may as well have ignored James.

Things were no better on the Sarkhyrian side. Prince Kaelas was a fuse just waiting to be lit. The dark cloud of his anger and hate for Zex hung over the group. The three guards rode in miserable silence, all of them seemingly afraid to be the one to set him off. Alaric was his usual stoic self, but Ishaan noticed that he put himself between Kaelas and Zex whenever he could, using himself as a buffer to his cousin's fury.

All in all, it was a miserable trip. They were moving faster this time, at least, as they weren't having to follow a vague pull and could return down the trail they'd made on the way up. There was none of the banter and camaraderie he'd come to expect from the reconnaissance team, though.

He'd hoped having Theo back, alive and safe, would lift everyone's spirits, but his continued silence dragged them all down.

Now they were less than a day's ride to Yrasea and everyone was ready for this nightmare to be over. Ishaan wasn't the only one who'd wanted to push through the night and arrive back as quickly as possible, but Captain Trieste had put his foot down.

"I've trained all of you better than that," he'd snapped when James had dared to protest. "You know the signs of bad weather. If we're lucky, we're going to get storms, but given how our luck has been going lately, it's cold enough to freeze and we're about to get snow. I have no intention of carrying you down the mountain when your stubbornness leaves you with broken bones."

Alaric had sided with the captain when Prince Kaelas started to argue. Ishaan wasn't sure who was more surprised: Kaelas or Trieste. But the surprising agreement was the spark to a hesitant truce between the two groups.

"Set up your shelters with the entrance facing east," Halbrig advised, possibly the first time she'd spoken anything but Sarkhyrian around them. "It will keep snow from blocking you in."

Irric offered to make food for everyone, and the young soldier, who said his name was Ereyan, volunteered to help.

"Everyone else, get your shelter set up and your horses taken care of," Trieste ordered.

"Will you share with me again tonight?" Theo asked, voice low, though he already knew the answer. Since they'd gotten him back, Theo and Ishaan had been sharing a tent. James now shared with Irric, leaving Naema and the captain together.

Ishaan nodded, avoiding James' piercing look. He didn't know how to fix things between the two friends when he didn't even know for sure what was wrong. After his breakdown in the clearing, Theo refused to talk about what had happened to him or how he was feeling. He'd shown interest in the new signs Ishaan had developed and they spent the evenings mastering those and coming up with new ones. It was the only thing that felt close to normal anymore.

True to Captain Trieste's prediction, snow started falling as they were finishing supper. Ishaan felt a whisper-soft kiss of ice brush his cheek and looked up to see tiny flakes of sparkling white swirling down toward them. He smiled faintly, tilting his head back and letting the flakes land on his face, melting away the moment they touched his skin. He'd seen snow before, of course, but only what fell through the thick canopy of the Morehan Forest. There was something about the dance of snow across the sky, filtered through the moonlight, that was hauntingly beautiful.

Theo had to urge him into the tent when they were done cleaning the dishes, and even then, he only went because he was getting cold.

"I hope it doesn't last. I don't want to spend a second longer in these mountains than we have to," Theo muttered as they got settled. Ishaan took his boots off, but otherwise stayed dressed as he was. It was warm and cozy in the spelled tent, but he was more concerned about something going wrong. Having Zex in the camp with them had put everyone on alert, even though the heavy manacles on his wrists never came off. Alaric had assured them all that the metal prevented Zex from using magic or shifting forms, and it seemed to be working, but then again... the man was a *dragon*. Ishaan wasn't sure what to believe anymore.

He settled on his bedroll across from Theo, already opening the notebook he'd retrieved. He'd learned never to leave it in his bag, instead carrying it in the pouch James had given him.

"The snow is pretty," he wrote, turning the page for him to see.

"Maybe, but it makes traveling difficult. I just want to get to Yrasea, drop off the lot of them, get our team, and go home to Nevarre," he sighed. Ishaan did a mental tally of the days they'd been on the road and realized there was a very good chance the missing members of the reconnaissance team would be waiting for them when they returned. Kellan had already been on the road when they left, and Lord Wyrenian had personally promised to retrieve Vesa and Kya from Esterdon.

"James or the captain might have an update on the team?" He was hesitant to show the words to Theo. It wasn't his place to attempt to fix the strained relationships between them all, but he felt like he had to try, anyway. James had helped him on the road and stood up for him when the captain wanted to leave him behind. He at least owed him this.

Theo saw right through it, of course, and shook his head. "I'll see them tomorrow."

"They're worried about you. They just want to know you're alright."

"They didn't seem so concerned when they left me, did they?" Theo's words carried a bitterness that Ishaan had never heard before, and the other man appeared to regret them immediately. "I don't want to talk about this anymore."

He reluctantly let it go, but even as they started reviewing the new signs they were working on, Theo's words wouldn't leave his mind. The very first night after they'd recovered Theo, Ishaan had written almost an entire page explaining why they'd gone to Yrasea instead of pursuing him. Theo said he knew orders were orders, and they had to obey the queen, so Ishaan had left it at that. He realized now that had been a mistake. Hopefully it wasn't too late to fix it, though he didn't know how to do so. All he could do was be there for Theo and hope it was enough.

The light from the campfire outside was dimming and the camp was quieting down at last when Theo heard footsteps crunching through the snow.

Beside him, Ishaan went still, his hands frozen and his head tilted slightly, listening.

"I'm coming in," a familiar voice announced just before the fabric that served as a door lifted and James appeared.

"We were getting ready to go to sleep," Theo said evenly, some of the tension draining away, but not all. Seeing James had never hurt like this. Every time he looked at his teammates now, relief and fury tangled together within him. He kept his silence because he knew he could never take back words said in anger.

"Then I'll make you a cup of coffee in the morning for keeping you awake," James shot back. "We need to deal with this. I can't take it anymore, Theo."

"I don't know what you're-"

"Don't! Just... don't. You know exactly what I'm talking about. I've known you for ten years, remember? I know when you're mad. I don't care what I need to do to fix this, but I'll do it. Do you need to yell and scream? Do you need to punch me? Whatever it is, just do it, because I can't handle my best friend treating me like I don't exist."

"I'm not going to punch you. And I'm not mad. I just want to go to sleep." Theo couldn't look James in the eye, but at least he was talking to him. Or at him. On the edge of his vision, he saw Ishaan edging away. He hoped it was to give them privacy, not out of fear.

"You're *furious* and lying to me won't change that," James hissed. "You think we abandoned you and you're angry. You have every right to be, too. I understand."

"No, you don't!" Theo pushed himself to his feet in the wake of his shouted words. His anger flared within him, finally burning through the last of his restraint.

"Theo..."

"No!" He interrupted James when the man tried to speak. "You don't understand. You can't possibly understand, James! He spent *hours* playing around inside of my mind with his magic, trying to find answers. You don't have any idea what it's like to have someone else looking at your memories, shifting them around and twisting them until you don't know what's real or not anymore. But I held on and fought back because I *knew* my team was coming for me. Even if the queen gave orders otherwise, I knew my best friend would come for me, no matter what."

James flinched back as though Theo really had struck him. His fair skin paled further and he took a step back, not that there was much room in the tent. "I wanted to," he managed, but all the fight had gone out of his voice.

"But you didn't, and I was stuck there with him. I thought I was going to die there and I didn't even understand why." His fury burned itself out as quickly as it'd come and he sighed heavily, just as tired and defeated as James. "I don't understand any of this. I wish we'd never taken on this cursed mission."

"I'm sorry, Theo. I didn't know what to do," James confessed, his voice thick with tears. "I wanted to come after you, but I didn't want to leave Ishaan behind."

That surprised him, and he finally looked up at his friend. "I thought the two of you didn't like each other? I would have thought you'd be happy to leave him behind."

"We came to an understanding. We both just wanted to find you. And I knew you'd never forgive me if I'd left to come after you and he'd gotten hurt."

It was true, much as Theo didn't want to admit it. Since the moment they'd met, Ishaan's safety had become Theo's highest priority. He looked over to where Ishaan sat against the wall and Ishaan frowned, reaching for the journal.

"James looked out for me and made sure the captain didn't leave me behind," he wrote. "But I'm not weak. You two don't have to look after me."

"I don't think you're weak," Theo promised, looking up from the words. "You wouldn't be standing here today if you were."

"No, definitely not weak," James agreed. Theo caught an odd note in his voice though, and the way he glanced at Ishaan was almost speculative, like he wasn't sure what he actually was instead. Before he could question James about it, though, the man turned his attention back to Theo. "You have every right to be angry. I just want to know how I can fix this. You've been my best friend since basic training and the only person who really knows me. I won't lose that."

Theo went quiet, but he didn't break eye contact with James. A heavy silence fell over the three of them, but Theo couldn't break it. Not yet. He had one chance to find the right words. If he wasn't careful, this would be the moment he lost his best friend. He could tell James was barely holding himself together as he waited for Theo to respond. It was so unlike the brash young prince he'd met in training.

"I hated you the first day we met."

James jerked, startled when Theo finally broke the silence, but he chuckled quietly. "I hated you, too. I thought you were competition."

"I thought you were a spoiled brat, just out for glory." A tiny smirk broke through and finally, he felt some of the tension ease. "I wasn't wrong."

"That's rude," James gasped. He was smiling, a shadow of his usual cocky grin, but there was a sheen of tears in his green eyes. "Good thing the captain knew better than we did and forced us to work together."

At the mention of Captain Trieste, Theo's tiny smile faded. "I always thought he had the answer to everything."

"He's not perfect, Theo. He's a soldier just like us and he has to follow orders, too."

"I know that. I do. But I can't change how I feel. I wish I could."

James reached for him and Theo hated himself for flinching at first. His shoulders were tense when James pulled him into a tight hug and it was several seconds before he let himself lean into it.

"I'm so fucking sorry, Theo," James whispered fiercely. "I should have stayed with you at Esterdon."

"There would have been a war if he'd taken you and you know it." Theo's shoulders slumped, his head dropping to rest on James' shoulder. "I knew what I was doing when I stayed to face them. I made that choice."

The realization dawned on Theo then. He *had* made that choice. He was angry at the captain and the team for leaving him to Zex's cruel ministrations, but he'd known it was a possibility when he'd turned back to face them. He'd expected to die there and it was a consequence he'd been willing to face if it gave his teammates enough time to get away.

He swallowed the lump in his throat and wrapped his arms around his best friend, hugging him tightly. He pretended not to hear the tiny sob that broke free before James could smother it, but he clutched him just a bit tighter.

Maybe this hadn't magically fixed everything. Anger and resentment still curdled within him, no matter how ashamed he felt of those feelings. His mind was still a mess, and they still had to deal with Zex and his soldiers. He didn't even want to think about the fact that the current prince of Sarkhyr and the traitor prince were both *dragons*. For now, standing here in the dark tent in the Darsheen Mountains with his best friend and a man who was possibly becoming something more, he let himself believe that everything would be okay.

Chapter 14

The graceful spires of Yrasea rising up to meet them had never been a more welcome sight.

Alaric breathed a sigh of relief as the castle finally came into view, its towers casting long shadows across the city as the sun began its descent. The snow had slowed them down, but with the mages at the head of the line to melt away the worst drifts, they hadn't lost as much time as he'd feared. Zex had helpfully reminded them he could have cleared the whole path at once, but he'd been promptly ignored. The threat of being gagged again seemed to work quite well.

To prevent any escape attempts, Alaric had ridden beside Zex the whole way down the mountain, with Halbrig and Ereyan on either side and Chrysaris behind him. Sharing a tent with the man had been the worst sort of torture, even with a guard beside him at all times. Even on the rare occasion Zex was silent, having to sit in a small space while those eerie eyes bored into him had left him on edge and eager for morning.

Once they were home safely, Kaelas owed him at least a week of leave for this.

A soft intake of breath beside him caught his attention, and he glanced over to see Zex sitting upright in his saddle, his gaze locked on the city. The pain on clear display in his silver eyes struck Alaric like a blow to the chest.

He realized then that Zex hadn't seen the city he'd once ruled in almost seven years. Not since the day he'd fled. He refused to feel any sort of pity for him, not after what he'd done to deserve it. But it was a surprising thing to see such naked emotion on the man's face instead of his usual sardonic smirk.

"Ereyan," Kaelas called, making the young soldier jerk to attention. It was the first time Kaelas had spoken since they'd left the campsite, aside from setting the mages to work clearing the path.

"Yes, your Majesty?" Ereyan managed not to stammer, but it seemed like a near thing.

"Ride ahead and apprise Hadiza of the situation. *Only* Hadiza," he stressed. "They'll know what to do."

Ereyan saluted and rode out, moving at a fast clip. Unlike higher up, the snow near the base of the mountains had already almost completely melted away, leaving the way clear.

"Ah, Hadiza is still in charge? Wise decision. They were the only one who could put up with you," Zex commented. He'd composed himself quickly and his smirk was back in place. It grew when Kaelas' jaw clenched, a sure sign of his irritation.

"Keep moving," was all he said, though, before picking up his pace to put himself in front of the group.

"Sir?" Halbrig turned to Alaric, clearly torn. He just shook his head.

"Ride with him, both of you. First and foremost, your duty is to protect him. I'll deal with the prisoner."

Then they were gone and he was once again alone with Zex. Well, aside from the Nevarreans, but they were keeping their distance. Their prince, though, the mage, was watching them and had been most of the ride. If all else failed, he was fairly sure he had at least one person of decent power who could back him up, even if the Nevarrean mages still relied on crystals and sigils.

"Finally, some peace and quiet."

Alaric slowly counted down from ten, reminding himself that patience and resolve were his strongest virtues. Only once he was feeling centered did he address the man riding beside him.

"If I were you, I would take this time to silently appreciate the open air. The windows in the cell you are going to are quite small, if I recall correctly."

Zex just laughed, as relaxed and carefree as a child on a silly adventure. It irritated him in ways he couldn't begin to understand. Someone who had done the things Zex had done should look and sound as evil as he was inside.

"Will you come visit me when I'm all alone in a prison cell? I find I quite enjoy your company, after all this time we've spent together."

Patience. Resolve. Another calming breath and he kept his eyes trained on the castle ahead when he spoke.

"The moment I walk away, I will never see you again, nor will I waste even a second thinking of you."

"Oh, really?" The man's voice was a dark purr, unexpected and unnerving. "That's a lie, Alaric. You're going to think about me quite often. There will be nights you lie awake, alone in your bed, and all you will think about is me."

The words, spoken in that low rumble, shocked him into silence. For once, he didn't have a quick comeback. No one had ever dared speak to him in such a way before, and he had no defense ready.

He knew Zex wanted a reaction, wanted him to turn and look, and he refused to give him that satisfaction. The longer the man was quiet, the harder it was to ignore him, though. Still, he refused to dignify Zex's dark whispers with a response.

His much-vaunted resolve cracked before they'd gone a mile.

Against his will, he glanced over at the man beside him, expecting a taunting smile or another rude comment.

The intensity in Zex's quicksilver eyes caught him off guard. The man was watching him intently, almost expectantly. When Alaric didn't immediately speak, Zex's lips quirked into a faint grin.

"Nothing to say? Or are you already thinking about it?"

His words were a dash of cold water to his shock. Alaric lifted his chin, removing all traces of emotion from his face as he stared Zex down. "Every word out of your mouth is a waste of the breath you took to speak them," he snapped. "I will gag you again and I will feel absolutely no guilt about it."

"I can think of something I-"

"Enough." Alaric cut him off before he could make any more lurid comments. "I assumed you'd wish to return to the city of your birth with what dignity a traitor can, but if you insist on making me muzzle you, I will."

Zex's smile dropped and he narrowed his eyes. "You don't have your little toy soldiers here to help you now. I promise you, it will not go well for you this time if you try."

"I may not have them, but I'm sure the Nevarreans would be more than happy to take their place. For five days, I've been the only thing standing between you and them. I imagine none of them would mind helping me put you in your place."

"And what is my place, exactly? Tell me, little mage."

"Your place is in a cell. For life. You're a traitor and a murderer. Imprisonment instead of execution is a kindness you don't deserve."

The words lingered between them in the silence, heavy and harsh. Zex studied him, his gaze making Alaric's skin crawl. When he finally spoke, his voice was utterly devoid of emotion.

"Maybe you're right. Everyone wanted Kaelas to kill me. Maybe this time, they'll succeed in convincing him."

An odd, sick sense of guilt settled in Alaric's stomach, but Zex was calm as could be as he settled in his saddle, eyes forward, bound hands resting on the saddle horn.

Alaric wasn't a fool. He knew 'execute' was just a nicer word for 'kill', but hearing it like that unsettled him. One word and Zex had slipped under his skin. While he may not exactly agree with execution, he knew some crimes were too great for any other punishment. The very worst traitors and murderers were executed. That was simply the way things were. But as horrible as Zex was, Alaric somewhat knew him now and the thought of Kaelas killing him just didn't feel right.

With that cloud hanging over them, neither one of them spoke another word all the way back to Yrasea.

Entering the city of Yrasea was a completely different experience than their first arrival. Ishaan rode on his own this time, for one. He still wasn't comfortable on a horse, but riding beside Theo helped. He could focus on the quiet soldier instead of the giant animal carrying him.

The biggest difference, though, was the people filling the streets of the city.

When they'd first come through, escorted by Alaric and his men, the city had been a ghost town. He'd been exhausted and lost in his own mind, but he hadn't missed how utterly deserted the place was. Now, people peered at them through windows and many were simply standing beside the road, staring.

Apparently, the Sarkhyrian guard who'd gone ahead couldn't keep a secret.

The few people Ishaan had met so far had been polite, but distant. Not unfriendly, but not going out of their way to speak to any of them. The crowd here was anything but. Their eyes were hard as they watched the procession, mostly varying degrees of fury when they spotted Zex. It was clear even to him that the people of Sarkhyr truly, deeply hated their former prince.

Zex, for his part, kept his head up and his eyes straight ahead. He didn't acknowledge the scowls directed at him or the smattering of harsh words thrown his way. Ishaan couldn't understand the words, but he knew the sharp tone of curses and insults.

"We're going to end up in the middle of a riot, if this keeps up," James muttered, barely audible over the seething crowd. He rode on Theo's other side, as he had since the two had made their tentative peace.

"Everyone stay close," Captain Trieste ordered. He slowed his horse enough to let the others catch up and the Nevarreans closed rank, with him and Theo in the middle. It cut them off slightly from the group ahead of them, but in this instance, it wasn't a bad thing.

Better them than us, Ishaan thought. It wasn't charitable, perhaps, but when it came down to it, he meant it. Everything that had happened, from the moment his parents had dragged him to the basement, right up to when Theo had been taken, could be blamed on the Sarkhyrians. He wasn't feeling particularly keen to help them in any way.

"Ishaan, if anything happens, I want you to stay close to one of us."

He pulled his attention away from the crowd and looked to find Theo watching him intently. It was the most focused he'd seen the tracker recently, telling him how serious Theo was.

Ishaan raised his open hand and tapped his index finger against his chin twice in the sign they'd come up with for 'I promise'. Anything was better than the endless nodding that made him look like a broken doll.

The soldiers kept a hand close to their weapons, but thankfully, it didn't turn out to be necessary. The presence of Prince Kaelas at the front of the line seemed to be enough to hold the people in check, at least for the moment. They made it safely to the entrance of the castle, where another crowd awaited them, along with more guards.

The person at the bottom of the steps was the first to move, bowing low.

"Prince Kaelas, I'm happy to see you have returned safely," they said in a strong, clear voice. Their eyes drifted to Zex and stayed there, studying the man. "It appears your mission was a success."

"Hadiza, it's good to see you," Zex drawled with a flash of his usual smirk. Ishaan felt Theo stiffen beside him when the man spoke and he reached over, lightly resting his hand on Theo's knee. He wasn't sure if he was crossing any boundaries, but a moment later, he felt a hand settle on top of his and squeeze.

"I wish I could say the same," Hadiza was saying, solemn now. "I had hoped that you would learn from your mistakes and stay out of trouble. I see now that some things never change."

"We can't all be as smart as you are, I guess. Although it's a surprise to find you still working for Kaelas, to be honest. I would have thought you'd be ruling this place by now, since you're the only capable person in this city since I left."

"That's enough," Prince Kaelas snapped, turning his mount and rounding on Zex. "This is not a homecoming. You are being remanded to the prison cells, where you will stay indefinitely."

Ishaan shared a startled look with Theo. This was news. He'd been under the impression that Zex was going to be executed. The stunned look in Theo's eyes said he'd thought the same.

"Your Majesty."

One of the women behind Hadiza stepped forward. Her clothing, threaded with silver and gold, marked her as someone important, but the way she looked down her nose at them told Ishaan everything he needed to know about her.

"Yes, Jaserra?" Kaelas reluctantly turned away from Zex to face the woman, who stepped around Hadiza to place herself before her prince.

"My deepest apologies for interrupting, but I feel it must be said. The one condition of former Prince Zex's imprisonment was that he remained in his cell for the rest of his days. Seeing as he escaped, instead, that puts him in violation of his sentencing, which we all agreed would result in his immediate execution. Considering the crimes he's guilty of, I don't see the need to waste the effort of warding a cell for him. I'm sure my fellow chancellors will agree. I don't wish to question you, of course," she tacked on belatedly, almost an afterthought.

Ishaan barely held back a snort. She was lying. Not about the first part, maybe, but the way she held herself, the faint gleam in her eyes, said she took great pleasure in questioning Prince Kaelas and his decisions in front of them.

"I am well aware of the terms of his punishment," Kaelas said coldly. Maybe he wasn't as big a fool as Ishaan had first assumed, if he was at least smart enough to realize she was testing him. "However, given the events that have occurred and the harm he's caused, it will take time to sort everything out. Until we know the extent of his plotting, we will hold him in prison. This is my final word on it."

Jaserra was an expert at the game and kept her face smooth as she bowed, barely more than a dip of her head. "Of course. My apologies again for interrupting." She stepped back to rejoin the group that Ishaan assumed must be the 'fellow chancellors' she had mentioned.

Prince Kaelas waited in silence until he was sure he would not be interrupted, then turned his attention back to Zex. "Nothing has changed. Once we've undone the damage you have caused, you will face the consequences of your actions."

"That doesn't give me much incentive to help you, now does it?"

The stares of everyone around them were likely the only thing that kept Prince Kaelas from dragging Zex out of his saddle. The way his hands clenched around his reins made it appear he wanted to throttle the man. Ishaan couldn't say he blamed him.

"We will deal with this inside," he growled, his golden eyes flashing with an unnatural fire that made the thing inside Ishaan want to curl up and hide. "Alaric, see that the Nevarreans are taken to their rooms. I will escort Zex to the prison." He turned back to Captain Trieste before continuing. "Once I have him secured, we will sit down together, alongside Lord Wyrenian."

"I'll apprise him of the situation," Trieste nodded stiffly. The crowd dissipated quickly when Kaelas, Zex, and their guards left. The chancellors were the last to leave and Ishaan didn't miss the lingering stares Jaserra was giving the two princes. Finally, though, she was gone, and they were left with Alaric and Hadiza. The two exchanged quiet murmurs, then Hadiza sketched a low bow and left, as well.

"I suppose a peaceful homecoming was too much to ask for," Alaric murmured, almost to himself, then turned to face them. "Please, allow me to escort you to your rooms."

"I'm starting to believe he's the only sane one in this country," James muttered to them as they followed Alaric through the maze of corridors that made up the Sarkhyrian palace.

"I'm certain you're right."

Ishaan couldn't help but note the way Theo's eyes darted everywhere as they walked, as though he were expecting an attack at any moment. Given what he'd been through, it was understandable. Ishaan, too, felt uncomfortable despite the luxury that surrounded them. The silver and gold dragons adorning the walls and ceiling no longer fascinated him. Instead, they felt almost threatening, now that he knew what he knew. The silver dragon in particular, the one that had caught his attention the most, now made him feel cold and sick inside, knowing it was the reason Theo had suffered and continued to suffer. The little ball of *other* inside his chest didn't agree, but Ishaan ignored it, shoving it down.

"Here we are." Alaric opened the double doors that led to the hallway they'd been using, though they'd only stayed the one night. "According to Hadiza, the missing members of your team have arrived safely. Lord Wyrenian and his apprentice are sharing a room to leave one for them. I assumed, hopefully correctly, that you would all want to remain near each other?"

"Yes, that's a correct assumption," Captain Trieste agreed quickly. Ishaan felt the energy of the group pick up immediately at the prospect of being reunited with the rest of their team.

Alaric stopped beside one door, standing slightly to the side of it. "Our healers have seen to them and they are doing well. Hadiza is having a meal prepared and once Prince Kaelas returns, your entire team is more than welcome to sit down with us. All of you deserve to know what is going on."

"Thank you, my lord," Trieste said, the words formal but short, betraying his eagerness to get into the room. He managed a quick bow before giving in to his impatience and hurrying into the room. The rest of the team was on his heels, not even glancing at the Sarkhyrian in their rush to get inside. Alaric seemed bemused, but also quietly accepting, as though he were used to being overlooked.

Something inside Ishaan's chest gave a little twist and this time, the feelings were his own. He knew too well what that felt like, to be in the background, overlooked and forgotten until needed.

Theo hurried into the room, his excitement lending him a bit of strength, but he paused when Ishaan stopped in front of Alaric. He waited until the man looked at him, a quiet curiosity in his gray-blue eyes.

Ishaan raised his right fist to his chest, just below his collarbone. He didn't want to simply mouth the words. He needed Alaric to understand how much he meant it.

"I'm afraid I don't..." He trailed off, apologetic but not pitying.

"It's the sign we made up for 'thank you'," Theo explained. Alaric glanced at him, eyes widening, then back to Ishaan, who nodded and made the sign again. Of all the Sarkhyrians they'd met so far, Alaric was the only one who seemed to actually care at all what happened to them.

"I'm glad I could be of service, in what way I could," Alaric said with an answering nod, but the corners of his mouth turned up into the smallest smile, barely perceptible. Something told him it wasn't often Alaric received genuine gratitude.

He could feel the tension in Theo, though, and knew how desperate he had to be to get back to the team, so he left it at that. He gave another nod, then allowed Theo to all but drag him into the room, leaving Alaric standing alone in the hallway as the door closed behind them.

Chapter 15

Theo's heart was racing as he all but dragged Ishaan into the room. His stomach clenched and his breath came in ragged pants. Irric must have heard them, because he stepped to the side and made space for them in the crowded room.

The first person he saw was Vesa. She was standing on her own, though Naema stood close by, ready to offer support. She was paler than usual, but already so much better than he'd last seen her. Kya was on her other side, whole and healthy, and he spotted Kellan a moment later talking to Captain Trieste.

Fear for his team had been his constant companion since the attack near Osirith. It was one thing to be told that Vesa was safe and alive, but the weight of fear he'd carried was so heavy that he nearly staggered when it disappeared. He slumped against Ishaan, his knees suddenly weak with relief. The movement caught Vesa's attention and she was moving before Theo could tell her not to.

"Theodric."

Her calm, soothing voice was something he'd desperately missed, and when she wrapped her arms around him in a hug, he didn't resist. Vesa wasn't one for overt displays like this, but it was like she knew he needed it.

"I'm glad you're safe," he whispered, his voice cracking. He was mindful of her injury, holding on as tight as he dared. Distantly, he was aware of Ishaan releasing him, and a moment later, another person had their arms around him.

"We were so worried about you!" Kya sounded near to tears as she held onto both of them. "Don't you ever do anything like that again!"

James, of course, had to chime in. "You know he won't agree to that. It's *Theo.*"

"Fine, but next time, I'll kick you in the knee."

Theo choked on a laugh and squeezed Kya as tight as he could. It was probably too much, but she didn't say a word of protest.

Having all of his team here, knowing they were safe, settled something inside Theo. An irrational part of him still clung to that edge of resentment that they'd left him. It had lessened after his conversation with James and Ishaan's reassurances, but he couldn't make it go away. Despite that, these people were his family. The eight of them had been together through the worst situations imaginable and had trusted their lives to each other. He needed them to be safe and whole.

He could have clung to them for hours, and he would have, but reality was creeping back in. Kya stepped back first. Vesa gave him another gentle squeeze, then she was gone, as well.

"Mages, ward the room," Captain Trieste said, breaking the silence. "We have a lot to talk about and I'd rather it stayed among us."

Kellen, James, and Kya were quick to set the sigils in the four corners of the room. A light touch on his arm got Theo's attention while they worked, and he glanced over at Ishaan. The other man nodded toward the table on the far side of the room, a questioning look on his face. As much as he wanted to prove to himself and the team that he was fine, he already felt the excitement burning off, leaving the fatigue that had plagued him all the way down the mountain.

With Ishaan's subtle assistance, they took two of the chairs at the table. Vesa and Naema perched on one bed with Karsa at their feet, while Irric took the other. There was no question that Kya would sit with him after she'd been away from her best friend for so long. The captain and lieutenant took up position by the door once the mages were done, leaving James to join them at the table. Once everyone settled, they turned their attention to their leaders.

"Before we get into anything serious, I just have to say how relieved I am to see all of you," Kellan said with that warm smile he was so known for. "The last few weeks have been some of the hardest we've ever faced, but I had complete confidence in all of you."

"At least someone did," Kya said under her breath. Kellan rolled his eyes and Irric nudged her in the side, but her comment eased some of the tension in the room. Even Captain Trieste seemed to relax a little when he took over from Kellan.

"I'll echo Lieutenant Sol and tell you all that I never doubted you. Even when Theo was taken and certain decisions had to be made, my belief never wavered. In that vein, I owe you an explanation." Trieste turned his full attention to Theo now. "No amount of explanation can make it better, but know that leaving your trail was not a simple decision. We are soldiers, however, and the queen's word is our law. She believed seeking help from the Sarkhyrian prince was the best option and she was right. As skilled as we are, we very well could have lost your trail in those mountains and if it had come down to a fight with Zex, we would have been no match for him."

"I understand. I do," Theo assured him, and he did. It just might take a while to fully convince himself and make that bitterness disappear.

"Speaking of him," James cut in, taking some of the attention off Theo, to his relief. "Are we going to discuss the fact that the prince of Sarkhyr is a *dragon?* And the man we've been hunting is not only also a dragon, but apparently used to be a prince of this country?"

There was a beat of silence. Predictably, it was Kya who spoke first.

"*What?*" She got to her feet, eyes wide. "How much did we miss? What happened in those mountains? And did you say he's a *dragon*?!"

"Sit down, Saleed," Trieste said firmly. Only once she obeyed did he continue. "To summarize what happened before you arrived: Prince Kaelas agreed to help us find Rhoan. When we finally found them, he apparently lost control and turned into a gold dragon. Zex then turned into a silver one and they fought. Kaelas was winning and I believe his only goal was to kill Zex. He may well have done so, but Ishaan ran into the middle of the fight for reasons I'm sure he'll be sharing shortly. The silver dragon protected him and in doing so, Kaelas overpowered him, ending the fight."

The table shook with the force of three rapid knocks, cutting Trieste off when he took a breath. Theo looked over at Ishaan, shocked by the sudden fear in the man's eyes. He'd gone pale, making the scars on his face stand out in stark relief.

"What is it?" Trieste asked shortly. He was not usually a man who tolerated being interrupted.

Ishaan's hands were shaking as he raised one vertically and rocked it back and forth twice in the sign for 'wait'. With the other, he dug out the journal Theo had given him and flipped to a clear page. He was fast, getting the words down in a messy scrawl, then shoving the journal toward James. Theo had already been reaching for it out of habit, and it shocked him how badly it stung when it went to James instead.

"I thought James protected me with a spell? It couldn't have been Zex. Why would he help me?"

James passed it back to Ishaan once he'd read it, then shook his head. "It wasn't me. Apparently, the Sarkhyrians can do magic without sigils and spells, but I can't. I couldn't get there in time. He grabbed you to keep Prince Kaelas from crushing you."

"But why?" Naema asked. "He's the enemy. Why would he try to protect one of us?"

"I wish I had an answer to that," Captain Trieste said. "It's another question I plan to ask this evening when we speak to Prince Kaelas and Alaric."

Theo kept quiet, stealing a quick glance at Ishaan. He was still pale, but the look in his silvery eyes wasn't the surprise that had been there a few moments ago. No, now there was a quiet, grim certainty that said he'd come to the same conclusion Theo was reaching. He had a feeling Captain Trieste was also thinking the same thing, if the way he changed the subject to this evening's meeting said anything.

Theo ignored him for possibly the first time in his entire military career, his mind racing as he watched Ishaan. Everything was starting to make sense now, but rather than ease his concern, the growing fear was threatening to choke him.

Somehow, Ishaan and Zex were connected.

If he was correct, almost everything Zex had done made sense, in a twisted sort of way. He hadn't been able to figure out why a man who'd fled justice would come down from the mountains and give himself away like he had. It didn't make sense... unless Zex had been looking for Ishaan. After seeing how quickly the two men had healed after their brutal fight as dragons, it explained how Ishaan was still alive. No one should have been able to survive the horrific injuries Ishaan had suffered in the fire. He'd not only survived, but had the strength to flee several miles before his body gave out. The way the burns had healed so much literally overnight and how he now looked as though the fire had been months ago, rather than weeks...

Ishaan may not be a dragon like Kaelas and Zex, but there was no doubt in Theo's mind that Ishaan's fate was closely tied to the two of them. Along with that realization came another that nearly made him sick just to think about.

If Ishaan was truly tied to the princes of Sarkhyr, there was almost nothing Theo could do to protect him.

CHAPTER 16

When summoned to supper, the entire team moved as a unit. Ishaan noted with concern how gingerly Vesa moved, but no one questioned her when she announced she was coming. He noticed that Naema stayed by her side, though, ready to support her if she needed. Only Karsa stayed behind, asleep on the floor beside Naema's bed. The dog had kept up with them all this time; she deserved a rest.

He wasn't looking forward to this. The uncomfortable truths that lay unspoken were dangerously close to coming to light, and he didn't think he was ready to face them. It'd been easy to ignore the things he didn't want to see when they were overshadowed by the hunt for Theo. Already he was exhausted just thinking about the evening to come. Then again, he felt exhausted most of the time anymore, so it was nothing new. His legs felt weighted as he walked beside Theo, and his muscles ached. Not the aches he was becoming familiar with after hard days of travel, but the kind he'd gotten as a child when he'd been ill. There had been no one then to comfort him and he knew there would be no one now, so he forced himself to push through. Maybe after everything was settled tonight, they'd finally be able to rest.

The soldier who had escorted them this far bowed and walked away, leaving the Nevarreans alone for a moment outside the doors.

"I'm sure I don't have to tell you all to watch yourselves tonight," Captain Trieste warned, looking at each one of them. "Be careful with your words. There's no need to give them any more information than they already have. If you have any doubts, silence is the best option." That seemed directed at Kya and James, in particular.

"What happens after tonight, sir?" Naema asked. "Are we going home? Do we have new orders from the queen?"

"We'll discuss everything once we know the full situation. For the moment, keep your eyes open and gather as much information as you can. This is what we do, soldiers. Don't let me down."

Lieutenant Sol pushed open the doors and together, they made their way into the same dining area they'd visited the night Kaelas agreed to help them find Theo. Ishaan was familiar with it, of course, but now it felt as though he was seeing it with fresh eyes. The double throne, the marble shot through with silver and gold, made sense now. Whereas the stunning stained glass window had left him in awe before, now it just left him cold. It was hard to see the beauty in the dragons' flight now that he knew their secrets.

"Please, have a seat," Alaric said, cutting through his thoughts. Surprisingly, only Prince Kaelas and Alaric awaited them. There weren't even any Sarkhyrian guards in the room.

Captain Trieste and Lieutenant Sol took the seats nearest the two men, allowing the team to spread out along the table. Ishaan found himself seated between Theo and James, with Kya across from him. Unlike the ones who had been here already, Kya was looking around with wide-eyed fascination.

"Will Lord Wyrenian be joining us?" Trieste asked once they were all settled.

Alaric glanced at Kaelas, then shook his head. "We hoped to keep as much information contained within this group as possible. We understand you will have to report back to Queen Isadore, of course, but I assume you see why we want to keep this quiet.”

“Do your own people know?” Lieutenant Sol asked. “About what they are?”

“One of 'them' is sitting at the table,” Prince Kaelas interjected, clearly annoyed. “I ask that you not speak of me like I am some animal.”

“I didn’t mean any offense, your Majesty.”

“And none was taken,” Alaric cut in, shooting a quick glance at Prince Kaelas. “Only those people that need to know have this information. The chancellors, of course, and a select few staff and soldiers. To most of the people of Sarkhyr, our princes being dragons is simply a legend.”

“In all that time, no one has given away that secret?” Trieste asked skeptically.

Alaric held up his hands. “I believe this is best told in order. Please, let’s eat first. I’m sure everyone is hungry after our travels.”

Ishaan didn’t want food nearly as much as he wanted answers, but Captain Trieste nodded, overriding any protests the others might have. Alaric went to the door and murmured something to whoever stood outside and, a few moments later, servers had the table filled with food. They were quiet as they worked and departed at a nod from their prince.

“Please, help yourselves,” Alaric urged, and the table fell silent as everyone filled their plates. The food was relatively simple, but hearty. Pots of thick, spicy stew, fresh breads, roasted vegetables, and grilled meat disappeared at an alarming rate as the soldiers ate. Most of them, anyway.

Ishaan gently nudged Theo under the table, drawing the man’s attention. When Theo looked at him, Ishaan nodded toward his plate, which held only a piece of flatbread and some vegetables. He knew Theo couldn’t have been eating well while with Zex, and on the ride back they mostly ate cold trail rations. The sight of Theo's untouched plate concerned him.

"I'm not very hungry right now," Theo murmured, leaning closer to Ishaan, likely to keep the others from hearing them. "I just want to get this over with and find out what's going on so we can go home."

Ishaan could understand wanting answers, of course, but he was also well aware that Theo needed to heal and get his strength back up. He raised his eyebrows expectantly, locking eyes with the stubborn soldier until Theo finally sighed and ladled some of the stew onto his plate.

"Satisfied?"

No, but it was a start, so Ishaan gave him a small smile and nodded. Perhaps that would be enough to whet Theo's appetite and go back for more. If not, Ishaan wasn't above nagging at him. After all the time Theo had spent taking care of him while he'd recovered from his burns, there was no way he wouldn't do the same in return.

The table was mostly silent as they ate. Kya struck up a quiet conversation with Irric at one point, but even that withered away as the tension in the room crept up. Ishaan pushed Theo until he finished everything on his plate, but when he tried urging him to get more, Theo just shook his head and pushed the plate away. It wasn't much, but it was enough for now. Once everything here was settled and plans were made, he was sure Theo would start to mend.

Prince Kaelas was the last to finish. Ishaan noticed the way everyone sat up straighter in their chairs when he put his spoon down. A nervous thrum built in his chest and he felt the *other* within him stir in response. Whispers of what it was, that strange thing within him, danced at the edge of his mind, taunting him. He ruthlessly shoved them back into the box of things he didn't let himself think about, locked away with the darkest memories of his childhood. Tonight was about getting answers. Everything else could wait.

"I hope you don't mind if I ward the room for privacy before we begin?"

Alaric's voice cut through the thick silence. Beside him, Theo flinched at the sudden sound. It was nearly imperceptible, but enough to raise Ishaan's concerns even more. The sooner they got Theo out of Sarkhyr, the better.

"My mages can assist you," Captain Trieste offered, but Alaric shook his head.

"There is no need, but thank you for your kind offer." He went quiet, his eyes oddly unfocused as he looked around the room. A moment later, the walls shimmered with the faintest hint of blue light, lingering a moment before fading away. "It is done."

"But you didn't set any sigils?" Kya looked stunned, half-standing as if she intended to go examine the walls for herself.

"Sarkhyrian magic is a bit different than what you've seen before. We have no need for spells and symbols and crystals," he explained in a far kinder tone than he'd used when James had asked a similar question. Ishaan was starting to think of this as Alaric's 'ambassador' side. He found himself wondering just how many different masks the quiet man wore.

"A conversation for another time, perhaps?" Lieutenant Sol suggested when Kya looked ready to launch into a slew of questions. The young mage reluctantly agreed, sitting back down, but Ishaan didn't miss the way her eyes lingered on the walls.

"I confess, I'm not quite sure where to begin." Alaric glanced over at his cousin as he spoke, but Prince Kaelas remained silent. It seemed he wouldn't be the one answering their questions this evening. Given what little he knew of the man, Ishaan couldn't say he was surprised.

"You could start by explaining to all of us exactly who Zex is and how we came to be in this situation," Trieste said, and the edge to his voice suggested that he was running out of patience.

"That will require learning a bit of the history of my country. I ask that you bear with me and allow me to tell it before asking many questions."

Only once everyone had agreed did Alaric speak again. He didn't bother to consult with his cousin this time, since Kaelas showed no signs of breaking his stubborn silence any time soon. He simply leaned back in his chair with his arms crossed over his chest, golden eyes staring straight ahead as Alaric began.

"Traditionally, Sarkhyr has always been governed by two rulers, each imbued with the power of the dragons. The dragons themselves choose their successors, usually while they're still children. They imbue the child with a portion of their power, usually less than half. It's done to prepare the child and let them grow accustomed to the power within them. Upon reaching adulthood, the dragons complete the transfer and the new rulers inherit the full power of the dragon. The time between is spent teaching the children to rule as a unit and create a bond between them."

"They're pair-bonded?" James asked, earning a sharp look from the captain for interrupting. Alaric glanced at the mage and nodded.

"Yes, in a unique way. The two aren't born bonded, but they're together from the moment they are chosen to allow the bond to grow."

"What's the criteria?" Lieutenant Sol asked. "Why do the dragons choose who they do?"

Alaric shook his head. "We're not entirely sure. They tend to choose their successors around the same time, usually no more than a month or two apart. There doesn't seem to be any sort of pattern. Several generations back, the daughter of a duchess and a boy found living beneath an old bridge ruled side by side. Each new ruler's powers and strengths and weaknesses differ from the one before them."

"Which isn't always a good thing," Kaelas muttered, the first time he'd spoken all evening. Alaric turned to him, but the prince had nothing else to add, it seemed. Ishaan wished Kaelas would simply leave and allow Alaric to handle this.

"It has its flaws, like every system," he conceded when it became apparent Kaelas wasn't going to continue. "And, like everything, there is always room for corruption to grow, but for the most part, it's a tradition that has kept us alive and thriving for most of our history."

"Most of your history?" Captain Trieste repeated.

Alaric sighed quietly. "Yes. As I said, no system is perfect. Several hundred years ago, our mages began to see a decline in their magic. It was only a slight change, but enough that they made note of it. As the years passed, the decline continued."

"That's around the time that the ability began to weaken for everyone, isn't it?" James interrupted. The captain made a move to silence him, but Alaric was already nodding.

"Yes. Before any of this happened, spells and reagents were only needed for magic of extreme complexity, or to bolster weaker mages. What I said in the mountains was true: dragons are beings of magic. Our legends say they gifted humans with the ability to use their magic, which makes our power bound to them. When their power began to decline, so too did the power of the human mages."

"What caused the decline, though, if the dragons clearly still remain?"

"Unfortunately, the prince and princess in power at that time were infamous for their rivalry. They were the first in our history to have a pair-bond that was weak and fragile. That weakness affected everything, including magic. The chancellors at the time urged them to push the dragons to choose their successors early, in hopes it would restore balance to our people."

Ishaan was watching Kaelas through this, rather than Alaric, and he caught the way the prince's eyes snapped to his cousin at the mention of the old rulers' rivalry. Something akin to pain was written on his face, his eyes burning with a sadness so profound it made his chest ache. It only lasted a moment, there and gone again in a matter of seconds, but Ishaan knew what he'd seen. It seemed the betrayals that had ripped Zex and Kaelas apart still had a tight grip on the prince.

"Can something like that be forced, though?" Kya asked. She appeared enthralled, like she'd forgotten this wasn't just a story.

"There is a way, but not only is it a closely guarded secret, it's also difficult and doing it risks angering two creatures older than we can imagine," Alaric said. "However, in this case, it worked. The dragons chose two young girls as their successors. Given the situation, the girls received their full power all at once, to avoid keeping the former rulers on the throne any longer."

"I'll bet this ends well," James muttered under his breath, so quietly Ishaan barely heard him. He agreed, though. Even without seeing firsthand the results of Sarkhyr's history, it sounded like a disaster in the making.

"The two princesses were raised together, but with the mages and chancellors taking the place of the old rulers. The magic stabilized and it seemed to be working, but it turned out to be a temporary solution. Their bond never grew as strong as the rulers of old, and once again, the mages saw their powers weaken. Even when the next rulers were chosen and raised the traditional way, taught by the two princesses, the power continued to decline. They could not overcome the weakness that the old rulers had introduced. It was decided then that Sarkhyr would close our borders until the problem was dealt with."

"It was a way to protect the people?" Lieutenant Sol asked. "If I recall my history correctly, a hundred years ago the entire continent was on the verge of war. The Gavarrian king was threatening invasion, Nevarre and Vaetreas were at odds, and the Canjiri were raiding everyone."

"Correct. The strength of our mages has always been the best defense for Sarkhyr and, with their power weakening, it was decided that we would be best served by removing ourselves from the growing tension. There were hopes that the next generation would bring more stability, but the cycle of weakness simply began again. When it came time for them to step down, there was little hope left that their successors could save us. But they surprised everyone. When Kaelas and Zex were placed together for the first time, their bond fell into place so easily that it seemed impossible. Never in the history of Sarkhyr have two rulers connected so quickly and seamlessly. Even as small children, their power surpassed all of their predecessors."

Chair legs scraping over stone pulled everyone out of Alaric's story. Kaelas had shoved his chair back and now stood a dozen feet away, his back to the group, facing the double throne of Sarkhyr. His shoulders were tight, his hands fisted at his sides.

"Kaelas?" Alaric stood and took a step toward his cousin, but stopped himself. "Do you need to step out?"

The man shuddered, and when he spoke, there was an inhuman rumble to his words. "No. Just get it over with."

Ishaan felt a hand on his leg and stole a quick look over at Theo. On the surface, he seemed calm and steady as always. The truth was in his eyes, though. The first thing Ishaan could recall seeing after the fire was the warm blue of Theo's eyes. Now they'd dulled, the warmth replaced with a pain and weariness that broke Ishaan's heart to see. Worse, though, was the fear. He would give everything and anything in his power to take that away, but all he could do was lay his hand over Theo's, twining their fingers together.

There was a long hesitation before Alaric finally spoke again. Kaelas stayed near the throne, but it was clear in the tense lines of his body that he was listening.

"As I said, Kaelas and Zex were like nothing we'd seen in recent history. They were in balance in a way everyone had started to believe was impossible. The two of them together were a perfect balance of magic and strength. Finally, the magic started to stabilize and even to grow. I imagine mages everywhere noticed that spells came easier and there were probably several years of sudden innovation?"

Lieutenant Sol nodded. "The last twenty years have seen more new spellwork than the last hundred, and I've noticed the newer generations of mages seem stronger than before." He directed that at Kya and James.

"Unfortunately, those changes will cease, if they haven't already," Alaric said softly. "Because the bond between the two princes was so strong, the consequences of breaking it were equally strong. When Zex betrayed our kingdom, he was also betraying Kaelas. The dragons had not been considering a successor yet and with the ravages of a plague sweeping through the country, there were precious few children being born. In their desire to ease the fears of our people, the chancellors called for Zex to be executed. However, without a successor, the silver dragon would die with him, which is why Kaelas insisted he be spared. Having him nearby would allow the bond to remain intact."

"What happened when Zex fled, though? Wouldn't the bond have broken?" Lieutenant Sol asked, his eyes now on Prince Kaelas. "I've studied pair-bonding. It was always theoretical for us, but every book I read says that the breaking of such a bond always ends in the pair either dying or losing their minds from the pain. Why isn't Prince Kaelas as affected as Zex seems to be?"

"That is one question I don't have an answer to, I'm afraid. With Zex here now, we will have to deal with him swiftly, before the situation can worsen."

"You're going to force the dragon to pass its power on?" Theo's voice was even when he spoke, but his grip on Ishaan's hand was painfully tight. "Or what's left of it, anyway?"

No.

The whispers that had been taunting Ishaan were straining the edges of the box in his mind, fighting to break free. He shook his head, pulling at Theo's hand, silently begging him to take his question back, but it was too late.

"What do you mean, Theodric?" Vesa asked, her voice unusually sharp. Theo had their attention now and Ishaan grabbed the man's forearm with his free hand, digging his fingers in, pleading with him. The box in his mind was breaking down and the thing that wasn't him was unfurling within him, as if sensing what was going on.

In the end, though, it wasn't Theo who tore Ishaan's world down. It was Prince Kaelas.

"He means that Zex has already begun the process of passing his power," the man spat, finally turning to face them. His gold eyes flickered with the inhuman fury of the dragon inside him as he prowled closer. "The only reason our fight ended so quickly is because half his power is already gone, forcibly passed over and hidden inside his successor." He leaned on the table, every ounce of his focus burning into Ishaan. "Inside of *you*."

CHAPTER 17

*A*round him, the manor burns. The fire is unnaturally hot, chewing *through metal and stone as quickly as wood. Dhanara is gone, even her bones burned away to nothingness by the molten rock. Doran is on his knees, his screams rasping and weak as smoke envelops him. His bond with his twin shatters and the agony of it is written on his tear-streaked face. The molten stone oozes toward him, but he makes no move to escape, waiting to rejoin his sister.*

Where his parents are, Ishaan doesn't know. They have the power to protect themselves. He knows they do. He has to run, to escape, but he's so tired. *He wants to stop, to let the flames take him, too, if only to make the pain end. His throat is raw, burning with every scorching breath he takes. He makes it to the front door, but his bloody fingers fumble the latch.*

This is it, *he thinks, sinking to his knees. He can feel the fire growing and growing behind him, devouring everything.* Maybe it's better this way.

His body jerks and he staggers back to his feet, but he didn't make the choice to move. His limbs are stiff, as though something is controlling him.

If you can't do this, I will.

The voice is familiar, the same one that spoke in his mind before the manacles on his wrists melted away. Something is inside of him, controlling him when all he wants to do is give up. He's tired. He's so tired.

He closes his eyes, ready for whatever fate has planned for him, but it's not to be.

The next time he opens his eyes, he's stumbling through the forest. It's dark. He doesn't know where he is, but the flicker of flames is no longer visible, and that's what matters.

Everything hurts. Every step he takes is excruciating. Breaths like razor blades eviscerate his throat.

Run or they'll find you. They'll take you back. They'll know it worked.

Fear of his parents, instilled in him from the day they realized he has no magic of his own, gets him moving again. Whatever this spell is, whatever this voice inside him is... if they know, he'll never be free of them. They'll take him apart piece by piece, studying him and the thing inside of him. Because whatever this voice is, it isn't him. It's something other. *Something that came from the strange artifact, the stone egg on the other table.*

The stone egg that looks like the one in Kaelas' book. Kaelas, who is both a prince and a golden dragon. Kaelas, who says part of the power of the silver dragon, of Zex, is now inside of him.

Yes. Yes, Zex! He is home, he is ours, he will help us! He is home home home home-

"Ishaan!"

Fingers dug into his shoulders in a tight grip, giving him something to focus on as Ishaan desperately tried to come back to the present. He felt the strange presence within him even stronger now, as though by acknowledging it, he gave it more power. Gave the *dragon* more power. Because somehow, he knew Kaelas was right. He could *feel* it.

"Ishaan, I need you to focus."

He closed his eyes, a deep shudder running through his body as he fought to latch onto that voice. Blindly reaching up, he gripped the man's wrists, and some of the panic receded.

Theo.

"I need you to give us some space," he heard Theo say, followed by the sound of scuffling feet. He felt the other man lean in a little closer, his voice a whisper just for the two of them when he spoke. "It's alright. You remember how to match my breathing, right?"

He managed to nod and felt Theo's hand move in his grip until it was reversed, with Theo holding Ishaan's wrist. He brought it to his chest, letting Ishaan's palm rest there, just over his heart. It was beating faster than normal, but his breathing was slow and steady.

It was startlingly easy to remember what to do. The nights they'd spent on the trail flashed through his mind. The nights he'd been injured still, sharing Theo's tent as they left the forest he'd grown up in. The nightmares came for him every time he closed his eyes, it seemed, but Theo was always there to talk him through it.

Slowly, his breathing steadied, and the memories lost their grip on him. They shrank back into the darkness, folding into the box buried deep in his mind.

As the fear eased, shame quickly rose to fill the gaps left behind.

Theo was captured, tortured, but he still has to comfort you because you're too much of a coward to face the truth, the spiteful little voice in his mind whispered. Unlike the voice he now knew was that of a dragon, this one was entirely his own. It had been his constant companion all his life and, unfortunately, it was usually right.

Ishaan drew another shuddering breath before finally opening his eyes. The first and only thing he saw was Theo, so close their heads were nearly touching. The concern in his eyes nearly broke him, but at least he didn't see pity there.

"Are you alright?" Theo asked softly, then shook his head. "Stupid question. None of us are. But are you with me?"

Always.

He nodded, his hand resting over the steady beat of Theo's heart as his breathing finally slowed and the panic faded away to nothingness.

"We don't have to stay. We can go back to the rooms right now and deal with this later."

Everything in him wanted to take Theo's offer. Exhaustion gnawed at his marrow, and all he wanted to do was go to bed and pretend none of this had ever happened. At any other time, he would have done exactly that, too. But now... now it was different. He had someone on his side for the first time in his entire life. Someone who was worth putting in the effort for.

Still, his stomach clenched when he shook his head. For once, he didn't want to be a coward. He didn't want to run away from his problems and hope to avoid them until they went away.

"If you're sure." Theo's free hand came up, hesitating only a moment before coming to rest lightly on his scarred cheek. "I'll be right beside you. All of us will. We'll figure this out as a team, alright?"

The touch was a soft, glowing warmth he'd never expected. It melted the edges of the ice he'd encased himself in for so long, but instead of fear, all he felt was a bone-deep relief.

They allowed themselves a few more moments of peace, but finally, Ishaan leaned away. Theo didn't release his hold on his hand, though, instead twining their fingers together beneath the table.

Somehow they were still in their chairs, but now they'd shifted closer to each other, their sides lightly pressed against each other. He assumed the sounds he'd heard were the team around him, but they were seated now, as well. A quick glance told him that Alaric appeared concerned more than anything else, while Kaelas simply looked annoyed at the interruption.

He's probably upset I interrupted his theatrics.

Ishaan kept that thought to himself, though the temptation to write it down to share with Theo was strong.

"Do we need to leave?" Trieste asked. He was watching the two of them, but without the frustration Ishaan would have expected. The simple show of support, as though he was just as much a part of the team as any of them, nearly shook him apart.

"No. We're okay," Theo replied. Ishaan nodded again to reassure him he was alright. He didn't quite believe it himself, but the others didn't need to know that.

"I'm sorry for the way Prince Kaelas told you that," Alaric offered. Ishaan looked over at him in time to see the man shoot his cousin an irritated look. As with every emotion Alaric showed, it was there and gone in a flash, his expression settling back into one of calm detachment. Ishaan wondered if *anyone* got to see behind that mask.

"I'd like to know why you think that's what's going on," Lieutenant Sol said. His usual friendly little smile was long gone, replaced by a look of such fierce protectiveness that Ishaan's chest tightened. Was that look for him? Had anyone ever looked at him like that in his whole life?

"Of course. We owe you an explanation." Alaric was quick to reply, cutting off Kaelas when he opened his mouth to speak. The prince glared at him, but subsided and motioned for Alaric to continue. "We weren't sure, at first, not until Ishaan pointed out the egg that was used in the spell."

"What egg?"

"What spell?"

Kya and Naema spoke at the same time and Ishaan abruptly remembered that most of them didn't know what had happened. Including Theo. Wincing, he tightened his grip on the man's hand in apology.

Captain Trieste and Lieutenant Sol exchanged a brief glance, but the captain was the one who finally spoke. "All of you have been on this team long enough to know that nothing being said in here leaves this room, but I'm going to reiterate it, anyway. I don't care how much you trust your partner or your children or anyone else. This stays here. Is that clear, soldiers?" Even after they gave the affirmative, he met their eyes one by one. Finally, he reached into a pocket, pulling out several pieces of paper folded into a small square. Ishaan recognized them as the pages he'd torn from Theo's journal, where he'd told James everything that had happened.

Well... almost everything.

Trieste looked them over once, as though to refresh his memory. "Ishaan, I'm going to summarize what's here. If you have anything to add, now is the time."

It wasn't an offer so much as an order. Trieste knew he'd kept parts of the truth back. Now that Prince Kaelas had announced what he knew, the gaps in the story he'd told James were more obvious.

"I'll keep it brief. According to Ishaan, his parents were obsessed with increasing their own abilities to use magic. They worked for King Kelstavar of Gavarria before he was overthrown and the new king took power and disavowed them. Somewhere during that time, they started practicing blood magic."

Theo's grip on Ishaan's hand tightened and he felt a shudder run through the soldier where they touched. His face didn't show his disgust, but Ishaan could see it in his eyes.

"Apparently, they became obsessed with the idea of stealing magic from other mages," Trieste continued. "They claimed to have proof that it was possible. Not long before we found Ishaan, they disappeared for months and came back with what I assume is this egg that you're talking about."

"We still haven't learned where they got it from-"

"But we're going to find out," Prince Kaelas cut in, interrupting his cousin and earning him another frustrated look from Alaric. Their interactions were starting to confuse Ishaan. One moment they were a united front, then the next they were at odds with each other. Alaric may claim to be just an adviser to the prince, but sometimes it seemed that he was the only voice of reason in this country.

"A problem for another time, though," Alaric continued, smoothing over Kaelas' comment. "Please continue, Captain."

Trieste glanced back and forth between the two Sarkhyrians, his gaze assessing. "Ishaan stated he had twin siblings who were powerful mages. Bonded, apparently. From what I can gather, the plan was to test the spell their parents found on Ishaan. They would transfer the magic from the egg into him and, if it worked and he survived, they would then attempt it on themselves. Is that right?" He looked at Ishaan, who nodded.

He was the one trembling now as he fought to keep the events of that night locked away. He felt Theo's hand slip free of his and almost panicked until he felt the other man's arm come around his shoulders, hugging him against his side. The warmth of Theo's body pressed against his cut his growing panic off at the knees and he all but melted against him, taking the comfort that was offered so freely.

"That sounds disturbingly familiar," Lieutenant Sol said quietly. He was watching the two of them with concern, but thankfully his dark eyes held no pity, only a quiet sympathy. "I stayed an extra day in Traelum to research before riding to Yrasea, but I couldn't find anything like that spell in the royal archives."

"I would be shocked if you had," Alaric said. "From what we have been able to discern, it's very close to the ritual that is used to force the transfer of the dragon's power from one ruler to the next. It's a closely guarded secret, though, so I would very much like to know how two mages from Gavarria knew it."

"We only share it with our successors when they reach adulthood and we complete the second part," Prince Kaelas offered, somewhat begrudgingly. "Every generation has at least one other who knows it, as a failsafe should anything happen. That person is chosen because we would trust them with our life. For this spell to be known to anyone else means that someone betrayed us at some point."

It didn't take much to surmise that Alaric was the one Kaelas had trusted with the spell, and Ishaan's gut told him he would die before giving up that secret. Had Zex told someone less trustworthy? Had one of their predecessors? Just how far down did the roots of this disloyalty reach?

"I will find out who gave this information to outsiders, no matter what it takes," Alaric said, looking to Kaelas, then back to Ishaan. "I would like to speak to you about that night soon, if you're willing?"

He said it like a question, but Ishaan was no fool. He had no say in this matter at all. He wouldn't have refused them, given what his parents had done, but he hated that, yet again, he had absolutely no say in his life. Deep down, he wondered if he ever truly would.

Of course, he couldn't say any of that, so all he could do was nod in agreement.

"I'll go with you," Theo murmured in his ear, which helped to ease some of the frustration. He may not have much power over his life or his choices anymore, but he had no plans to let the tracker out of his sight for the foreseeable future, if at all possible. The thought of losing him again made him feel ill and he knew without a doubt that it would break him this time.

"Thank you," Alaric continued, oblivious to his inner turmoil or Theo's whispered promise. "Captain Trieste, I take it that the spell backfired and that is when your team found Ishaan?"

Trieste nodded. "Given how quickly his injuries healed, we knew magic was involved even before he woke up, but we had no idea what could have caused it. My lieutenant and I only learned the full extent of the story recently, ourselves."

It was hard not to dart a quick glance at James, but Ishaan managed. In a way, it made sense that they didn't mention that a prince of Nevarre knew the entire story. He was sure it would cause some kind of political issue, even if he wasn't versed enough to understand exactly why.

"Why didn't you share any of this information the night you arrived?" Prince Kaelas asked sharply. The way he tilted his head and fixed his golden glare on the captain reminded Ishaan of a cat hunting prey, but Trieste didn't flinch.

"Probably for the same reason you didn't tell us the full story of Zex. We were protecting our own."

"I was not protecting Zex!" Kaelas snapped. His fury overrode the brief flash of warmth Ishaan felt at the captain's words and he flinched instinctively, pressing harder against Theo. The dragon inside of him stirred, perhaps in response to his unease. Now that he'd acknowledged what it was, he could no longer make himself ignore it and its emotions. He couldn't imagine what it would be like if he'd received the full power. With any luck, they could undo this spell quickly so he could forget about the dragon and get on with his life.

"Whatever the reason, it is done," Alaric said, raising his voice to cut off any further arguments. "We all know the full story now and we can move forward. I believe I've come up with a plan, or at least the beginning of one."

What that plan was, they would never find out. A brisk knock at the door was their only warning before it opened and a guard stepped through. Ishaan thought he looked vaguely familiar.

"What is it, Grayan? I asked that we not be disturbed." Alaric was polite, but there was an edge of impatience in his voice. The guard's expression hardened and that's when Ishaan placed him. He was the one that had been guarding the door when they'd arrived, the one who seemed oddly interested in the prince's cousin.

"I understand that, sir, but it's Hadiza. They're demanding entrance and won't be turned away," he grumbled. "They said it was urgent."

"Let them in," Prince Kaelas ordered, rising to his feet. The guard scowled, as if he'd been looking forward to the chance to turn someone away, but stepped out and a moment later, Hadiza stepped in. They waited until the door was closed firmly before speaking, though.

"I'm so sorry to interrupt, Prince Kaelas," they said, then paused, looking at the Nevarreans and Ishaan. "An urgent situation has come up. May I speak freely?"

"Is it related to the matter we were discussing with Lord Wyrenian?"

"Yes."

Kaelas looked at them, then he and Alaric had one of those silent conversations again. It was only a few seconds, but Alaric nodded once and Kaelas turned back to Hadiza. "This may involve them, so go ahead. I'll have their ambassador explain the full situation later."

Hadiza seemed hesitant but unwilling to disobey their prince. "Lady Heraldra has been found."

"Alive?" Alaric cut in, but the hope in his eyes died a moment later when Hadiza shook their head.

"No, sir, I'm sorry," they murmured. "She was found with a young soldier, though. He is alive, but barely."

"We need to get to him quickly, then." Prince Kaelas stood and turned to Captain Trieste. "Lord Wyrenian will bring you up to date on the situation. One of us will come to find you as soon as we have more information. Now that we know the full story, I'm beginning to believe it's all connected. Have one of the guards escort you back to your rooms if you don't remember how to get back. Hadiza, take us to him, please."

With that, the Sarkhyrians swept out of the room, leaving them alone at the table and even more confused than when they'd sat down. The silence lingered as they tried to sort out what was going on, but Kya was finally the one to sum it all up quite neatly.

"We're not going home anytime soon, are we?"

Chapter 18

"Is it safe to leave the Nevarreans unattended, sir?" Hadiza asked as they hurried through the back hallways, with Kaelas and Alaric close on their heels.

"The guards know to keep a discreet watch on any guests. They've been doing so for Lord Wyrenian and his team, remember?" Alaric tried to ignore the ache in his chest as he followed Hadiza. Lady Heraldra was one of the kindest people he'd ever known. Or had been, rather. Why anyone would hurt her was a mystery, one he intended to solve with haste.

"Tell me about this soldier she was found with. Who are they?" Kaelas asked.

"I'm not entirely sure, sir," Hadiza admitted. "He's quite young, so I thought perhaps a trainee, but the wear on his sword indicates someone with experience. I believe he's either a mercenary or..."

"Or what?"

"Or one of Zex's men," Alaric said suddenly, the pieces settling into place in his mind. "You think he might be one of the traitors who sought Zex out after he ran?"

"I believe so." Hadiza came to a stop outside a locked door, well away from any populated areas of the castle. "The guards who found the two are under strict orders not to speak a word of this to anyone. There were only two, so if word does get out, we know who to find. I warded the doors to keep out anyone but me after I let the healer in."

"Thank you, Hadiza. But what makes you think he's anything but a trainee?" There was an edge to Kaelas' voice when he spoke, a sliver of pain that Alaric was growing far too familiar with already. Having Zex this close to Kaelas was only going to make things worse. They needed to deal with this as quickly as possible.

"His armor, sir. Our soldiers wear blue and gold, not black and silver, which is what this young man was wearing," they explained.

"Which means you're most likely right," Alaric sighed. "We need to try to speak to him. I can only hope the healer has managed to help."

They stood back to let Hadiza undo their wards, then followed them into the room. It was an old storeroom, but the two tables no longer held cleaning supplies or old linens. Those lay on the floor and the tables had moved. One stood against the wall, where the body of Lady Heraldra lay covered in what looked to be an old tablecloth.

Grief welled up within him again, but he couldn't concentrate on that. His attention went to the second table and the young man currently lying on it, with a healer at his side. The extent of his injuries dragged a soft gasp from Alaric's lips before he could stop it and he moved a step closer, careful to stay out of the healer's way.

Deep slashes crossed his face and he felt bile rise in his throat when he realized the soldier was missing an eye. The same gashes crossed his bare chest and Alaric saw a hint of bone near his ribs. The silver touches on his black pants were stained red with blood and a small puddle was forming beneath him as it dripped off the edge of the table.

"How is he still alive?" he breathed, horrified.

"He may not be much longer. I don't know that even my magic can sustain him much longer." The healer sounded winded, as though she'd been running for miles. "It's almost as if something is blocking me. I've never seen anything like it."

Alaric quickly looked over at Kaelas, only to find his cousin already looking at him. "Could blood magic do something like that?" he asked quietly.

"I don't know, but I wouldn't put it past him to find some way to protect his followers from magic," Kaelas said with a sigh.

Alaric watched the healer as she struggled to keep the young man alive, his mind racing. He had magic of his own, but healing was not his specialty and odds were, he'd only make the situation worse by attempting to jump in. Kaelas could heal himself quickly thanks to the powers of the golden dragon, but it wasn't something he could extend to others. Unfortunately, that left them with very few options.

"We need Zex here."

As expected, Kaelas immediately shook his head. "Absolutely not. He's locked up and he's going to stay there until we deal with him."

"We need answers, Kas, and we can't get them if this man dies!" Alaric forced himself to breathe, to bury the flash of anger rising up at his cousin's stubbornness. "We need Zex to tell us what he did, so I can undo it and let the healer do her job. There's no time to argue about this!"

"You don't know what he's capable of, Alaric. You don't know him like I do."

"No, but I do know that we have no clue what happened to Lady Heraldra. She didn't deserve to die like this and we need to find whoever did it before they come for someone else. To do that, we need this man alive, which means we need Zex."

Kaelas' eyes burned so brightly they were glowing as the dragon within him raged. Alaric kept quiet for a moment, knowing how short his cousin's temper had grown in the years since Zex left. The delay ate at him, but in the end, Kaelas ruled Sarkhyr and it was his decision.

It felt like an eternity passed, but finally the glow died away and Kaelas simply looked resigned. "Fine. But he is to remain under your direct supervision at all times and the manacles do not come off. Not even for a second."

Alaric was out of the door almost before Kaelas finished speaking. He could feel the healer's power draining by the second as she fought to keep the man alive, and he knew they were running out of time. The only bit of good luck they had was that they were near the entrance to the underground area that served as a prison. It hadn't been used as such in ages, not since the prison on the edge of the city had been built, but they'd wanted to keep Zex close, in case anyone came looking for him.

He was out of breath by the time he reached the door and the guards looked at him with alarm.

"Sir, what's wrong?"

"Let me through, please," he managed, panting softly. "I have direct orders from Prince Kaelas to bring the prisoner with me. It won't take long."

They looked confused and more than a little alarmed, but they did as ordered. They offered to come with him, but he waved them off and hurried inside.

Zex was in the last cell at the very end of the short hallway. Magelights lit the area, embedded in the ceiling and out of reach of the cell doors. It was enough light for him to see Zex as he lounged against the wall, seemingly at his ease.

"I knew you wouldn't be able to resist coming to see me. I just didn't expect it to be so soon," he purred when he spotted Alaric. His smirk dropped the moment their eyes met, though, and he rose to his feet, coming to the door. "What happened?"

"Do you use blood magic to protect your soldiers?" He hated that Zex could read him so easily after all the years he'd spent working to keep his emotions from showing, but there was no time to worry about it.

"What do you-"

"Blood magic! Are your soldiers protected from outside magic by you?"

Zex frowned, clearly debating telling the truth, but he finally nodded. "Yes."

Alaric slid the key into the cell door but stopped short of turning it, locking eyes with Zex. "You are going to come with me and if you even attempt to escape, I will end you. Is that clear?"

"I believe I like this side of you, Alaric," Zex murmured. He nodded once. "I'm far too intrigued to attempt an escape at the moment. Please, lead the way."

He didn't believe the man for a second, but he had no choice. As he'd told Kaelas... they needed him.

The key disappeared into his long jacket the moment after he unlocked the door and he stepped back, motioning for Zex to go first. "Walk to the door and don't dawdle."

To his shock, Zex did exactly as ordered and they made it back to the old storeroom without incident. There they had to wait a moment to allow Hadiza to take down the wards again to let them in.

"I haven't been over here in years. I'm surprised anyone still remembers it exists. Maybe later, you and I could—"

The words died on his lips when the door opened and he spotted the soldier lying on the table. Alaric was watching him for any sign he was about to run, only instead, he saw the way the blood drained from Zex's face. The man didn't wait for Alaric, but ran into the room, manacles jangling wildly.

"Elias!" he cried, stopping beside the table. "What happened to him?"

"That's what we're trying to find out, but our healer's magic is being blocked. You need to tell me what you did so I can undo it." Alaric ran to his side, putting himself between Zex and Kaelas before his cousin did something rash.

"You can't undo it, that's the whole point!" Zex spat. He didn't look away from the young man, apparently called Elias. "Release me and I can save him."

"Absolutely not." Kaelas tried to shove past Alaric, hard enough that he had to use his magic to push him back. "I told you he would try something like this."

"I don't care what precautions you have to take to make yourself feel better, but let me save him!" Zex turned to them, his silver eyes wild and his hands trembling so hard the manacles were clinking together. "He's not even twenty years old. He's going to die if you don't let me help him!"

"The second those chains come off, you're going to kill us all and run away. I know you and I'm not letting you do this again!" Kaelas pushed at the barrier Alaric had erected to hold him back, clearly spoiling for a fight.

"Tell me what to do, Zex. Let me help him. The healer can't hold him much longer," Alaric pleaded, but Zex shook his head.

"I would if I could, but the protection can only be revoked by the one who placed it. I wanted him safe." He turned his full attention to Kaelas for the first time since the two had seen each other across the field. "Kaelas... please. Let me save him."

Alaric couldn't be sure which part was most shocking: that Zex had said 'please' or that his voice had wavered when he's said it. Whoever Elias was, he was important to Zex.

"I'm losing him," the healer gasped from behind them and Zex went pale as snow. Alaric saw it all play out in an instant in his mind. Kaelas would refuse, the man would die, and they would immediately lose whatever sliver of a chance they had at Zex cooperating with the forced transfer of power. The silver dragon would die with him and so, too, would Sarkhyr and the remaining magic in their world. In that brief second, he had a choice to make, and there would be no coming back from it.

"I'm sorry," he whispered. A moment later, Kaelas was across the room, trapped within an invisible barrier of Alaric's magic. Holding him back would be a struggle, and he knew he only had a few seconds.

"Betray me and you won't live to regret it."

Zex's manacles fell to the ground before the other man could process the words, but the weight of the metal leaving his wrists snapped him back to action. His eyes shot to the door, but only for the tiniest of moments. He spared a grim nod for Alaric, then turned to the table.

"The moment you feel my magic touch him, you need to let go," he ordered, and the healer nodded. Sweat dripped from her forehead and she looked ready to collapse. Zex looked around for something and didn't seem to spot what he needed. His eyes never left Elias as he brought his own arm to his mouth and bit deeply, until crimson blood welled past his lips. Instead of running down his arm, though, it ran *up* to pool in his hand.

Disgust and a primal sort of horror welled up in Alaric, but so did a strange, morbid fascination. He'd never seen blood magic performed, of course. It was not only highly illegal but also taboo, a topic no one wanted to talk about. He couldn't help but be intrigued, even as everything he'd been taught told him he should stop this.

"Alaric, let me out this instant!" The magic muffled Kaelas somewhat, but there was no disguising the unbridled fury in his voice. He was fighting hard, and it was taking most of Alaric's concentration to keep him at bay. He had to focus what energy he had left on making sure Zex didn't try to escape.

Zex ignored all of them, searching for something on Elias' body. Alaric spotted a tiny black mark on the man's forearm and looked up in time to see Zex holding his hand over it.

"Let go when I say," he murmured to the healer. He closed his fist and a drop of blood slipped free, building on his skin until it grew too heavy and began to fall. "Now!"

The healer stepped back just as the blood hit Elias' skin. It lingered for a moment, then disappeared into him, as though the mark had consumed it. At the same time, a ragged gasp fell from his lips and he jerked on the table, his back arching.

"Stay with me, Elias," Zex whispered. "Stay with me." He raised his fist further up and Alaric could only watch as droplets of blood fell into the young soldier's open mouth. Whatever Zex was doing, it didn't seem to be working. A growl slipped free and he clenched his hand even tighter, more blood swirling up from the wound to his hand and falling more rapidly.

Two things happened at once.

Alaric felt his barrier slip, then shatter as Kaelas finally broke through.

Elias cried out, echoing in the empty room, and the wounds across his face began to knit themselves back together.

The shock of his magic breaking made Alaric slow to react, and he could do nothing as Kaelas charged for Zex. Zex, however, didn't move. He held his other hand up and just the threat of his magic brought Kaelas up short.

"If you interrupt me now, he will die. Do you want his death on your conscience, your Highness?" Zex didn't look up, keeping his eyes on Elias and making sure the blood didn't miss his lips.

"You're going to kill us all anyway the moment you save him, so what does it matter?"

"Then, by all means, stop me now and see what happens."

Alaric finally recovered and took a step forward, putting himself between the two men. "Kas, we talked about this."

"We are going to have a lot to talk about if we survive this," he hissed, attention diverted for a moment. "*Never* do something like that again."

"I did what I had to do and I will accept the consequences of my actions. But you need to do the same. We can talk about everything else later. I can contain Zex once this is done, but not if I have to worry about you, too."

Tension flared between them, the feeling foreign and uncomfortable. He'd never felt anything but trust and affection from his cousin and this hurt, but he'd known this would happen the moment he'd made his decision. It was a consequence he would have to live with.

Kaelas was clearly fighting the instincts of the dragon, the edges made raw by the other half of his broken bond being so near, but in the end, his human side won and he took a step back. It allowed him to fully see Zex as the man worked, while also silently giving Alaric permission to continue.

Relieved not to be fighting a battle on two fronts, Alaric gave his full attention back to Zex and Elias. Already, the young soldier was looking better. The wounds on his face were closed and the gashes on his ribs were slowly healing as well.

"A few more moments and your healers will be able to do the rest."

It was startling to hear Zex's voice so soft. None of his usual bravado or flirtation was evident and for a moment, Alaric had a glimpse of the prince Zex could have been, had things gone differently.

The moment ended quickly, though, as the last gash closed. The injuries were still raw and even magic couldn't save his eye, but Elias was going to survive.

Zex pulled his hand away and turned to Alaric. He was instantly on guard, prepared to fight, and so was left speechless when Zex held out his wrists. It took Alaric a moment to move and replace the manacles, effectively locking Zex's magic down again.

Despite losing his magic, he appeared calm as could be as he examined Elias. The way he held himself so stiffly, though, told Alaric that the effort had exhausted him. There was blatant concern in his eyes as he looked at the young man. It disappeared when he turned to Alaric and Kaelas, however, hidden behind his mask of sarcasm.

"I don't suppose I could get a bandage of some sort?"

Chapter 19

No one spoke until they were back in the hallway of rooms they'd been given. Captain Trieste nodded toward his own room and they all followed him inside, with Theo bringing up the rear. Ishaan stayed at his side, his head down. Theo could feel him withdrawing into himself, mentally pulling away from the mess of a situation Prince Kaelas had dumped on them before disappearing.

The mages wasted no time in warding the room while everyone else got settled. Theo hadn't released Ishaan's hand since he'd taken hold of it at the dining table, and he didn't let go now. He tugged him down to sit on the edge of the bed with him, keeping them pressed close. They were going to need each other if they were going to get through this.

"I thought we were going to talk to Lord Wyrenian?" James asked the moment the last ward was in place, granting them privacy to speak.

"We will shortly," Trieste replied. "I want to make sure we're all in agreement before moving forward. First: are the pair of you alright?"

Theo suddenly found himself and Ishaan the center of attention, the entire team turning to them. Their concern came from the affection they all had for each other, but he hated how it set them apart, leaving them exposed and vulnerable.

"I'm fine. We both are," he added after a quick squeeze of his hand from Ishaan. "We have other problems to worry about." Trieste didn't seem completely convinced, but to Theo's relief, he let the matter drop. For now, at least.

"We do. So, our top priority is getting information from Lord Wyrenian to figure out what's going on. After that, we'll work with the Sarkhyrians to undo whatever spell was done on Ishaan, so we can all go home."

Beside him, Ishaan finally raised his head, his silvery eyes scared. He shifted, gripping Theo's hand, and he had a feeling he knew what was bothering the younger man.

"You'll come back to Nevarre with us, unless you have somewhere else you'd like to go?"

Ishaan shook his head, and there was no mistaking the relief on his face.

"I'd assumed that would be the plan was all along," Kellan offered, giving Ishaan a warm smile. "You're part of the team now."

Theo had a feeling Ishaan wasn't fully convinced, but they had time now. He'd take as long as needed to show him it was true.

"Moving on," Trieste continued. "I've said it before, but nothing we discussed tonight needs to be shared with Lord Wyrenian and his party. I've known him for a very long time and I know he's trustworthy, so I have faith the others will be as well. However, the fewer people who know, the better we'll be able to contain the information. So we keep the focus on the other issue."

"Do you think that's what they were dealing with when we arrived?" Naema suddenly asked. "Remember? Alaric was the one to greet us when we arrived, instead of Lord Wyrenian and Prince Kaelas, because they were dealing with some sort of problem. Could that be it?"

"There's only one way to find out. Escort Lieutenant Sol to Lord Wyrenian's rooms and ask him to join us, if you would. The rest of you, make sure there's room for him to sit. I assume he'll bring his apprentice with him, possibly his guards as well. Except you, C'Van." It was Vesa's turn to be the center of attention, and Theo saw her getting ready to get up from the chair she'd taken.

"Sir?"

"You are to stay seated and not move any more than necessary. The healers have done a lot to mend your wounds, but you still need to rest. I won't have you re-injuring yourself."

She didn't look happy at the coddling, but took her seat again, anyway. Naema and Kellan left to go fetch the ambassador while the rest of them shuffled over to make room.

"You two are going to have to share," James announced, right before squeezing himself in on Theo's other side. The seat was already small, just two cushions, so adding another fully grown man meant all three of them were squished together.

"There's room on the floor, you know," he pointed out, voice dry.

"I can't imagine that's very comfortable, but if you really want to, you're more than welcome. Ishaan and I wouldn't mind the space, I'm sure."

He felt Ishaan laughing beside him, little jerks that he tried to suppress but couldn't quite contain. The playful banter was so familiar it made his chest ache and helped to bury the last dregs of bitter resentment that had lingered. He loved his entire team, but James had been his best friend for years. The tension between them had hurt almost as much as Zex's blood magic.

"I leave the two of you alone for a little while and suddenly you're teaming up against me? I wasn't sure I'd ever see the day."

He hadn't realized how much guilt and tension James had been carrying until he smiled and some of the shadows in his eyes fell away. "That's what happens when you decide to be a martyr. See that you never do something like that again, otherwise you might come back to find the two of us married or something."

Ishaan leaned to the side and tilted his head, nose wrinkling a little as he looked James up and down. One eyebrow came up before he shook his head in a very clear negative.

"That's rude. Let's see if I ever help you up into a saddle again." James' tone was annoyed, but another smile hovered on his lips despite his best efforts to hide it.

"Why were we so eager to have the both of them back together, again?" Irric grumbled, shaking his head. Beside him, Kya just laughed. Theo didn't miss how she'd glued herself to Irric's side since the team had reunited. It looked like she'd missed her best friend.

Footsteps echoing down the hall brought them all up short, reminding them they still had business to attend to.

"Do you need some room in case you have to write?" he murmured to Ishaan. He knew the other man had the journal still, but it really was cramped on their seat.

Ishaan dug it out and put it on his lap, testing, then shook his head and raised his right fist to his cheek, running it down to his chin. It was one he'd come up with without Theo, but he'd been practicing with them and remembered after a moment, a simple sign to say he was alright or to ask if someone else was.

"Alright, but if you need me to move over, just let me know."

The room was quiet as Kellan and Naema returned, along with Lord Wyrenian. As the captain had predicted, he'd brought along four others with him. Three were easily distinguished as guards, given their armor, but the fourth was a bit of a surprise. While he knew Canjiri immigrants were scattered all over the kingdom, as was the case with Vesa's family, it was unusual to see anyone of Canjiri descent among the nobility. There was no denying the young man's distinct Canjiri features, though.

"That's his apprentice, Sir Embry Falloran," James murmured in his ear. Another surprise. That was not a Canjiri name. "The other three are their guards. The tall one is Jayakatong Ny. Rhea Mennez is the mage beside him. The shorter one is Yann Dulara. He looked out for Ishaan the first time we were here."

That raised his opinion of the man already, without even needing to speak to him. His gut was telling him the same thing James was, that they were good people.

"You must be Theodric." Lord Wyrenian took a seat on a small couch across from Theo, leaving room for Embry to join him. "I'm so thankful we have you back with us. I'm sure you're tired of being asked how you are, so I'll leave it at that."

"I-I'm glad to be back, sir," he managed. He certainly hadn't expected the man to speak to him with everything going on.

"We were told you could fill us in on whatever situation we walked into a week ago," Captain Trieste said, somewhat impatiently. "I don't mean to interrupt, but it seems fairly urgent. Apparently, someone named Lady Heraldra has been missing?"

"Did they find her?" Sir Embry asked quickly, sitting up straighter.

"Someone did, but I'm afraid she didn't survive whatever happened." Kellan used what Theo privately thought of his 'mother voice', gentle and soothing, but there really was no good way to tell someone about a death.

Lord Wyrenian and Sir Embry exchanged a quick glance, but the younger man said nothing else.

"I had a feeling it would end like this, but I had hoped otherwise," Wyrenian murmured.

Theo had to bite back a growl of frustration. He empathized with them, he really did, but he was growing very tired of being left in the dark. He wanted *answers*.

"Who was she, my lord?" Kellan prompted, still in that gentle tone. "What happened?"

Lord Wyrenian's sigh was a weary one, and he took a moment to compose himself before speaking. "She was a rather powerful mage, even by Sarkhyrian standards. I assume you've noticed by now that their magic differs from ours?" He waited for them to nod before going on. "She disappeared right around the time our party arrived in Yrasea. We offered our assistance, which Prince Kaelas accepted, but we weren't able to locate any trace of her. There were very faint traces of an unknown magic, but nothing we could follow. It was clear she didn't leave willingly, given the state of her rooms, but that's all we know."

"If she was truly that powerful, then whoever attacked her must have been even more so. How many mages in the area would have that kind of power?" Trieste asked. Theo knew he was already planning to offer his own help, if only to assuage his curiosity.

"Only a few, but all of them are accounted for and have multiple witnesses as to their whereabouts that night. The more concerning part is that she wasn't the first one to go missing."

That brought them all up short. The captain frowned, dark eyes narrowed. "How many have disappeared in a similar manner?"

"She's the third in a month. The first was a mage living outside the city, on a small farm. He was found dead the same day another mage disappeared. This one owned a fairly popular shop on the southern edge of the city. His husband found his body—"

"The day Lady Heraldra disappeared?" Trieste guessed.

"The very same day. She was within sight of the castle, where she should have been safe, but no one saw a thing."

"Whoever's doing this has been moving further and further into the city," Theo murmured, and the ambassador nodded.

"We noticed that, as well. The first two were strong mages by our standards, but mid-level at best by Sarkhyrian measures. Lady Heraldra was the first one of true power to be taken."

"Are there any suspects at all? Any clues or trails or anything?" Trieste prompted.

"I hate to admit it, but we couldn't find anything. But from the brief conversation I was able to have with Prince Kaelas before he left with you, I believe he suspects whoever this 'Zex' person is."

No one reacted, at least not on their team. Captain Trieste's warning to keep what they knew to themselves still rang in Theo's ears. But one thing struck him.

"I don't think it was him."

Suddenly, he once again found himself the center of attention. At least there was no pity to be found now, only curiosity and confusion. Still, the gentle squeeze Ishaan gave his hand helped center him.

"What do you mean? According to Prince Kaelas, he has that kind of power," Captain Trieste pointed out, edging around the truth.

"Maybe, but the timing doesn't fit. If she disappeared a week ago, he could have taken her, but unless he killed her immediately and left her to be found, he couldn't have done it. He was with us for the last five days." There was no sense hiding the fact that Zex was here. No one gossiped worse than soldiers, so the entire castle would know by morning.

"I take it to mean you apprehended him, then? Good," Wyrenian nodded. "We will need more information from Prince Kaelas, but the first two were killed shortly before they were found, so they were being held captive somewhere."

"So if the pattern stays the same, there's no way Zex could have been the one to do it. So who does that leave us with?" Trieste asked.

"One of his fighters, perhaps? Believe me, I've been thinking about this constantly since we arrived, but Zex was our best suspect to date. If it's not him... we're back where we were when this all started."

"Then it's a good thing finding information is why our team exists," James declared when a heavy silence fell over them at Wyrenian's words. "If this is something we can help with, of course," he added quickly, glancing toward Captain Trieste and the lieutenant.

"We're ready and willing to assist you in any way we can, Lord Wyrenian," Trieste said. "It *is* what we're best at."

"I won't refuse any help I can get right now. It's a Sarkhyrian matter and they're also working on finding this killer, but if we can help them, it would go a long way toward strengthening the relationship between Sarkhyr and Nevarre."

It was always politics, in the end. Theo knew it was necessary, and he didn't look down on those who chose to get involved, but he had no patience for political maneuvering.

"Once Prince Kaelas returns, we can all sit down together and come up with a plan. You're more than welcome to wait here with us, if you'd like?"

Thankfully, Lord Wyrenian was canny enough to recognize the empty gesture for what it was and shook his head. "Thank you, but I believe we'll take the time to eat and gather what information we've come up with. It will help to have it all in one place when we meet."

Pleasantries were exchanged, but Lord Wyrenian's party was out the door in short order. The wards were refreshed, and Captain Trieste was back to business as he faced his team.

"I want all of us to be focused on this for the moment. I don't know what Kaelas meant when he said he believed this was all connected, but it affects us, so I want everyone at their best. We need every scrap of information we can get our hands on, and I want to know every secret they're trying to hide from us. Is that clear, soldiers?"

"Yes, sir!" A grim conviction wrapped its fingers around Theo as the team made plans. Kaelas was right. Everything really was connected, creating a tangled web of lies, secrets, and magic. And, if his gut was correct, Ishaan was at the very center of it.

CHAPTER 20

Prince Kaelas never returned that night.

The team waited up for hours, but the summons never came. They used the time to catch up with each other after being separated so long. Ishaan stayed seated beside Theo even after James moved to a different seat, but he kept himself out of the conversations flowing around him. It was easy enough, though Theo tried to draw him into it. After the second time Ishaan refused with a shake of his head, they left him alone.

Neither he nor Theo acknowledged the fact that they were still holding hands.

Honestly, he was grateful for the comfort. Everything he'd learned today was churning in his mind, and he needed that anchor to keep him steady. Zex and the dragon were at the forefront of his every thought, and he was still trying to figure out what he could possibly do when the group split up, heading to their rooms.

"I can share with Irric and Kya tonight, if you want?" James suggested, nodding toward their joined hands.

"No, it's fine," Theo said, and Ishaan nodded in agreement. Now that the team was back together, everyone had split into their usual sleeping arrangements: Irric and Kya, Naema and Vesa, Captain Trieste and Lieutenant Sol. Except now, he broke up the symmetry. He refused to break up James and Theo's usual routine, though.

"Well then, someone is sleeping on the floor or two of us will have to be alright with sharing." The mage opened the door to the room and Ishaan was abruptly reminded that each room only had two beds in it.

"We'll figure it out, James," Theo sighed. "If you're going to shower tonight, do it now or I'm going."

"You take too long. I'm going first."

James' antics were almost enough to draw a smile, but even that wasn't enough to distract him from the thoughts racing through his mind. He kept his head down as he took off his boots and socks, following Theo's example and putting them near the door.

"Hey."

Theo's voice was soft, almost too soft to be heard over the sound of water running in the washroom. Their eyes met, and Theo gave him a tiny smile.

"How are you doing? The last few days have been a lot to deal with."

Would he ever get used to the feeling of someone actually caring about his well-being? He hoped not. It was something he never wanted to take for granted.

He shrugged, then pointed to Theo, lightly tapping the man's chest and raising an eyebrow in question.

"I'm fine," he said airily. Ishaan tapped his chest again and Theo sighed, relenting. "Really. I'm as fine as I'm going to get right now, I think."

The words he needed he didn't have signs for yet, so Ishaan motioned him to wait and retrieved the journal. He was quick, writing just a few sentences before handing it over.

"What can I do to help? You've been helping me since we met. I want to do the same."

"Just you being here is helping. I'm serious," he said when Ishaan scoffed. "I get stuck in my head sometimes. Something makes me think of what happened and I panic. I..." He hesitated, glancing toward the washroom as though worried James could somehow hear him. Ishaan reached up, lightly touching Theo's face and guiding him back until their eyes met. The pain he saw there nearly broke him.

"I don't want the others to know," he whispered. "The captain would likely pull me from duty, but I think if I don't stay busy, I'll break."

"I promise," Ishaan signed, bringing his free hand up and holding it open, tapping his index finger to his chin twice. It was one he'd taught Theo on the road back to Yrasea.

Theo leaned forward until their foreheads touched. "I keep losing track of time," he admitted, barely more than a breath of sound. "I'll be fine for hours or even a day or two, but it keeps happening. It's almost always at night, when everyone else is asleep, but when we were riding back, I would blink and suddenly an hour or two had passed. I don't remember anything about what happened in the time that disappears. It's just a big hole in my memory."

The two of them were so close that Ishaan could feel the tiny tremors wracking Theo's body. The man was terrified, holding on by a thread. It was a feeling Ishaan was far too familiar with.

He closed the remaining distance between them, wrapping his arms around Theo in a tight hug. He felt a shiver run through the other man's body, a moment of tension, then he melted against Ishaan, hugging him back with all his strength. It only took a few seconds for Theo to break down, burying his face in Ishaan's shoulder as the tears he'd been holding back finally came.

Ishaan held him as tight as he could, resting his head against Theo's and doing his best to be his anchor, the way Theo had been for him since the moment they'd met. His heart ached as he held the soldier. He'd give anything, *anything*, to take this pain away from him and fix everything for him, but he didn't even know where to begin. The magic that had done this was forbidden for a reason, and he had a sneaking suspicion that the only person who might be able to help was the man locked in the dungeon.

For now, all he could do was try to hold them both together. He squeezed Theo a little tighter as tiny sobs shuddered through him, giving him a safe space to let go of the pain. It was only a few minutes before the man in his arms quieted, but neither was willing to let go. Not yet, anyway. They held each other for countless minutes in the silence, broken only by the sound of falling water from the washroom.

"Thank you," Theo whispered when he finally lifted his head. His beautiful blue eyes were red-rimmed and heavy with exhaustion, but still he managed a soft, tiny smile for Ishaan. "I think I needed that."

Ishaan again lifted his hand, lightly bringing it to rest on Theo's cheek. He nodded once, attempting an echo of Theo's smile. He wasn't sure how well he succeeded, but it seemed to be enough for the other man. Their eyes locked and Ishaan's chest squeezed again, but it wasn't pain or worry this time. An unfamiliar fluttering had taken up residence in his stomach and he could feel a flush working up his face as they held each other's gaze.

He didn't know who moved first, only that it was so slow he almost didn't realize they *had* moved until their breaths mingled and their noses brushed. His heart was racing and a breathless anticipation hung thick in the air between them as Theo's head tilted ever so slightly and Ishaan leaned in a little closer. His breath caught as their lips brushed, a tiny touch that sent a shiver down his spine.

"Is this okay?" Theo whispered, sounding just as breathless as Ishaan felt. He immediately nodded, his other hand coming up to Theo's face. He hadn't shaved in days and the beginnings of a beard were coarse beneath Ishaan's hands, a gentle scratching sensation that grounded him and assured him that this was really happening. They were so close he felt more than saw Theo smile, and a wisp of excitement curled through his stomach.

This time they moved as one, closing the scant distance between them in a kiss that set Ishaan's body alight and turned his whole world upside down. He felt Theo's hands on his arms, a gentle touch that brought them closer together, as close as they could get. If his inexperience showed, it didn't seem to matter. Theo kissed him as though Ishaan was the very center of his universe, as though nothing else existed but right now, this moment.

The ember of attraction and affection that had slowly been building within him for weeks now burst into gentle flame. He didn't have a name for this feeling, not yet, but he knew what it *could* be, if he could find the courage to let it grow.

It only lasted a few seconds, that first soft kiss, before they broke apart. Ishaan was panting softly, and it gave him a deep sense of satisfaction when he realized Theo was breathing heavier, too. He was still gently cupping the soldier's face as they leaned against each other, heads touching while they settled themselves.

Ishaan would have happily stayed like that for the rest of the night, but they weren't alone. The shower in the washroom finally stopped, and Theo gave him a rueful smile.

"I never thought I'd wish James would take *longer* in there," he huffed, and Ishaan couldn't help but laugh. It turned into a tiny gasp when Theo brushed another tiny kiss against his lips before releasing him. Even the few inches of space between them now felt like too much after that, but that did nothing to smother his tiny grin.

"The shower is free!" James announced grandly as he swept out of the washroom. The two of them took a step away from each other and Ishaan was irrationally pleased to see that Theo also looked reluctant to move away.

"Ishaan, you can go next, if you'd like?" Theo offered and he nodded in agreement. He needed a few moments to pull himself back together, but he already knew he'd spend more time than he should reliving his first kiss. He didn't know what it meant for the two of them in the long run, but right now, he was going to hold tight to this happiness for as long as he could.

The door to the washroom had barely closed behind Ishaan before James turned to Theo, a huge grin on his face and a look in his eyes that made Theo groan. It did nothing to chase away the warmth still filling his chest, though. Those few moments with Ishaan had managed to push down the fears plaguing him and he wanted to hold on to this peace for as long as he could. For that, he could endure a little teasing from his best friend, and James didn't disappoint.

"It's about time!"

"I have no idea what you're talking about," Theo sighed, turning to his bag to grab a change of clothes and a towel. He knew he was still smiling. He couldn't help it.

"Theo. I've been your best friend for years and I know you better than anyone, so don't even try. I'm not blind, you know. I've seen how the two of you look at each other, so be honest with me."

Unfortunately, James was right. There really was no one who knew him so well. He set his bag aside and faced his friend, completely unsurprised by the triumphant smile James gave him.

"I'm not going to talk about what did or didn't happen until I talk to Ishaan first. As my best friend, that means you're not going to tell anyone else what you might know, either, right?"

"You take the fun out of everything," James groaned, but Theo knew it was just as act. James was a lot of things, but a gossip wasn't one of them. Not about personal matters, anyway. "I won't say anything, you know that. I'm just happy for you. You'd have to be blind not to see that there was something there between you two. I was starting to think I was going to have to kick your ass to get you to take the first step, though.”

Theo arched an eyebrow. “Time hasn't exactly been on our side, if you recall.”

“I'll give you that, but I hope this means you're done wasting time.”

“Wait a moment. I thought you didn't even like him. I know you looked out for him on the way here and I appreciate it, but can I ask what made you go from being suspicious of everything he did to wanting me to explore this with him?”

James didn't answer straightaway, but took a moment, gathering his thoughts. When he did finally speak, he was unusually serious. “Honestly? I'm still a little suspicious of him. Don't get mad,” he protested when Theo immediately opened his mouth to defend Ishaan. He subsided, motioning for him to continue. “All I mean is that the timing is suspicious, how of all this is happening at once. How many coincidences have to happen before it's no longer a coincidence? But... I trust that he has your best interests at heart and that's what matters to me.”

“So let me get this straight. You don't trust him, but you trust him with me?”

“Basically,” he nodded.

In a twisted sort of way, Theo supposed it made a measure of sense. As his best friend, he wasn't surprised James would want to look out for him. He most likely would have done the same, were their roles reversed. It was also very much something James would do, to put his friend's happiness above his own misgivings.

“You're still going to be watching him, aren't you? Until you sort all this out in your head?”

James scoffed. “Of course. I'm a scholar, Theodric. I don't like not knowing something and everything about Ishaan is one big mystery. I'll support you both, but I'm not going to let this go until I find out all the facts."

Theo glanced over to the washroom door, hesitating a moment. He could still hear the shower running, but Ishaan never took long in there. With that in mind, he leaned in a little closer to James, lowering his voice.

"I need your help protecting him." It burned to admit he couldn't do it on his own, but he had no choice. "He's tied in with this whole mess here in Sarkhyr and I'm afraid it's going to end badly for him. I know the captain and the team will keep an eye on him, but I don't want him out of sight of one of us until we leave. Promise me, James."

"Of course. You don't even have to ask, but I swear to you, I will do everything in my power to make sure nothing happens to him. Not here and not when we get back home."

Theo breathed a tiny sigh of relief, letting a little of his concern pass over on to James' shoulders. As both a powerful mage and a prince, having his friend's protection settle over Ishaan was one of the best things he could do for the other man.

"Thank you." He gripped James' shoulder, stopping just short of hugging him.

"You're my best friend. You know I'd do just about anything for you," James vowed, but a tiny smirk broke through the serious facade he wore. "I'm still going to tease you incessantly about this, you know."

"Forget it. I'm going to go ask Irric."

A pillow hit him square in the face before he could even pretend to turn to the door. Of course it was war after that, a chaotic mess of thrown pillows and laughter. It was all well and good until James managed to snag one on the edge of the lighting fixture, sending a shower of down and feathers raining over them. That was, of course, the moment Ishaan walked out of the washroom. He froze in the doorway, his mouth open and eyes wide, staring at the two of them. He and James glanced at each other and the second their eyes met, they both burst into laughter. Theo's ribs ached and he had to lean against the wall for support, he was laughing so hard.

After a moment, he saw Ishaan start to laugh, too, still confused but caught up in their antics. It was such a simple moment, really, but it was enough to give him hope that in the end, maybe, just maybe, everything might be alright.

CHAPTER 21

It was well after breakfast when they finally reconvened. Extra chairs were added to the same table in the throne room to make space for the full reconnaissance team, Lord Wyrenian and his group, Prince Kaelas, Alaric, and Hadiza. The sheer amount of people at the table was a little overwhelming. Ishaan found himself sitting near the head of the table, with Theo on his left and Lieutenant Sol on his right. Captain Trieste was beside his lieutenant, putting him across from Alaric. Prince Kaelas sat at the head, as usual. Beside Alaric was Hadiza, then Lord Wyrenian. His apprentice was beside him, as always, while the soldiers ranged out along the other half of the table. He was a bit surprised to note that the two groups had mingled somewhat: Yann Dulara sat between James and Kya, while Vesa and Naema sat with Rhea, the mage. Jayakatong and Irric were at the other end, keeping an eye on everyone in silence.

He would have preferred to be at the far end with them, but Prince Kaelas hadn't given him that option. At least he had Trieste and Theo to shield him somewhat.

"Now, I presume everyone knows where we stand so far, so I'll only summarize," Kaelas began without preamble. "Lady Heraldra was the third person to go missing recently. Like the others, she was found dead a week later. Unlike the others, she wasn't alone. We also found a young soldier not far away from her and he was able to be saved."

His tone was unusually harsh for having found a survivor, and for some reason, Alaric's shoulders tensed and his eyes darted away from his cousin. Ishaan watched, but that was the only hint of any discord between the two. Still, it was unnerving, to say the least.

"The soldier needed time to recover a bit before we could speak to him, hence why we are meeting so late this morning. I apologize for the delay," Alaric said, once again calm and confident.

"Was he able to identify who did this?" Lord Wyrenian asked. "We've been trying to come up with something, but so far there doesn't seem to be a viable suspect."

"His account wasn't as helpful as I would have hoped, but we were able to get a few new details. Namely, that the man who did this isn't a Sarkhyrian."

Prince Kaelas' words sent a buzz through the table and an icy chill down Ishaan's spine. He didn't know why, but an odd foreboding wrapped around him, a choking miasma of dread that made no sense but felt all too real just the same.

"Given how isolated your country has been recently, it's surprising that a foreigner could go undetected for so long," Captain Trieste said with a frown.

"Did the soldier have any idea *why* these people were taken? I can't seem to find any connections between the three, other than being native-born Sarkhyrians." Lieutenant Sol asked the question that had kept Ishaan wondering half the night. It also neatly distracted Kaelas, whose eyes had narrowed at Trieste's words, like he thought the man was accusing him of something.

"They were all mages," he said, somewhat begrudgingly. "There were sigils on their bodies, which says to us that they were involved in some sort of spell before their deaths. The spell may well have been the cause of death."

"I know you're going to ask, but we don't know what the spell or ritual was," Alaric cut in and Ishaan saw every mage at the table sit up a little straighter, curiosity and determination burning in their eyes. Personally, he wanted absolutely nothing to do with anything that involved magic, especially if it killed people.

"With respect to Lady Heraldra, would it be possible to examine the sigils?" Lieutenant Sol asked carefully.

"I have drawn out what we found on each body," Hadiza said, speaking up for the first time. They waited for Prince Kaelas to nod his permission before opening a slender leather folio. Ishaan hadn't even noticed it sitting in front of them. Sheets of paper bearing copies of the sigils were passed to Lord Wyrenian and Captain Trieste, who promptly gave it to Lieutenant Sol. Ishaan shifted until he was pressed against Theo's side, as far as he could get from the paper. That irrational sense of dread wouldn't leave him and it was all he could do not to flee the room.

"We had hoped you may be able to help us shed some light on this," Alaric continued. "Such sigils are rarely used here, but I'm aware they're more common in the southern kingdoms. We have several books that may help, but if you can assist, it would greatly speed up the process."

"Rhea, would you mind?" Lord Wyrenian gestured to his mage. Sir Embry immediately stood, allowing Rhea to take his chair. He lingered behind Lord Wyrenian, though, studying the page alongside the two of them. On their side of the table, James and Kya didn't wait for an invitation, both making their way over to Lieutenant Sol.

"A few of these do look familiar," James said, frowning. "This one is used for stabilizing energy and the jagged one there is an amplifier."

"The one on the bottom left is used by healers. I've used it myself, to help a soldier with a chest wound to breathe until an experienced healer could arrive," Rhea added. "Whoever performed this spell appears to have been attempting to keep the victim alive."

"They clearly failed," Kaelas pointed out. As if they had somehow missed that fact. Ishaan managed not to roll his eyes, but it was a close thing.

"I think if we can figure out what the rest of these mean, we'll be able to figure out what caused them to die," Lieutenant Sol said. "Unfortunately, I don't recognize any others, but if you will allow us access to those books you mentioned, we can find them. There are over a dozen of us, which means we should be able to find our answers quickly."

"And if we can find out the purpose of these spells, I'd bet it'll give us a good idea of who did it," James added. Even from a few seats down, Ishaan could see the gleam in his eyes. For a moment, it reminded him of his brother. Doran used to get that same look in his eyes when presented with a mystery. Unfortunately, that curiosity had also extended to the spells their parents used to test on Ishaan. His brother may have been the least awful of his family, but Ishaan still buried the memory of him as deep as he could.

James is not Doran or Dhanara or our parents, he sternly reminded himself.

"I'll bring them in here. Hadiza, keep me informed of anything urgent that comes up. Until we find who's responsible, this is my top priority," Kaelas said. "I'll speak to the guards and quietly heighten security in the city. No need to cause a panic, but extra soldiers patrolling may serve as a deterrent."

"Yes, sir," Hadiza replied, getting to their feet. They bowed low before leaving, making sure the door was shut tight behind them.

"I'll assist you, Kas," Alaric murmured. "If the rest of you have any supplies or anything you feel would be helpful, please bring it here. We'll meet again in an hour?" He looked to Kaelas, who nodded.

In moments, everyone was standing to leave, the room buzzing with conversation. Ishaan stuck close to Theo, nearly crying with relief when he felt the other man's hand slip into his and twine their fingers together.

"What's wrong?" Theo murmured in his ear. No one seemed to hear, but Ishaan shook his head. He couldn't explain it with simple signs, anyway. He raised his free hand upright and rocked it back and forth twice in the sign for 'wait'. It was the best he could do at the moment.

Theo left it at that until they were back in their room with James, the captain's orders to gather their things and meet in his room ringing in their ears. While James dug through his bag, which contained far more books than Ishaan had realized, Theo lead them to the far side of the room.

"Can you tell me what's bothering you? Other than this entire situation?" he asked quietly. They were close enough to touch and Ishaan's worries scattered like ashes in the wind, replaced by memories of last night and that kiss. From the way Theo's eyes darkened, he was having similar thoughts.

"Behave. We don't have time to get sidetracked," James called, cutting through the moment like a knife. Ishaan laughed softly, and Theo shook his head with a rueful smile. That left space for the worry to come back, though, and his laugh faded into a quiet sigh. He pulled out the notebook and answered the question, turning it so Theo could see.

"I don't like magic, especially when it's been used like this. I'll help with research, but it reminds me of being back at the house I grew up in. I can't promise it won't affect me, but I'll do my best."

"You don't have to get involved. You have enough going on right now without adding this on top of it. No one is going to force you to do this."

Ishaan was tempted. He was ashamed to admit it, but he really was. He was ignoring the entire issue of apparently holding the power of a dragon inside him, but once the mages of Sarkhyr were safe again, Ishaan knew Prince Kaelas would turn the full force of his scrutiny on him. *He* would be the next mystery for everyone to solve, and he had a strong feeling it would not turn out well for him.

So no, he didn't want to dive into magical spells and sigils again. Years of his childhood were lost to learning the secrets of magic. Whenever they could find him, the days he didn't hide well enough, his parents had always tasked him with helping them research. Knowing that he'd helped find the spells they later tested on him just added an extra twist of cruel irony.

At the same time, he'd made a promise to himself. Before they'd gone into the mountains in search of Theo, he'd promised himself he would quit running away from his problems. He would never be as brave as the soldiers he'd fallen in with, but he could at least be less of a coward. So, as much as he wanted to lock everything away in the box in the back of his mind, he knew he couldn't.

"I'll do it. Will you stay close?" His hands shook as he wrote, but the words were still clear. Theo read them and leaned in close again.

"I'll stay with you," he breathed. James was still digging through the books now spread across his bed, and Ishaan's heart raced with anticipation when Theo closed the distance between them. "Is this okay?"

Ishaan didn't hesitate to nod. It was probably a little too eager, but he caught a glimpse of Theo's smile, so maybe it wasn't a bad thing. Then Theo was kissing him, and all his thoughts and worries fled his mind. Somehow, it was even better than the first time. Warmth slid over him, sinking into him until the ice he'd protected himself with melted away.

It was quick, since they had company in the room, and Ishaan was already yearning for a few moments alone with Theo to explore this new feeling. It felt effervescent, making his head spin and his stomach flip. He didn't know exactly what it meant between them, whether it changed everything or nothing, and he didn't care. He'd never felt like this before, and he just didn't want it to end.

"We should probably help James sort his books or we'll never get this over with," Theo laughed softly, resting his forehead against Ishaan's. "I'm here if you need me, alright?"

Ishaan tapped Theo's chest twice in response, giving him a pointed look. Theo may be there for him, but he was going to be there for Theo in return. Then and there, he made himself another promise. No matter what happened, no matter how much he wanted to run, he would always be there for Theo. No matter what.

Chapter 22

"You would think with over a dozen of us working on this, we would have found meanings for more than just four symbols."

Kaelas' words echoed what Alaric and most likely the entire group were thinking. Alaric pushed away the book in front of him and rubbed his eyes, fighting a yawn. It was hours past sunset and they'd been searching all day. To have found less than half of the sigils in the books they'd been poring over went beyond frustrating and into infuriating. The four they'd found were simple, discovered within the first hour of research. It had given them all a false sense of hope that they would be able to resolve this quickly.

That rapidly proved to be wrong when they didn't find a single other symbol in any book over the next nine hours. Lunch time had come and gone, barely noted as they rode the excitement of finding the first four so easily. By evening, that excitement was long forgotten. They'd eaten a cold dinner delivered by Hadiza's assistant, eating while they worked.

"Perhaps we should call it a night?" he suggested. "Everyone is exhausted. We can come at the problem with fresh eyes tomorrow."

Lord Wyrenian nodded immediately. "I think that's a good idea. It's been a very long day."

Kaelas looked at the stacks of books spread out across the table and Alaric knew he was weighing his choices. Kaelas never had much use for books, even as a child, according to what he'd been told. That was likely the deciding factor for him.

"Very well. Alaric will ward the room to keep everyone out but us until morning. We'll meet here for breakfast and get back to work. I don't want to give this man any more time to hurt anyone."

The Nevarreans were gathering their things almost before Kaelas finished speaking. Alaric noted that Ishaan and his soldier, Theodric, were out the door before anyone else. He couldn't blame him, given what had come to light recently.

He waited until they had all left and it was just himself and Kaelas in the room before letting out a tired sigh. "We're running out of books, Kas. I don't think we're going to find anything in the ones we have left."

"I'll send someone to the city library to get anything we don't already have here. We have to find out what these mean. I need our people to be safe. I can't let them survive a plague only to lose their lives at the hands of some foreign mage gone mad."

"I understand. Believe me, I do," he assured him. "I was just thinking that perhaps we *do* need fresh eyes on this."

Kas looked at him as though *he* were the one who had gone mad. "That's why we sent everyone to rest. They left just a few moments ago, in case you somehow didn't notice."

"I'm well aware of that. I'm not blind," he snapped, exhaustion getting the better of him and loosening the reins on his temper. "But have you stopped to consider that we have possibly the most knowledgeable magic-user in the world sitting downstairs?"

The change in Kaelas was instant. His golden eyes burned a fiery bright gold and his face hardened into a deep scowl. "No."

"Kas, we should at least consider-"

"No!" Kaelas shoved himself to his feet and suddenly the force of his fury was directed at him. Unfortunately for Kas, Alaric was one of the few people in the kingdom who refused to be intimidated. Not by Kaelas, at least. But the golden dragon, the being whose very nature was to be uncontrollable? He could admit that he didn't want to cross it, not so soon after using his magic to hold his cousin back.

"It was only a suggestion. I apologize," he murmured. He kept his eyes averted until the heavy pressure in the room dropped and the glowing gold faded from Kaelas' eyes.

"It was a foolish suggestion. Even if he did know what they were and he decided to share his knowledge, we'd never be able to trust what he says. He's a liar, Alaric. He's a liar and a traitor and I want you to forget that thought ever crossed your mind."

"You're right, it was a bad idea. Let's just take a break like the others are and get some sleep, alright?" he suggested, giving his cousin a small smile. "We're both exhausted. We'll figure this out tomorrow. I know we will."

"I hope so. I can't take many more days like this." Kaelas stretched, his slow movements giving away just how tired he was.

"Go ahead. I'll set up the wards, then head back to my rooms."

Kaelas agreed and let himself out, leaving Alaric alone. He went to each corner of the room, focusing his magic and allowing it to seep into the marble walls. He'd done this same thing in here before, so the walls seemed almost to recognize him and the wards were up in moments.

Yawning, he paused by the table on his way out, studying the stacks of books and pages of notes written in over a dozen different hands. He already knew tomorrow was going to be a waste of time, no matter what he'd told Kaelas. His gut was telling him they were looking at this whole situation wrong, but he didn't know what the right way was.

However... he knew someone who might.

Alaric didn't give himself time to second-guess his decision. He took a copy of the sketched out sigils, slipped it into his pocket, and hurried out the door before his common sense could take over and tell him what a mistake this was.

That little voice of reason was still trying to talk him out of this, even as he approached the guarded doors leading down to the cells. The two soldiers on duty stood up from the small table they'd been seated at, quickly coming to attention.

"No need to trouble yourselves, it's just me," he assured them. The months he'd spent perfecting the demeanor of a calm, controlled adviser served him well here and the tension bled from their bodies.

"What can I do for you, Lord Alaric?" one of the women asked.

"Prince Kaelas had a few questions for the prisoner, so I offered to come in his stead to keep the peace," he lied. "It won't take very long."

"I'll escort you," the other woman said, but Alaric shook his head.

"No need for that, Lahri, but thank you. He's well-contained and I can protect myself."

Lahri hesitated, glancing at her partner. "We were told he was extremely dangerous and to keep everyone out."

But they hadn't been told who, exactly, the prisoner was, otherwise they wouldn't even be considering this. He didn't doubt that the gossip would reach them sooner rather than later, but for now, it worked in his favor.

"I'll keep my distance from the bars, I assure you. I checked his restraints personally and I promise you there is no danger to me. The questions we have for him are somewhat sensitive in nature, otherwise I would gladly accept your offer of an escort." The smile he gave them was warm and almost apologetic. It usually worked when dealing with stubborn chancellors and seemed to have the same effect on protective soldiers.

"I'll leave the door cracked," the first guard conceded. "We won't be able to make out words, but if there's any hint of a disturbance, we'll be there in a matter of seconds."

It would have to do. "That's an excellent idea. Thank you for being so conscientious about my safety." He lowered his head in a shallow bow of gratitude, earning him a warm laugh from both women. Staying on the good side of the palace guards was always a wise move.

He left them standing in the doorway and proceeded down to the row of cells beneath the castle. Through that entire exchange, part of him was screaming to turn back. Lying to guards and going behind Kaelas' back was not who he was. It went against the image of himself he'd spent years curating. For once, though, he'd made his own decision and ignored that part of himself. Lives were on the line. He *had* to do this.

"I do hope your visit this time is for more pleasant reasons."

Zex's low voice slid out of the darkness and across Alaric's skin, leaving an uncomfortable prickle of awareness behind. Taking a slow breath, he shoved it away and donned the persona of 'Alaric, adviser to Kaelas' as he stopped in front of Zex's cell door.

The man was lying on his bed, reclined on his elbows, with one foot resting on the floor. His dark curls were tousled and framed his annoyingly handsome face. It would appear he'd just woken from a deep sleep, but the sharp interest in his silver eyes said he was wide awake.

"I have a few questions to ask you." Alaric kept back from the door, as he'd promised the guards he would. The deliberate move seemed to amuse Zex. The man didn't move from his comfortable position on his bed, merely raised an eyebrow.

"What a coincidence. I have some questions for you, as well," he drawled.

Of course he did. "I'm not here to have a conversation. You're going to answer my questions and then I'm going back upstairs."

"As simple as that?" The man had the gall to smirk and Alaric had to work to smother a flash of irritation. "Tell me, Alaric. Why should I help you? What do I get out of this?"

"You get to continue staying here, in a heated cell with plumbing and soft pillows. I promise you that the alternatives are not nearly as pleasant."

"I know the standard of prison cells in my own castle, though, and the worst of ours is still far above the best the southern kingdoms have to offer. You're going to need a better threat than that."

"It's not, though."

Zex tilted his head. "Pardon?"

Alaric let a tiny smirk of his own break free for a moment. "You said you know the standards of your own castle. But it's not your castle, is it? Not anymore."

He knew he should probably feel guilty about such a sharp dig, but instead all he felt was a tiny surge of triumph when Zex's eyes hardened and that infuriating grin finally fell away.

"Perhaps not, but that changes nothing. I know what you're threatening and I'm not intimidated. I'm also rather uninterested in answering any questions you might have, so I'll bid you a good night."

With that curt dismissal, Zex laid back down, eyes closing as though he really intended to sleep.

This is why you don't lead with your emotions, he silently scolded himself. He had one last card he could play, though.

"You aren't willing to help me in exchange for an update on the young soldier, then? I believe you said his name was Elias?"

The tension in the cell suddenly thickened, growing heavy. It was similar to the sensation he felt when the golden dragon within Kaelas was close to the surface and he was abruptly reminded that a pair of tourmaline-laced iron manacles were the only thing keeping the silver dragon from rising and wiping them all out.

Zex pushed himself upright and rose to his feet, moving until he was at the bars and standing directly in front of Alaric, with only a few feet between them. "Leave him out of this," he growled, eyes narrowed. "He has nothing to do with this."

The vehemence took him by surprise. "I was only offering to let you know how he's faring."

"Not very well, I would imagine, judging by what your people already did to him." His silver eyes had taken on a distinct glow, but the manacles did their job for the moment.

"Wait a moment." Alaric frowned, taking a step forward. "We did nothing to him except save his life."

"You saved him after torturing him. How kind of you," Zex spat back. His hands were gripping the door of his cell now, the metal links of the chain between his wrists clanging against the reinforced bars.

"I swear to you, we did nothing to hurt him. We found him like that, and our soldiers brought him back to our healers in an attempt to save him. We didn't know he was one of yours until we discovered your protection on him."

Suddenly, the easy way Zex had surrendered after healing the man made sense. Alaric had assumed it was arrogance, but now he wondered if it had been the man's attempt at protecting Elias from more of the torture he believed they'd done.

"Then who did that to him? He was in perfect health when I last saw him in the mountains." Some of the fury in Zex's eyes eased, but he didn't step back from the cell door.

"That's what we're trying to find out. That's the reason I'm here at all. We discovered clues but haven't been able to interpret them. I had hoped you might have more insight."

Zex tilted his head again, the last of his anger replaced by that sharp interest of earlier as he studied Alaric. "Kaelas agreed to let you come down here and question me?" he asked, voice thick with skepticism.

"My cousin trusts me to make the best decision about the welfare of our people and our country."

The snort of laughter that answer earned him made him jump. Zex shook his head, smirking again. "Spoken like a true politician. I take that to mean he doesn't know you're down here. If I know him as well as I once did, he directly forbade you from coming to see me, and yet here you stand. I knew there was more to you than you let show, but I confess, I didn't think you had it in you to defy Kaelas."

"We may not always completely agree on what course of action should be taken, but everything I do is in service to Sarkhyr and Kaelas." Guilt tried to gain a foothold, kindled by Zex's words, but he refused to let that ember grow within him.

"I'm sure he'll accept that when he finds out," Zex said dryly. "He's always had quite the temper. I can only imagine how much worse it's become since I left and our bond became what it is now. I assume he's been relying on you to keep him from falling apart completely?"

Alaric did a better job keeping his reaction hidden this time, despite how hard those words hit. Zex was dangerously close to a truth known only by two people in the entire world: himself and Kaelas.

"I have no idea what you're talking about," he said, draining any hint of emotion from his tone. "I didn't come here to answer your questions. My terms are simple. Assist in deciphering the clues we found, and I will update you on your young friend."

"It sounds like I was right. That's not surprising, really. But fine, I'll play your little game. Show me what you've found and I'll help you if I can."

This was quite possibly one of the worst ideas he'd ever had. He was well aware of that, but it didn't stop him from extracting the notes he'd taken.

Pulling just one page, he handed it over to Zex. He had to get close enough to the cell door to give it to him, which also put him within arm's reach of the man. Kaelas would have a fit if he knew, but Zex simply took the page and glanced at it.

"I assume this is a test, then?"

"I have no idea what you're talking about. Can you decipher it?"

Zex scoffed. "A toddler with a picture book could decipher these. They're basic enhancement sigils, meant to give a boost of power to whatever working the mage is doing. They're a bit obscure, yes, but I know for a fact there are books in the castle library that explain all of them. If Kaelas were working alone, I could well believe he wouldn't figure it out, but not you. You're smarter than this."

It *had* been fairly obvious what he was doing, he supposed. "Yes, it was a test. I wanted to see if you would be truthful with me. You'll understand if I don't blindly trust your word for it."

"You wound me. Why would I lie to you?"

"Why would you tell me the truth?" he countered, earning another laugh. He hated how much it humanized Zex.

The man shrugged. "It's in my best interests to cooperate with you. At least at the moment. Now, are you actually going to let me help, or are we going to waste the time you've stolen by sitting here bickering? Not that this hasn't been very enjoyable for me."

"If I find out you're lying about anything I show you, I won't wait for Kaelas and the chancellors. I'll deal with you myself."

"So fierce. I think I like you, Alaric."

"I'm honored," he said, letting every bit of disdain show as he spoke. Unfortunately, Zex was right. It was only a matter of time before someone realized he wasn't where he was supposed to be. He could only hope that the someone wasn't Kaelas.

He stepped closer to the bars, barely a foot between them now, and held out another page to Zex. He wasn't foolish enough to release all of them and the tiny smirk Zex shot him said he hadn't missed the deliberate move. The page of copied sigils stole his attention before Alaric could comment, though.

"Where did you say you found these?" He frowned, tilting the page toward the magelight in the corner.

"Does it matter?"

"Yes, it actually matters quite a bit." Zex raised his head, bristling with annoyance. "I recognize a few of these, but their purpose varies wildly depending on how they're placed. Were they on paper? Written in the dirt? Sketched onto an altar?"

Kas is going to kill me.

It really was too late to back out at this point, though. No matter what happened now, his cousin was going to be furious. Might as well make the coming argument worth it.

"They were on the body of a dead woman," he said with a sigh. "Carved into her skin. The healer I spoke to believes it was done while she was still alive."

Predictably, Zex didn't even flinch, just tilted his head and studied the page in his hand. "I assume you're here because you haven't caught the person doing this? That's not surprising. Whoever they are, they're powerful. Not only that, if they're using these on a living person, they don't care about collateral damage."

"But what *are* they? They're not in any of the books we can find."

"I should hope not. If you think blood magic is so awful, this sort of spellwork would give you nightmares." Zex turned the paper so Alaric could see the sigils. He pointed to each in turn as he spoke. "This one is a binding of sorts, to build a bridge between two mages. It started as a way to share power in battle, but it took roughly a week for someone to corrupt it and use it to force the binding and steal power. A concerted effort was made to strike it from every book of magic that exists, though clearly at least one was missed."

Building a bridge to share power. That was eerily similar to what Ishaan had described.

"What about the rest?"

"This one I don't know, but practitioners of blood magic use the one beside it." Zex paused, as though expecting some sort of comment from Alaric, but he wasn't in the mood to interrupt. He gestured for him to keep going. "Alright. Weak mages use it to strengthen their intent. It has to be fed with blood, so whoever did this chose the easiest route."

"You wonder why everyone finds blood magic so repellent when you tell me of things like this?" Alaric couldn't help himself. The very idea of it revolted him.

"I was wondering how long it would take for you to start lecturing me on the wickedness of my ways."

"I'm not going to lecture you, but... you have to know how *wrong* that is."

"You say that as though I were the one doing this. I'm not a weak mage. I don't need such crude workings to bolster my magic."

Alaric gaped at him. "That's what you take offense with? The fact that you think I insinuated that you're weak, and not that the sigil was *carved into someone's skin?*"

"Of course, it's awful what was done to the poor woman." The distinct lack of emotion in Zex's voice said everything Alaric needed to know about the man's sincerity. "I simply meant that I'm not the one doing such things and I never would. I know you think of me as a depraved monster, and you're not completely wrong, but you seem to forget what I used to be. I was once a ruler, just like your precious cousin. One can't rule a kingdom without caring about the people at least a bit. Neither I nor my followers are doing this."

There was that emotion that had been missing a moment ago. His gut told him that Zex wasn't lying. Not about this, at least. It helped that they'd all but eliminated Zex as a suspect, of course.

"Then help me decipher the rest so I can find who truly is doing this before they hurt someone else."

Their eyes met, but he didn't back down, silently challenging Zex to put proof to his words and help him. The moment dragged on, but finally, the other man nodded.

"Very well, but you had better hold up your end of this bargain."

"I'm a man of my word. Help me and I'll answer any questions you may have about your young friend."

"Do you have another page of these symbols?"

Alaric nodded. "I do, actually. I'll give them to you one at a time."

"At least show them to me from there," Zex demanded, clearly irritated. "This last sigil doesn't make any sense on its own, so I need to see what others were with it. It would help quite a bit if you remembered which one was found right beside it."

"Fine." Alaric pulled out the other two pages of notes he'd borrowed, studying them a moment before holding them up to face Zex. "These are the rest of the sigils we found. The one on the far right, in the bottom corner, is the one that was directly beside that one."

"You're absolutely sure it was that one?" For once, Zex was deadly serious, no trace of amusement in his quicksilver eyes. Whatever this was, it was somehow even more dire than Alaric had imagined.

"I'm sure. They were the only two placed that close together, so I noticed them immediately. Why? What are they?"

Zex studied the paper in Alaric's hands, then the one he held, a deep frown marring his features. "They are serious trouble for all of you," he finally said. "This first one here is another binding, but it's different from the others. This one is meant to be a permanent bond, controlled by the caster. Depending on the symbol it's placed with, it can be used for any manner of spells, from stealing power to stealing someone's very life."

An icy chill crawled up Alaric's spine. "What does that mean? Stealing their life? You mean killing them?"

"Yes, but not just killing them. The caster, if they're strong enough, can steal their victim's life for themselves. I don't know how this person could possibly know about it. To the best of my knowledge, there was only one book in the entire world that held that spell in its pages and I personally destroyed it years ago."

"Just a moment. I'm not boasting when I say my magical knowledge is quite vast, but I've never even heard of such a thing. It's not possible."

"I've never heard of it actually being used," Zex admitted. "But all these other symbols are for binding, controlling, and strengthening. All of them combined may just be enough to actually work."

"We thought the victims were killed by accident, but you're suggesting their lives were stolen to... what? Lengthen the perpetrator's life?" Even to his own ears, his voice sounded faint.

"I believe you're right and these people *weren't* killed on purpose. It's likely the mage was attempting to use his victims as a sort of power source, to either gradually lengthen his own life or to help him heal from any injuries. Doing all this work only to kill them quickly doesn't make any sense."

"None of this makes any sense, Zex!" The words slipped out as almost a shout, shock and disgust loosening his restraint. He immediately regretted it when he heard clattering on the stairs.

"Lord Alaric! Are you alright?" Lahri stopped at the end of the hallway, eyes narrowing when she spotted how close he was standing to Zex.

"Everything is fine. I'm sorry, I got a bit heated while questioning the prisoner. It's nothing to be concerned about," he assured her, easily slipping back into the guise of a calm, controlled politician. He even managed a gentle smile. "Thank you for coming to investigate so quickly. I promise I won't be much longer."

"I can stay," she offered, still watching Zex suspiciously, but he shook his head.

"Thank you, but no. My reasons from earlier still stand, I'm afraid. Only a few more minutes and then I'll leave. I promise you I will be alright."

She didn't appear to be convinced, but she didn't argue further, slowly heading back up the stairs. Alaric noticed she kept the door cracked open, though. With a sigh, he let the mask fall and turned back to Zex, only to find the man staring at him intently.

"What now?"

"Who *are* you, Alaric? Truly? Do you even know, yourself?" The question slid under his skin despite his attempts to ignore him.

"I don't have time for games. I only have a few minutes before the guards get anxious and I'm forced to leave, so let's finish this."

"You won't be able to hide from me forever," Zex murmured, his eyes glowing silver for a moment before settling back to normal. "Very well. Let's finish this, then. In my opinion, the mage you're looking for is incredibly powerful, but either severely ill or injured. He would have to have a deep understanding of the intricacies of magic and years of experience with combining sigils. Foreign, perhaps Vaetrean or Gavarrian. As for why he came to Sarkhyr to do these spells, I would imagine he has somehow learned some of our secrets and knows our mages are stronger."

"You know all that just based on the spells he used?"

"Most of it is fairly obvious once you know what the spells are for. I believe him to be foreign only because our own people have little use for sigils and rituals. We've so rarely needed them that they're not common practice, which means our mages don't study them. You didn't, did you?"

"Not much," Alaric admitted. He was tired, worn down by the amount of knowledge he was trying to take in. "More than my peers, but clearly not enough."

"It wasn't meant as a slight against you or your skill. It's simply the way it is. I can't begin to fathom the reason he's doing this, but no one resorts to such means unless they are truly desperate and have no care for the lives of anyone but themselves. If you plan to go after him, which I assume you do, I would advise you to take the strongest mages you can get your hands on. Or me, of course." Zex smirked, and it was enough to shake the fog of shock from Alaric.

"I would have to be as insane as our killer to even consider that, so I wouldn't get your hopes up."

"The offer stands," he said with another shrug. "Now, your turn. I helped you. Tell me what happened to Elias."

It wasn't exactly what he'd promised, but he owed Zex more than he cared to admit. They never would have figured this out on their own. "Our soldiers found Elias not far from the woman who was killed. He hasn't regained full consciousness yet, but we believe he may have been attempting to defend her. Perhaps he stumbled across the killer. We don't know for sure. After what you've told me, my guess is that the person doing this was planning to use Elias as his next power source, until it became obvious Elias had no magic ability. It appears he was left for dead and our soldiers found him in time to save him."

"He's healing, though? Even though he hasn't woken?" Zex pressed. He was against the bars now, resting his elbows on the supports. His hands were outside the cell as far as the chains of his manacles would allow, the page of symbols Alaric had given him held loosely in front of him.

"The healer believes it won't be much longer before he regains consciousness. He's healing well now that we're able to fully work on him. That protection you had on him was quite strong. You must care about him quite a bit." Alaric could admit that he'd been curious about that. Who was the young soldier to Zex, for him to be so well-protected? He wasn't surprised when the other man deflected.

"That's good to hear. I suppose the odds of me speaking to him once he's awake are slim." It wasn't a question.

"More like nonexistent, but I will let him know you were worried about him."

Zex tilted his head again, something Alaric was starting to think was a gesture he wasn't even aware he was doing. "That's oddly generous of you, Alaric. What is it going to cost me?"

"You helped me far more than you had to. I'll pass the message along and consider us even." He held out his hand for the paper, but Zex didn't even attempt to hand it to him. He stayed where he was, the page dangling in front of the bars while those eerie eyes dared him to take it. Alaric had never been the one to accept pointless challenges from the other children growing up, knowing he had nothing to prove to them. He had nothing to prove to this renegade prince, either, but something in him refused to let him back down. He closed the distance between them again, never breaking eye contact as he plucked the page from Zex's loose grip.

"Thank you for your assistance. I will handle it from here."

Zex moved faster than he should have been able to, with the bars and manacles working against him. Before he could blink, Alaric was pressed against the bars, his face barely an inch from Zex. Hands gripped his shirt, giving him no room to escape. They were so close he could feel the other man's breath on his cheek, but oddly enough, he felt no fear.

"Let go of me," he ordered calmly.

"Don't go after this man alone," Zex demanded, barely more than a whisper.

"I had no intention of going alone. I'll be with Kas and several powerful mages. Now let go of me."

"He'll kill you without hesitation. Take me with you. I can protect you."

That startled him enough to break through the veneer of calm that had settled over him. "Why would you do that, though? I'm nothing to you and you are nothing to me. What happened here tonight will never happen again."

"And yet, I believe what I said when you brought me here was correct. Will you be thinking about me when you leave here, Alaric?" The dark growl when Zex said his name made Alaric shiver, but he couldn't name the emotion that accompanied it. Or rather, he didn't want to name it.

"I plan to forget about you the moment this door closes behind me. Release me or I will *make* you release me."

A heavy silence fell between them, their eyes locked in silent battle. It felt like eons passed before Zex finally released his hold, allowing Alaric to take a step back and gain space between them. He stayed where he was, once more resting against the cell door, only this time, his hands were behind the bars.

"I would warn you never to touch me again, but I will never see you again after this moment, so that hardly seems necessary." Alaric pulled the mask back on, a cloak to hide how much Zex had rattled him.

"I meant what I said. Whoever this mage is, he's stronger than you and doesn't have your qualms holding him back." Zex stared him down a moment longer, then slipped back into the lazy, arrogant stance that Alaric was coming to realize was just as much a mask as the one he wore. "Pass my message along to Elias."

Zex stepped back from the bars and returned to his bed, lounging comfortably as though the last several minutes had never happened. Alaric stood watching him a moment longer, then turned on his heel and left. He almost made it to the top of the stairs before Zex's voice caught up to him, his words making his stomach clench.

"I'll see you soon, Alaric."

Chapter 23

The sound of angry shouts echoed down the hallway to greet them when Theo and his team arrived to begin research the following morning. They paused a few feet back from the door to the throne room. The guards standing outside looked distinctly uncomfortable, but they weren't rushing inside, so there clearly wasn't any danger.

"It's too early for this, captain," Kya whined and Theo had to agree. Breakfast was waiting on them past those doors, along with coffee and tea, but he had no desire to get dragged into a fight when the sun had barely begun to rise. Beside him, he heard Ishaan sigh, and he glanced over to find the younger man half-asleep on his feet.

"Ishaan," he murmured and Ishaan blinked a few times as though waking from a deep sleep. "Are you alright?"

Theo didn't believe the nod he got in response even for a moment. Ishaan had been the first one to fall asleep last night, barely even touching his pillow before he was out. He'd slept straight through the night until James' grumpy complaining had forced him to wake. It had been an exhausting day, but it still seemed a little unusual.

"Let's get this over with," Captain Trieste said with a sigh, and Theo put his concern aside for the moment. He did make a point of slipping his hand into Ishaan's, though. He believed the little smile he got far more than that nod.

"Is it just me or does that sound like Prince Kaelas and Alaric?" Naema murmured as they approached the door.

"I didn't think they had separate thoughts on anything," James said. "Or that Alaric would allow himself to sink so far as to yell."

"Let's cut the chatter and focus," Kellan said quietly, and they fell silent. The guards appeared to be trying very hard not to listen as they opened the doors. Theo was the last inside with Ishaan, and the moment they crossed the threshold, the doors closed behind them.

He paused, assessing the situation as quickly as he could. Given how loud the two men were being, it wasn't that difficult.

"I don't care what information you have! You disobeyed a direct order!" Kaelas was shouting. He was toe-to-toe with his cousin, using his few inches of extra height to loom over Alaric. The younger man wasn't backing down, though.

"You may be the prince of Sarkhyr, but you're being irrational!" He wasn't quite shouting, but it wasn't far off. His fair skin was flushed with anger, a rare display of emotion from the stoic man. "I got the information we needed. Why does it matter where it came from?"

"Because you lied to me! You told me to my face that you were going to do the wards and go to bed. Instead, you did the *one* thing I directly told you not to do! Since when do you lie to me, Alaric?"

Even from across the room, Theo could see a faint golden glow from Kaelas, and he turned to Captain Trieste in alarm. "Captain? Should we be here? If he loses his temper and shifts form, he's going to crush us."

"I think we're safe for the moment," Trieste said to them, then raised his voice to reach the two Sarkhyrians. "Prince Kaelas? Alaric?"

"I did what I had to do!" Alaric went on as though Captain Trieste had never spoken. Theo doubted they'd even heard him. "You refused to even consider-"

"Because you don't know what you're doing!" Kaelas' shout echoed across the room, unnaturally loud.

"I found out what almost all the sigils are *and* what they do! I have an idea of who this murderer is and what his goals are. We have a real chance at tracking him down and you won't even *listen* to what I found!"

"Because you got it from *Zex!*" Kaelas spat the man's name like a curse and Theo froze, disgust curling in his gut. Just hearing that name was enough for the edges of his vision to blur. Only Ishaan's tight grip on his hand kept him grounded, but it was a struggle.

"Wait, did he say he knows what all those symbols are?" Kellan asked over the sound of the continued argument. "If that's the case, this argument is wasting time we could be using to find the mage who did this."

"We can't believe a word out of that man's mouth," Theo spat. "He lies as easily as the rest of us breathe. Besides, why would he help us with anything? I hate to say it, but I agree with Prince Kaelas."

"We'll deal with who's right and who's wrong later. First, I need to cut this off before it gets truly out of hand. Stay put," Trieste ordered. He strode across the room until he was beside the two men. "Prince Kaelas. Lord Alaric."

Finally, the two acknowledged they weren't alone. Alaric took a step back, and Theo watched all the emotion drain from his face. He couldn't hide the flush of color high on his cheekbones, though.

"I apologize, sir. I didn't realize you had arrived. Please excuse the noise. My cousin and I were having a slight disagreement."

That was a bit of an understatement. Theo turned his attention to Kaelas. Unlike Alaric, it was taking the prince far longer to back down from his anger.

"We wouldn't be having this 'disagreement' if you hadn't decided to commit treason," Kaelas growled and Alaric turned on him.

"Treason? I'm doing everything in my power to save Sarkhyrian lives while you have a temper tantrum because I went behind your back!"

The doors opening behind them announced the arrival of Lord Wyrenian and his team, much to Theo's relief. An ambassador was exactly what they needed at the moment.

"Dare I ask what we missed?" Wyrenian asked, his voice low. Beside him, Sir Embry kept his focus on the arguing men.

"I'm very glad you're here. I think this is beyond our capabilities." Kellan quickly filled the ambassador in on the argument, which had resumed, leaving Captain Trieste trying in vain to intervene.

"I've noticed Prince Kaelas can be quite particular when it comes to Zex," Lord Wyrenian murmured. He watched the two for a few seconds, but rather than join the captain to intercede, he turned to his apprentice. "Embry?"

"Yes, sir?"

"Arguments like this are quite common among everyone, not just the nobility. Why don't you see what you can do to smooth the waters?"

Theo bit back a groan. He had nothing against Embry. The young man had worked well with them as they'd spent the day researching, but he would have much preferred the more experienced ambassador to get involved. He'd hoped they would get this resolved sooner rather than later. It wasn't his place to say so, though, so he held back his reaction. This was Lord Wyrenian's domain.

"Are you sure, sir?" Embry asked, his dark eyes studying the two Sarkhyrians.

"The result of this situation is important, but not world-shattering. What better way to practice your skills than this? I fully believe you can handle this."

"I will not let you down." Embry raised his chin and Theo saw nothing but quiet confidence as he made his way across the room. He murmured something to Captain Trieste, too quiet to hear from this distance, but whatever it was, the captain seemed to agree with. He left off trying to be heard over Prince Kaelas' shouting and rejoined the rest of the group.

They probably should have left. Theo could only assume that having such a large audience for his first attempt at peacemaking wouldn't make this any easier for Sir Embry, but despite that, he was curious to see how this turned out now.

"Lord Alaric. Prince Kaelas." The young man didn't raise his voice, but something about him must have caught Kaelas' attention, because he stopped mid-shout to glance at Embry.

"Whatever it is, it will have to wait." The prince was abrupt, but not overtly impolite.

"I understand this situation with Lord Alaric is important and I hate to interrupt, but I did just want to ask one question, if I may?"

Kaelas hesitated and Theo knew the argument was about to start all over again when he caught a glimpse of glowing gold in Kaelas' eyes. Just in the few days he'd known him, he'd become more than a little familiar with his temper.

Instead, though, he shocked everyone and nodded. Even Alaric looked stunned, his eyes widening and brows shooting up as he stared at his cousin. Embry, though, remained as calm as ever.

"What are your priorities, Prince Kaelas?"

Now Kaelas mirrored the rest of them, the anger fading into confusion and shock. "Excuse me?"

"Your priorities as the prince of Sarkhyr. I have never met royalty before, so I was curious as to what your top priority is?"

"Where's he going with this?" Irric muttered behind Theo, who just shook his head. He genuinely did not know.

"I think I know. Just watch," James urged him.

Kaelas considered it for a few moments before he spoke. "Keeping the people of my country safe and well. That should be the main purpose of every ruler. It's why we exist."

"I wish every leader had your dedication," Embry said with a faint, warm smile. "I doubt many would do as you have done and taken the time to personally hunt for someone who poses a threat to your people."

"Then they don't deserve to be in charge. A leader is supposed to lead. I can't sit back and let others deal with something like this. It wouldn't be right."

"And now that we seem to be so close to finding out who this person is, I can only assume that you will want to use this new knowledge to finally track them down before they can hurt anyone else. I can see why your people speak so highly of you, Prince Kaelas."

"I just do the best that I can," Kaelas shook his head. "You're right, though. I wouldn't risk sending anyone after a dangerous mage without being there to protect them." He paused, then turned to Alaric. "We'll continue our discussion later. Right now, we need to focus on verifying as much of this information as we can and figure out a way to use it to track this mage."

"Of course." Alaric actually stuttered the first word, the most non-plussed Theo had ever seen the usually stoic man.

"I will help in any way that I can, of course. Thank you for taking the time to speak with me," Embry murmured, drawing Kaelas' attention back to him.

"It was my pleasure."

Embry gave a flawlessly executed bow, his movements so fluid it was almost a dance, then turned to rejoin the group. He didn't seem to be aware of the golden gaze that followed him the entire way.

"Excellent work, Embry." Lord Wyrenian was careful not to let his expression give him away to the Sarkhyrian prince, but his pride in his apprentice showed in the way he gripped the young man's shoulder. "I had no doubt at all that you could handle this."

He may not have, but Theo was still trying to understand exactly what he'd just seen. With only a few sentences, the young man had cut the prince's temper off at the knees. At the same time, he'd convinced him to use the new information while making it seem like it had been Kaelas' idea all along.

Theo was left gaping at him, only now realizing just how badly he had underestimated Sir Embry Falloran.

The young man in question just gave that same tiny little smile and looked around at the others. "Shall we get to work?"

Even with the new knowledge given to them by Zex, the list of suspects remained stubbornly blank. The knowledge that they were using information given to them by the man who still tormented Theo's thoughts sat wrong with him, but in this case, what choice did they have? He was a man of his word, and he'd vowed that he could handle this.

He felt a light touch on his knee and glanced up to see Ishaan watching him, clearly concerned. He wasn't sure why at first, until he realized Prince Kaelas was staring at him expectantly.

Theo bit back a curse. "I'm sorry. I was caught up in reading. What did you say?"

"I asked you if you recalled anyone else in Zex's party that hasn't been accounted for yet," he said, in a tone implying that he was surrounded by incompetence. He wasn't the only one who caught it, if the way James bristled was any indication.

"No, there were only the ones I mentioned and I don't think any of them would be capable of this type of magic," he said quickly, to forestall another argument.

"We still have no one, then," Alaric sighed.

Another light touch, and Theo saw a scrap of paper slide in front of him. Ignoring Kaelas' huffy response to his cousin, he focused on the note.

"Did you lose track again?"

It was a simple question, but a cold sweat broke out, and Theo had to fight a shudder. Even though no one was watching them, he didn't dare speak the words out loud, so he nodded once. Following Ishaan's lead, he wrote his response and passed it back.

"The last thing I recall us talking about was if some of the sigils predate even the Caranish language. How long ago was that?"

"About an hour."

Three words. He'd never realized just how much power words held until that simple statement filled him with a fear unlike any he'd ever known. The other times this had happened, when he'd lost time, hadn't been like this. Hours of riding through the mountains or in his bed at night, he expected his mind to wander. Here, though? Surrounded by people, with conversations going on all around him, some of which he'd been actively listening to? How had he managed to lose himself again?

"I don't think anyone noticed," Ishaan assured him, the note crammed onto the last remaining space on the little slip of paper. It calmed one fear, at least, but not enough. When Ishaan's hand slipped into his, he held onto it like the lifeline it was, trying to ground himself in the here and now.

Desperate for something to focus on, he tuned back in to the conversations happening around the table and abruptly realized that Captain Trieste was speaking to Prince Kaelas. Or arguing, rather.

"I understand your concerns, but we need more information. We're getting nowhere with this."

"While I appreciate your help, this is still a Sarkhyrian matter. My very best mages are scouring the scene where Lady Heraldra was found. What do you think your team will find that they can't?"

Trieste was not a politician, and it had never been more obvious than now. Even to Theo's untrained eye, he looked ready to start another fight.

Luckily for them, Lord Wyrenian *was* a politician, and he smoothly inserted himself into the conversation before it could get out of hand again. "The captain means no insult to your people, Prince Kaelas. Considering we are looking for a mage, though, perhaps it would be prudent to have every mage working this case be familiar with the energy left by the perpetrator? I confess I know little about magic, but Rhea tells me it leaves something behind?"

"Yes, sir," she nodded. She didn't hesitate, and Theo wondered how long the ambassador's team had been together, for them to work so seamlessly. "It isn't a trail or anything we could use to find who did this, unfortunately, but every mage has a unique energy that tends to linger. For a simple spell, it would dissipate in mere seconds, but for something of this magnitude, that energy could feasibly linger for days or longer."

"Lady Heraldra wasn't killed where she was found, though. We don't know where it occurred," Kaelas pointed out.

"You're right, but I believe magic like this would leave its stain wherever it is," Kellan said. He gave Rhea an apologetic smile for interrupting, but she nodded for him to continue. "It will not be as strong as the scene of the crime, but if we can familiarize ourselves with this mage's energy, we would know it again when we sense it."

"Meaning that if it's anyone in the city, we would know them the moment we were close enough," Alaric finished. "Kas, it's a good idea. We should go now, while we still have a chance of finding a trace."

Kaelas was quiet for a few moments, considering it from every angle, but Theo had a feeling he would agree and wasn't surprised when the prince finally nodded.

"Very well. I will take the mages to the scene," he decided. "The rest of you will keep researching."

Kya's chair clattered and almost toppled from the speed at which she stood up. Being still for this long had to have been wearing on the young mage. For a moment, Theo almost envied her, but as curious as he was to see the scene and attempt to find some sort of trail, he was just as happy to sit this one out until he could be sure he wouldn't lose track of time again.

"Saleed, Delphine, stick with Lieutenant Sol. No wandering off," Trieste ordered, his dark eyes specifically locked onto James as he said it.

"That applies to you, as well, Rhea," Wyrenian echoed. "This is fact-gathering only."

"Yes, sir." She rose and joined Kellan, Kya, and James near the head of the table. Alaric rose, too, but Kaelas still sat.

He had only a moment to be confused before the prince's eyes locked onto Ishaan and Theo immediately knew what he was going to say.

"I would like Ishaan to accompany us," he said, but it wasn't a suggestion.

"For what purpose? He's not a mage," Trieste protested, and Theo felt Ishaan's grip on his hand tighten.

"He is, though," Kaelas pointed out, eyes never leaving Ishaan. "He holds half of Zex's power within him and while I am loath to admit it, Zex is one of the most powerful mages in generations. Given the circumstances, this would be an ideal time to find out if that power is dormant or not."

The grip on his hand went slack and Theo turned to find Ishaan frozen, eyes wide with shock. Like Theo, Ishaan hadn't truly put the pieces together in his mind until they were so bluntly laid out by Kaelas.

"Taking that into consideration, I would think the best option would be to have him here, safe in your castle," Trieste pointed out, but he didn't even finish before Kaelas was shaking his head.

"I would like to say I trust every person living and working here, but I'm afraid I cannot. I know rumors have spread that he is here and should anyone connect the two of them, I would prefer to have Ishaan where I can see him."

Theo couldn't fault that logic, as much as he wanted to. There was no way he was letting Ishaan out of his sight again, though. Not after last time.

"Rhoan, you will accompany us," Trieste ordered, just as Theo opened his mouth to speak. He caught the captain's eyes and caught a spark of grim amusement there. "As a safeguard, should anything go wrong."

Theo expected Kaelas to object simply for the sake of objecting at this point, but to his surprise, the prince nodded.

"Fine. Let's get this done. Meet at the stables in ten minutes. The sooner we get there, the sooner we can get answers. Send for Hadiza if anything happens while we are away," he said to the soldiers remaining. "They will know what to do. And do not go anywhere near the dungeons or Zex. No matter what. That is an order."

Kaelas left at that, with Alaric on his heels. Only once the door closed did Trieste speak, and even then, it was in a low voice. "Keep your eyes and ears open, mages. Treat this like any other job. You know what to do."

"Yes, sir," Theo nodded, echoed by the mages.

"The rest of us will do the same. Take note of anything you see, even if it doesn't seem consequential. We'll meet when you return. Now get moving."

As the group splintered, with him and Ishaan accompanying the mages to grab equipment while the fighter stayed behind, Theo felt his chest tighten. The last time the group had split up, Vesa had nearly died and he'd ended up in the hands of Zex. He didn't want to leave them again. Something was going to happen. Something bad. He just knew it.

A soft, rhythmic sound worked through the panic building within him and he latched onto it, allowing it to distract him as he tried to figure out where it was coming from.

It was only after several seconds that he realized it was Ishaan. It was a very faint sound, like he was clicking his tongue, and it stopped the moment Theo looked at him. The concern in his eyes was obvious, though not to the others, as they all hurried to their rooms to get what they needed.

"Thank you," he whispered. "I'm alright now."

Ishaan raised an eyebrow, skeptical, and it was enough to get a faint smile from him. "I promise. Having something to focus on helped. Thank you."

It was enough to appease Ishaan, and the two of them entered their room to find James stuffing his bag full.

"James. We're only going for a few hours. You won't need every reagent you possess," he pointed out. The mage scoffed.

"But what if we need something and I don't have it? I'd rather be prepared."

"James. We're going with the lieutenant, Kya, Rhea, and Lord Alaric. If there's something you don't have, one of them will. Just get your usual supplies and maybe two or three of the less usual. It'll be fine."

Ishaan surprised him by lightly smacking his arm at the same time that James let out a loud groan.

"Why would you say that?" he all but wailed. "You've just guaranteed that this is going to be a disaster."

"You're both overreacting. It's a quick trip and we're not even leaving the vicinity of the city. We'll be back in just a few hours. Let's just get our things and go."

The anxiety threatened to well up within him again, but Theo ruthlessly shoved it down. Ishaan was doing a good job of hiding it, but it was clear he was scared, which meant it was up to him to protect the younger man. He firmly believed that this really would be a simple in and out trip, but he had to believe his own words. It was going to be fine.

CHAPTER 24

Theo's words lingered in Ishaan's mind as the group rode out from the city of Yrasea. He desperately hoped that everything really would be fine, that they would find the information they needed and be back before supper, but his gut was telling him it wouldn't be that simple. Something was going to happen. He just didn't know what.

He kept to the rear of the group with Theo, putting distance between himself and Kaelas while also allowing them to watch over the group. It had the added comfort of putting them out of sight of the others unless they turned. Given what had happened earlier, when Theo had lost time again, Ishaan preferred keeping out of the center of attention as much as possible.

When Alaric fell back to ride beside him, he felt a flicker of alarm, but the man seemed calm enough and as relaxed as he ever seemed to get, which wasn't very much at all. Still, relief washed over him when he felt Theo edge a little closer.

"Your protection isn't necessary against me, Theodric, no need to glare. I only wanted to talk."

He was getting familiar with how intense Theo could get when he was being protective, and Ishaan fought not to smile. The tracker didn't come off as overly threatening, so when he got serious, it was a bit of a shock.

"You can talk with me here."

If he wasn't mistaken, it seemed like Alaric was the one holding back a smile now. He managed, though, and nodded once. "I wouldn't dream of attempting to do otherwise. I simply wanted to check on the both of you. The last few weeks have been difficult, to put it mildly, and more so for you two. Finding a moment to speak to you alone has proven to be nearly impossible, so this will have to do."

The Nevarreans didn't trust Alaric. None of them had come out and said it, but it was obvious in the way they held themselves back from him and never volunteered pleasantries or information. He could understand, of course. Being the adviser to the prince meant anything said to Alaric would most likely find its way back to Kaelas, so they were simply being cautious.

Ishaan knew almost nothing of politics, but he did know how to read people. Growing up, it was the only way he'd managed to survive. His instincts were telling him that Alaric was a good man. Even more than that, though... he could see something of a kindred soul in him. Even had he not been watching everyone, it was impossible to miss how often Alaric was ignored or shuffled to the side until he was needed. It was something Ishaan was unfortunately familiar with, as was the loneliness that came with always being an afterthought.

Alaric hid it well, but Ishaan got the impression that he was very much alone. He didn't appear to have any sort of friends or even acquaintances outside of Kaelas and Hadiza. He seemed to know just about everyone in the castle by name, at the very least, but no one sought him out. Even the one strange guard only ever watched him, if a bit too intently for comfort. He knew how awful that was, to feel so alone even with others around, and he didn't wish that on anyone.

He straightened in his saddle and held the reins out to Theo. He seemed to understand, because he took them and guided Ishaan's horse so Ishaan could pull his journal out of his bag. Honestly, he could have dropped the reins and most likely have been fine. The horse he was riding was the same one he'd taken up the mountain. It simply wanted to follow the group and would continue to do so until told otherwise. Still, it made him feel a little more secure to have Theo as a safeguard.

"We're as alright as we can be. Some days are harder than others," he wrote, showing it to Theo before passing it to Alaric. The other man had likely been expecting the usual vague promise that they were fine and the honesty seemed to surprise him, if the way he hesitated before passing the journal back said anything.

"I'm truly sorry for the suffering you both have endured in Sarkhyr, for whatever that is worth." There was no one else near enough to easily overhear, but Alaric still spoke quietly, ensuring the conversation stayed between the three of them. "If there is anything at all I can do for either of you, if it's within my power, I will. It doesn't make up for what's happened, but it's the least I can do."

Ishaan shook his head, quickly writing a response while Theo replied. "You don't have anything to apologize for. None of this is your doing."

"Still, I—"

He was interrupted when Ishaan pushed the journal at him. He waited impatiently until Alaric took it and read his response.

"This whole mess started before we came here, and what happened to Theo wasn't your fault. We'll be alright. We're working on it together."

The words drew a soft, somewhat sad smile from Alaric. "I can see that. I am very grateful that you have each other for support. But my offer still stands. If there's ever anything I can do for you, or anything you need, simply tell me."

An idea struck, and Ishaan waved his hand to interrupt Theo when the soldier started to speak. He had no doubt Theo planned to demur and he could see why, but the idea in his mind had latched on. He scribbled it out as quickly as he could, trying to keep his writing legible.

"I'm not asking this because I think you owe me anything. I heard you mention once that there was a proper language of hand signs. Do you know it? Could you teach me?"

Alaric's whole face changed when he really smiled. His gray-blue eyes lit up and a tiny dimple appeared in his cheek, making him look as young as he truly was for once. "I do know it, though it's been awhile and I would likely need to refresh my skills, and it would be a pleasure to teach you. To teach both of you," he added, nodding at Theo.

"Thank you. I appreciate you, Alaric," Ishaan wrote, and the way Alaric's smile grew spoke volumes about how often anyone told him he was appreciated.

"When we're done here for the day, I will find the books I learned from and we will find time to practice. I promise."

"I'm looking forward to it." Theo echoed the words Ishaan had written, and he even sounded sincere about it.

"As am I." Alaric's smile faded a bit when he realized Kaelas was watching them, but at least it didn't go away completely. "I should check in with Prince Kaelas, but I really am looking forward to working with you both."

The vibrant smile disappeared in the blink of an eye and Alaric was once more the serious adviser he'd made himself into when he rode up to rejoin his cousin.

"Was this a good idea?" Theo murmured once they were alone again. "He's not what I expected, but he's still Prince Kaelas' cousin."

"I trust him," Ishaan wrote, and he meant it. His instincts had rarely failed him in the past, not when it came to people. "And he could use a friend, I think."

"It *would* be nice to have an easier way to communicate than you having to use this journal all the time," Theo conceded. "If you trust him, then I'll give him a chance as well."

It was no small thing, given Theo's history with the Sarkhyrians, and Ishaan gave him a little smile when he made the sign for 'thank you'.

"I don't plan to extend that courtesy to Prince Kaelas, though," he admitted. "I'm not sure what it is, but there's something about him I just don't trust. Is it just me, or do you get the same feeling about him?"

Ishaan studied the prince for a moment. Kaelas and Alaric were deep in conversation and whatever it was about, Kaelas didn't seem very happy. His cousin seemed unperturbed, though. He supposed it made sense, if Alaric had been dealing with Kaelas for years now.

"I think I know what you mean," he finally responded. He'd gotten fairly well-practiced at balancing the journal on the saddle horn so he could write legibly. "Maybe this is how he always is, though. Sometimes people are just angry a lot."

Theo considered it, then shook his head. "We only spent a few minutes with those chancellors of his and honestly, I remember very little of the day we arrived, but I don't think they'd be willing to put up with a ruler who's always upset and arguing. Nor would Alaric, for that matter."

Which meant something had to have changed recently. Something had shifted in Sarkhyr. He didn't know what it could be, but he had a strong feeling it involved Zex, which meant it involved him.

That thought wasn't one he cared to think about right now, though. Or ever, but especially not right now. He pushed it to the back of his mind as best he could and turned to Theo, jotting down a quick note for him.

"We still have some time until we get there. I've heard you joking about how you and James met. Will you tell me the story?"

Ishaan's heart clenched in his chest when Theo broke into a grin. Finally, he saw a hint of the man he'd met in the forest all those weeks ago. His bright blue eyes lit up with amusement and he sat up a little straighter in his saddle.

"He'd probably kill me if he knew I was telling you this. He likes to jump in and try to defend himself." Theo's smile turned a little mischievous. "We hated each other when we first met. I was sure Captain Trieste was going to kick one or both of us off the team with the way we behaved. In the end, though, he figured out a way to force us to trust each other."

Ishaan didn't have an actual sign for any words that would urge Theo to tell him more, but the way he was flapping his hand around seemed to get his point across. Theo leaned a little closer, unable to contain his grin.

"He sent us on a mission to track down a Florys Bog Dweller."

Ishaan frowned and shook his head, confused. Nothing like that existed. The name sounded vaguely familiar, perhaps from an old storybook, but no such creature existed in the real world.

"You're thinking it's not real, right?" Theo guessed, then laughed. "We did, too, but Captain Trieste assured us it was, though, and sent us after it on our own. It was the smelliest, most miserable three weeks of my life, but it was a success. Not for us, of course, but for the captain. We came out of it as friends and he didn't have to go through the hassle of recruiting a new tracker and mage."

Ishaan could imagine it too well, the younger versions of Theo and James bickering as they trudged through a murky bog. Laughter bubbled up in him until he was clinging to his saddle to steady himself.

"If you ever really want to get James, ask him about the incident with the frogs."

For some reason, that set him off all over again, and he laughed until his ribs hurt. It felt good to release some of the fear and tension he'd been holding onto for so long, and he grinned up at Theo. Seeing the happiness in the man's eyes made his breath catch and his heart stutter.

The feeling that crashed into him was big, too big to put a name to. It was exhilarating, but also terrifying. Then their eyes met and he saw a hint of that same feeling looking back at him. It eased some of the fear, but he still didn't know what to do with it.

As always, though, Theo came to the rescue. He leaned across the distance between them, stopping a breath away. Only once Ishaan nodded did he close the gap and brush his lips across Ishaan's in a gentle kiss.

They still had obstacles in front of them, some too big to even think about, but the way Theo looked at him just then gave him hope that somehow, some way, they would make this work.

Ishaan couldn't say what he'd expected to find when they arrived at the scene of Lady Heraldra's murder. Prince Kaelas had spared them the more gruesome details, but he was all too aware that the symbols they were researching had been cut into the poor woman's skin. He tried not to imagine what else she must have suffered, if this was the gentler version.

The area they rode into didn't look as though a dead woman had lain there. Prince Kaelas brought them to a small building, seemingly out of place in the emptiness surrounding it. The landscape was rough and rocky here, well off the beaten path, with nothing to block the bitter wind. It seeped around the edges of his cloak in a sharp reminder that winter was fast approaching.

"What is this place used for?" Kya asked. The cold didn't seem to bother her, at least. She sat perched in her saddle, head turning this way and that as she studied their surroundings.

"It's an outpost of sorts for soldiers and guards," Alaric explained. "I'm sure you've noticed, but it gets quite frigid this far north. Magic can only do so much, so we have buildings like these scattered around the perimeter of the city. This one is roughly halfway to one of the old mountain passes. Very few come out this way anymore, since an avalanche buried that passage. It was pure luck anyone passed by this way."

"One of Zex's soldiers made it this close to Yrasea?" Lieutenant Sol asked. At Kaelas' low growl, he raised his hand. "I meant no offense, of course, but I have to wonder what brought him here. I assume anyone that sides with him is also considered a traitor, or at least a criminal, so what would bring him this close to the city?"

"And what are the odds of him not only being here, but being here at exactly the right time to catch a murderer in the act?" Rhea spoke up. She and Lieutenant Sol had spent most of the trip in quiet conversation, but Ishaan hadn't spent much time around the mage.

"I'm afraid I don't have answers to any of those questions. With any luck, one of you will be able to find something that was missed."

Alaric's suggestion seemed to irritate Kaelas even more. He swung down off his horse and walked away from the group. "They were found over here," he called over his shoulder, leaving everyone to scramble off their horses and hurry after him.

"That man would be much more tolerable if he cut back on the theatrics," James muttered under his breath, and Ishaan was inclined to agree. He'd nearly fallen on his face in his hurry to slide out of his saddle. Only a quick move on Theo's part had kept him from completely humiliating himself.

"Perhaps it's related to the dragons, because Zex was the same way," Theo said, and Ishaan looked up at him in surprise. This was the first time Theo had spoken the man's name without flinching. It had to be a good sign.

"No wonder they don't get along. They both want to be the center of attention."

Ishaan snorted out a laugh, unable to fully suppress it. He clapped a hand over his mouth before anyone else noticed, but James shot him a cheeky grin and a wink. He truly was incorrigible.

"Eyes up. Looks like we're here," Theo murmured, and the smile instantly slid away. It was almost unnerving how quickly James went from a laid-back joker to a hardened soldier. The two of them moved until they flanked Ishaan, one on either side of him. Part of him wanted to protest that he didn't need protecting, but the larger part of him took comfort in having them look out for him.

The space just a few hundred feet from the outbuilding was much closer to what he'd been expecting. The grass was brown and dead here, making the dark red-brown bloodstains stand out. He winced at the sheer amount of it that had soaked into the ground, spreading out from a darker stain.

"The other two scenes weren't like this," Prince Kaelas said, finally turning to face them. "We believe they were killed in one location and their bodies left in another. Perhaps that was the plan here, as well, but when Zex's soldier found them, most likely the killer had to leave her here to avoid detection."

Ishaan raised his hand until Kaelas looked at him, then grabbed his journal and wrote out a quick question, giving it to Theo to read.

"Why would he have done the spell here? Is it important?"

Alaric shook his head. "I wish we knew. Nothing about this makes sense."

"I have one theory," Rhea said. "From what Alaric could find out, this was some sort of spell to drain power, correct? In that case, perhaps it was happening slowly?"

"What do you mean?" Lieutenant Sol asked, dark eyes slightly unfocused, his mind clearly racing, as though the pieces were coming together, but they weren't quite there yet. If so, he was in a much better position than Ishaan. He had no idea where she was going with this.

"What if some of the sigils we can't identify yet are used to keep a line of power open between the mage and the victim? He could have been attempting to get to something or someone in the city while continually draining her power to bolster his own."

"Being discovered could have thrown his plan off-track, if he had to divert some of that power to protect himself from the soldier who found them. In that case, he could very well have lost control of the working and killed her in the process."

"The backlash would have weakened him. In that case, the smart decision would be to retreat and recoup," James said, nodding. He was staring at the bloodstained grass, alight with a keen interest that made Ishaan's blood run cold.

James is not Doran. He is not like my parents, he reminded himself, clinging to that thought to ground himself. Logically, he knew James and the other mages only seemed excited because they were one step closer to solving this puzzle. None of them would do something like this. They were good people. He *knew* that, but he couldn't stifle the shiver of fear that ran down his spine.

"If he had to flee in a hurry, we may be able to find a trail," Theo said, and already Ishaan could tell he was focusing on the task. His eyes were darting around the site, looking for any hint of a track, but he stayed where he was. Relief warred with the knowledge that they needed to find the man who'd done this. He wanted Theo to stay near, but he also knew the soldier had a job to do.

Reluctantly, he touched Theo's arm to get his attention. "It's okay," he signed, then pointed toward the ground. The rest of his team, along with Rhea, had already spread out. Perhaps they were searching for some sort of magic trail? Only Kaelas and Alaric remained, heads bowed together in a heated conversation.

Still, Theo hesitated. "I don't feel comfortable leaving you here. We don't know if he's still in the area."

Ishaan huffed and repeated the sign, then pointed again and honestly, he hoped Alaric was sincere about helping him learn more hand signs, because being unable to fully communicate what he meant was getting very frustrating.

"Fine, but stay put, okay? Stick close to Alaric, if you can. Promise?"

He didn't leave until Ishaan nodded his agreement and once more pointed away from them. He'd never truly seen Theo in his element, and Ishaan could admit he was a little fascinated. The soldier's steps were silent and his sharp gaze didn't miss a single detail as he scoured the area. The uncertainty and hesitation that he'd been carrying since his rescue seemed to melt away as his training came to the forefront.

"They may be awhile." Alaric's quiet comment startled him, earning him a faint smile from the man. "Kas has gone to help the mages. Prince Kaelas, that is," he amended. "I'm afraid this isn't my area of expertise."

Ishaan pointed to himself and shook his head ruefully. He had the journal on hand, just in case, but Alaric seemed to understand what he meant well enough.

"To be honest, it's not Kaelas', either, but he can't abide standing by and doing nothing while others are searching. I fully expect him to lose patience and take to the sky to go searching. I'm hoping he can restrain himself, though."

The questions tumbling around in Ishaan's mind at that couldn't be easily signed, so this time he did use the journal. "Do your people know what he is? How could something like this stay secret for so long?"

Alaric took a moment, considering his answer before he spoke. "Our people know dragons are real, but not that Kaelas is one. Most believe the dragons have gone extinct, a rumor we don't discourage. It's difficult to explain, but those who don't know the truth have always viewed our rulers as a sort of representation of the ancient dragons. Figureheads, in essence. Does that make sense?"

Ishaan nodded. "So they know dragons exist and have managed to keep it hidden all this time?"

"Who would believe us if we told them?" There was a spark of mischief in Alaric's eyes. "As there are only ever two at a time and the secret is highly guarded, gaining proof is nearly impossible." His faint smile dimmed. "There are ways to hide it if someone finds out who shouldn't know, though."

He was silent long enough that Ishaan touched his arm, growing concerned. Alaric sighed.

"I wasn't there when it happened, but I've heard stories of the day they arrested Zex. He changed and became the silver dragon in front of a dozen guards. Those that survived had to be made to forget what they'd seen. It's the sort of magic no one ever wants to use and the knowledge of how it's done is granted to very few. Usually less than five mages in a generation and only the most trusted have the knowledge."

"You know it." It didn't take much to figure that out. As far as Ishaan could tell, there was no one in the kingdom Prince Kaelas trusted more than his cousin. "Am I allowed to know that?"

"Kas would not be happy," Alaric admitted. "However, given how tangled you've become in our mess, it doesn't seem right to keep secrets from you. I get the feeling we are going to be spending a lot of time together once we solve this current debacle."

As though summoned, he felt the thing within him stir. The dragon. It still didn't feel real. "Why did Zex do this? Is there a way to get his power out of me? I don't want it." His handwriting was small, cramped, betraying his fear.

"I won't lie to you, Ishaan. This situation is completely unprecedented. The transfer of power has always been from one ruler directly to another.

It's only been done by force the one time that I'm aware of. Until we have time to sit down and fully investigate what happened, I can't say how to proceed. We may very well have to consult with Zex at some point to find out what he did and why."

No. The idea of even looking at the man who had hurt Theo so badly felt wrong. He shook his head, adamant, but Alaric kept going.

"I know you don't want to, and it may not even come to that. We may figure it out on our own, especially if the Nevarrean mages are willing to stay. Our mages in Sarkhyr are powerful, but none of them know about the dragons. We will have to limit that knowledge as much as possible, which means we will need the aid of your friends. I just wanted to prepare you in case we need to include him."

He still didn't like it, but he begrudgingly admitted that Alaric had a point. The other man seemed to realize he'd pushed as far as Ishaan was willing to allow and let silence fall between them. Given they were still virtual strangers, it was a surprisingly comfortable silence. He hadn't been lying when he'd told Theo that he trusted Alaric. Something about the Sarkhyrian felt almost familiar, though they'd never met before. He couldn't explain it and didn't care to examine it too closely. Not right now, at least. He had enough to worry about as it was.

Over an hour passed before the others returned. By then, Ishaan and Alaric had moved away from the scene of the murder and settled on the dry grass, cloaks wrapped tight against the cold. Alaric had offered to do a small spell to help keep him warm, which he'd immediately refused. It was nothing personal, but the last thing he wanted was any more magic done on him. He made do with his cloak, but part of him was grateful for the chill in the air. Now that he'd settled, the constant exhaustion he'd been battling was creeping over him again, weighing him down. The brisk bite to the air kept him alert, if uncomfortable.

Alaric was quiet beside him, appearing lost in thought, and Ishaan wasn't in the mood to freeze his fingers to write in the journal just for idle conversation, so they'd let the silence linger while they waited.

Lieutenant Sol was the first to arrive back, with Kya at his side. Ishaan quickly got to his feet and turned to offer Alaric a hand up, as well.

"Oh. Thank you." He seemed almost surprised. Because Ishaan had offered assistance or because *anyone* had offered assistance, Ishaan wasn't sure.

The two of them made their way to the two mages. "Any luck?" Alaric asked, though it was clear from the frustrated look on Kya's face that they hadn't been successful.

"We found a few odd traces of magic, but they died away before we could follow them," Lieutenant Sol said, shaking his head. "It's difficult to tell if the traces were weak to begin with or the mage altered his tracks somehow."

Kya huffed, tossing her braid over her shoulder. "I don't see how Theo does it. Tracking is so boring. It felt like all we did was walk around in circles."

"Now you see why specialist groups are made up of mages *and* soldiers. Theodric and the captain likely feel the same way about magic that you do about tracking."

"A great deal of a mage's time is spent reading and studying," Alaric said quietly. He so rarely interacted with the rest of the team about anything but the bare necessities, but to Ishaan, it appeared the man really was attempting to be friendly.

"That's true, but it's reading and studying about magic. That's more than worth it," Kya said after a beat of silence. "It beats staring at dirt and mud for hours, that's for sure."

"Even when staring at dirt is useful?"

Ishaan perked up when he heard Theo's voice, trying to hold back a smile as the tracker joined them, along with James. He hadn't even heard them approaching. Theo's chilly hand slipped into his and the smile broke free, though he quickly ducked his head to hide it. He wasn't sure how successful he was, if James' quiet chuckle said anything.

"Does that mean you found something?" Lieutenant Sol asked, and Theo nodded.

"I think so. I found faint prints leading away from the city. It could be the mage we're looking for. The steps were uneven, as though the person was limping. I followed them for a while and they seem to be on a fairly straightforward path."

"Do we follow them?" Kya was up on the balls of her feet, blatantly ready for some action, but Ishaan didn't share her excitement. Too many things had gone wrong the last time the team split up like this and the fear was already creeping in.

Surprisingly, the first person to agree with his unspoken protest was Alaric.

"I don't believe that would be wise," he said, shaking his head. "We do not know where this mage is going and what resources he has available. Most likely he is working alone, but if he has help, we'll be going in blind and your team is missing all but one of your fighters."

Lieutenant Sol nodded. "I agree with Lord Alaric. We have a trail and a direction. We should regroup and come up with a plan before we go blindly charging in."

Kya visibly deflated, her shoulders slumping, but at least she didn't protest.

"The rest of you can return to the city, if you'd like. I'll wait for Prince Kaelas to return."

Ishaan shook his head and squeezed Theo's hand at Alaric's offer, silently urging him to speak up.

"I'd prefer we all go back together, if that's alright, Lieutenant?"

Lieutenant Sol nodded in agreement. "We're safer as a group. We'll wait with you, Lord Alaric."

"Please… just Alaric," he cut in. "There is no need for titles between us. And I would be grateful for the company. I don't believe he'll be gone much longer."

Ishaan smiled up at Theo when the other man glanced over at him, grateful he'd understood. His instincts were telling him that if he could break through Alaric's walls, he would find a friend in the man. Given the rocky road ahead of him, he had the feeling he was going to need all the allies he could get.

Chapter 25

The Nevarreans continued to impress him.

Once Kas had returned, thankfully in his human form, they'd returned to the city to regroup. Within an hour, both Captain Trieste's team and Lord Wyrenian's team were fully informed about the situation, and a plan was made. They agreed that the knowledge of Kaelas and Zex and the dragons needed to be kept as limited as possible and had volunteered to help before Alaric could even ask.

From there, the plan was relatively simple. Both teams would follow the trail, armed and prepared for whatever they would find. Lord Wyrenian would stay behind with Sir Embry, his guards, and Captain Trieste's injured soldier, Vesa. Together with Hadiza, they would monitor the city, in case the killer had any accomplices in Yrasea.

The only argument came when discussing when to do this. Kaelas argued to leave immediately, but Captain Trieste argued that they were already losing the light and venturing into the mountains in the darkness, this close to winter, with no idea where they were going, was madness at best.

"He's right, Prince Kaelas." Alaric knew he didn't imagine the dark look his cousin shot his way, but he couldn't blame him. Until the incident with Zex, he had never disagreed with Kas. Not in public, anyway.

"Fine. But we leave before first light tomorrow morning," Kas agreed, sullen and almost pouting. "I want us to be on that trail by the time the sun rises."

He'd stalked out with that pronouncement, leaving the rest of them to sort out any remaining details. The Nevarreans surprised him yet again by asking him to join them for dinner, an offer he'd accepted. Alaric had never had much luck befriending anyone in Sarkhyr, where they all viewed him as an extension of his cousin, but the Nevarreans didn't seem to have the same problem. A few of them were still a bit guarded around him, but for the most part, they were far more welcoming than he would have been in their situation. Particularly Ishaan and Theodric, the two that had the most reason to hate anything related to his country.

They retired for bed early and Alaric was surprisingly content as he made his way back to his own rooms. He needed to rest and prepare for the long day tomorrow, so he didn't know why he was hesitating in the main hallway.

Going to the right would take him to his rooms.

Going to the left would eventually take him to the door leading down into the prison cells.

He had no reason to go down there. He had all the information he needed from Zex. Most of the sigils were deciphered, and they had a solid lead to follow come morning. Going down that hallway would not provide any new information and would only play into Zex's hands, somehow. He knew the man would find some way to get under his skin and twist every word around until he had no idea what was true and what wasn't.

Alaric took a breath to fortify himself. He would go to his room, prepare for tomorrow, then get a good night's sleep. He had no time for rogue princes with too-knowing eyes and a permanent smirk on his handsome face. It was best to walk away and do his best to forget about him altogether.

He couldn't even pretend to be surprised at his own actions when he went left.

The guards let him pass without question this time, though one of them couldn't hide his concern. He seemed familiar, but it took Alaric a moment to recognize Grayan, the uncle of Ereyan. It seemed he'd finally been cleared for light duty again after his injury.

"I'll be safe, Grayan. The prisoner is secured and I know you both are only a shout away," he promised, but it didn't appear to reassure the man. So long as they didn't come down, though, Alaric wasn't too concerned.

Still, he hesitated once he reached the bottom of the stairs. His common sense was telling him that this was utter foolishness. There was no further information needed from Zex and on top of that, Kaelas would be furious when he found out Alaric had come back down here. All his life, he'd always done the smart thing, the safe thing. Now, though, his curiosity had dug its claws into him and wouldn't let go, and he found he didn't want to push it down. For once, he wanted to do something for himself.

"I can hear you, you know. How long is it going to take you to pluck up your courage and come down here?"

Zex's voice cut through the dim hallway, challenging him, and Alaric's hesitation disappeared. He steeled his spine and walked to Zex's cell at the end of the hallway, stopping well out of arm's reach. Just like last time, Zex lay stretched out on his cot, reclining on his elbows. His dark curls were rumpled, though, as though he'd truly been asleep just moments ago. For some reason, that little detail struck him hard.

"How did you know it was me?"

"Who else would come down to visit me? Certainly not Kaelas." Zex stretched, pushing himself up to sit cross-legged. "So, what brings you here, Alaric? Some new information you need me to translate again? Or maybe you've decided to release these manacles and let me go?"

Alaric scoffed. "That's never going to happen, and not just because Kaelas would murder me if I did. You may have helped me with one issue, but you're still here for a reason, as you well know."

"Ah, yes. The chancellors, in their infinite wisdom, have dubbed me a traitor. How could I possibly forget?"

"They declared you a traitor because you killed people, Zex. There's no way to explain that away."

"There are occasions where such a thing is justified, you know. After all, everyone here is doing their best to see *me* killed, if you recall," he said, sounding supremely unconcerned about his own possible execution.

"Even barring that, you used forbidden magic," Alaric said. He didn't understand this driving urge to prove Zex guilty when he'd already been convicted. "You kidnapped that Nevarrean soldier and tortured him. To what end?"

"He thinks that was torture? I was as gentle as I could possibly be with Theodric. I needed information rather urgently and he was being uncooperative, so I gathered it the best way I knew how. There was no malice behind my actions, and if there had been another way, I would have taken it. I'd extend my apologies, but I'm fairly sure I know exactly what he would tell me to do with them."

Zex was probably right. Alaric had no doubts that Theodric wanted absolutely nothing to do with Zex and his apologies. The fact that he'd even considered it was surprising, though.

"Still, when you look at your history, it doesn't paint you in a very good light."

"You seem to be working under the assumption that I care what anyone thinks about me. I have and will continue to do what needs to be done. If that makes me a traitor, then so be it."

Alaric hesitated a moment, then took a small step forward. He was still out of reach, but it was a little easier to make Zex out in the dim lighting.

"Even if everyone thinks you're a traitor? Did you ever care for your people or your country at all?"

Finally, his words had an effect on Zex. His smirk slid away, and a darkness seemed to surround him, his silver eyes dimming. "What do you care, Alaric? I'm nothing but a fallen prince in your eyes, right? A disgrace to my title and my country."

"Zex..." He wrapped his hands around the bars separating them, not even realizing he'd moved until he felt the cold metal against his skin.

The man looked away, the silence so loud it seemed to echo within the stone walls. The longer it lasted, the more his common sense reasserted itself. This was why he shouldn't have come. There was no point. He was being a reckless, impulsive idiot, and it was long past time for him to forget all of this and go back to bed.

He'd already taken two steps backward before Zex replied, his voice merely a whisper of sound. "I cared more than you could ever possibly imagine. Everything I did, I did because I *cared*." He spat the word like it was a curse. "This is where it got me. Chained in a dungeon, branded as a traitor and a murderer, with an entire country that wants me dead."

The raw emotion in his voice sent a shudder through Alaric and he moved in closer again, unable to resist. There was a world of anger and resentment and pain in Zex's words, deeper than he could fathom. He was curled in on himself, his fists gripping the chains of his manacles so tightly his knuckles were white. There was no reaction when Alaric stepped up to the bars. Zex seemed lost in his own memories, a world away from the shadowy prison cell.

Nothing about his posture or the hurt in his voice seemed fake, and Alaric suddenly found himself questioning what he thought he knew. Had things truly happened as he'd been told? Who were the witnesses who had seen these things? Was it possible they'd made a mistake or missed some crucial detail? There had to be more to this story. He just knew it.

"What happened?"

His question was little more than a breath, but the response was immediate. The darkness fell away from Zex and that hated smirk slipped back into place, hiding away any emotions.

"It's a little late to be reminiscing, Alaric," he purred. "I can think of so many better uses for our time than reliving old memories."

"Don't. Don't do that."

"Do what? I'm simply seeking a more enjoyable topic of conversation to pass the evening with."

Alaric huffed out a sigh, venting his frustration. "Don't hide behind sarcasm and flirting. I just want an answer."

"But sarcasm and flirting are the bulk of my personality. If you want a serious, boring conversation, you should seek out one of the chancellors. I'm sure they'll be more than happy to tell you anything you'd like about me."

"But would it be true?"

"How would you know if anything *I* told you was the truth?"

"You are one of the most infuriating people I've ever met in my life and I deal with politicians all day," he snapped.

Zex chuckled, low and dark. "I choose to take that as a compliment."

"Of course you would." He shook his head. "I shouldn't have come down here. I'm going to forget this ever happened and go to bed. I have an early start tomorrow."

"Off dealing with more politicians? I wish you the best. I always preferred to pass that duty off to Kaelas."

"I'd rather deal with a few angry chancellors than spend all day in the mountains chasing a killer, but we can't always get what we want." He wasn't sure why he'd told Zex that. There was no reason for him to know what they were doing. It'd just slipped out, his tongue loosened by his anger.

"Chasing a killer?" At least Zex's smirk was gone, replaced by a frown. "You're going after the mage that used those sigils you had me translate, I assume?"

"I shouldn't have told you even that much. Just forget about it."

"No. No, I don't think I will," Zex said. He got up and walked to the bars, putting him mere inches from Alaric. "A mage who can use magic like that is dangerous and unpredictable. Who are you taking? I know you're not stupid enough to go alone."

"We have a team prepared. Whoever he is, he'll be no match for this many of us. We can't very well leave him be to go wherever he pleases. We need to catch him before he kills again."

"Why do you need to go, then, if there are so many already? You're not a fighter."

That stuck under his skin, and Alaric scowled. "I am more than capable of taking care of myself, as you well know. I am the strongest mage in Yrasea and one of the most powerful in Sarkhyr. I am going because I am needed and because I *want* to go. Your concern is neither wanted nor needed."

Zex surprised him by grinning. It wasn't his usual sardonic smirk, but an actual, amused smile. "When you get angry, you get very formal. Did you know that? I can tell how mad you are by how elitist you sound."

"You are utterly infuriating."

"But you like it. Don't you, Alaric?" Zex slipped one hand through the bars, his fingers brushing against Alaric's hand and sending a jolt of awareness across his skin. He quickly jerked away, but it was impossible to banish what he'd felt.

"I'm not playing these games with you. I'm going to my room to prepare for tomorrow. Sleep well, Zex. Or don't. It doesn't matter to me." He turned on his heel to walk away.

"Alaric," Zex called before he'd gone more than three steps. Cursing himself for a fool, Alaric turned back to him.

"What, Zex?"

The man was leaning against the bars, watching him, unusually serious. "Be careful tomorrow. I'd hate for anything to happen to the only interesting person in this city."

Alaric had to bite back the urge to smile, for some insane reason. Only once he had himself under control did he nod. "I will. I'll..." He sighed. "I'll let you know how it went when we return tomorrow."

"I'm looking forward to it. Sleep well, Alaric."

"Sleep well, Zex."

He lingered a moment longer, then hurried down the hallway and up the stairs. His heart was beating as though he'd run the entire way, and his stomach was tight and jittery in a way he couldn't allow himself to acknowledge. He was so lost in his thoughts that it took him a moment to realize someone had said his name. Turning, he spotted the two guards. One had taken a step toward him.

"I'm sorry, Grayan. I was caught up in my own mind. Could you repeat that?"

"I was just checking you were okay, my lord," the guard said with a frown. "You look a bit flushed. Would you like an escort to your room?"

"I'm quite alright, but thank you for your concern. I can make it on my own," he assured him. He forced himself to breathe slowly, hoping to settle his emotions.

"Are you sure, my lord? It's no trouble at all," Grayan insisted. He took a step closer and reached out as though to take Alaric's arm. Startled, he stepped back from the guard.

"I'm sure, soldier." His voice was perhaps a bit harsher than he'd intended, but the guard had taken him by surprise.

Grayan's expression hardened and, for a moment, something flashed behind his eyes that sent a shiver through Alaric. It was there and gone so quickly, though, that he wondered if he'd imagined it. Perhaps being around Zex had gotten under his skin more than he'd realized.

"I apologize, my lord. It's not my place to question," he muttered, chastised, and Alaric felt a little guilty for how sharp he'd been.

"No, it's fine. I thank you for your concern, but I assure you I'm alright, just a bit tired. I'll retire to my room now. Thank you, though." He gave what he hoped was a convincing smile and excused himself, leaving the two guards at their post.

By the time he made it back to his room, the incident was forgotten, his sole focus returning to the mysterious man in the prison cell. How much of what Zex had said was the truth and how much was designed to gain his sympathy? How could he possibly ever know? The man lied as easily as he breathed. Who was he to question the word of Zex's victims and the few who'd survived that day years ago?

His thoughts ran in circles in his mind long after he should have been asleep, tripping and tangling over themselves until all that remained was a knot of confusion. It was hours before Alaric could finally fall asleep and when he did, his dreams were filled with flashes of a fallen prince with quicksilver eyes.

CHAPTER 26

"Have you seen the captain this morning?"

James' question pulled Theo from the haze of routine and he paused in securing his saddlebag to glance around. There had to be at least two dozen people in the stables, possibly more, all moving in and out of stalls as they prepared to leave.

"I didn't realize he wasn't here, honestly," he admitted. "Between our team and the extra Sarkhyrians, it's hard to keep track."

"Which leads me to my second point: has anyone seen Prince Kaelas this morning?"

That drew him up short. "I know I've seen Alaric," he said slowly. "But now that you mention it, I haven't seen him, either. Have you?" He directed that question to Ishaan, who was standing just outside the stall. The younger man frowned and looked around, then shook his head. The concern in his eyes spoke louder than any words could have.

"Maybe they're just going over last-minute details?" he suggested. "Or the captain had to check in with the queen. Either way, it's most likely not a big deal."

James grimaced and clapped him on the shoulder. "You're a terrible liar. As your friend, I feel like I have to make you aware of that."

Rolling his eyes, Theo shrugged off the mage's hand and lightly shoved him out of the way. "Go finish getting ready. We're leaving soon."

"Fine, but keep an eye out, alright? Something doesn't feel right."

With those somewhat ominous words, James left them to finish getting ready. Theo immediately moved around his horse so he could see Ishaan, already knowing he'd have questions.

"James is a worrier. Don't let it get to you. I'm sure it's just some details that need to be taken care of. This is a fairly major operation. It's going to be fine."

Ishaan looked as skeptical as Theo secretly felt, but he was at least willing to play along with the best-case scenario and shrugged. It was the closest thing to acceptance he was likely to get, so Theo let it be and got back to work.

Now that James had pointed out that the two were missing, though, he couldn't get it out of his mind. Even Lord Wyrenian and his team were in the stables, helping with last-minute preparations. The ambassador would remain behind with his guards, apparently as a sort of liaison between Queen Isadore and Hadiza, who would act as leader until Prince Kaelas returned. It made sense, even with what little he knew of politics. In the past, he'd always left it to James to give him a summary of things like that.

Nothing to do for it but wait and see, though. He finished securing his belongings and turned to Ishaan, only to find the other man reaching for him with a slight frown on his face. He instinctively scanned their surroundings for a threat, confused when he realized the stables were half-empty. It wasn't until he saw Kya walking her horse outside beside Irric that it made sense.

"How long did I lose?" he whispered, pained. Ishaan quickly shook his head, holding up one finger. It was a routine he was unfortunately getting used to, but at least this time it had only been a minute or two. Ishaan closed the distance between them and leaned in, resting his forehead against

Theo's. Hidden by the walls of the stall, they stole a moment of peace to allow him to gather his thoughts together.

"I'm glad you're coming with us." The confession was barely a breath of sound, almost lost when his horse stamped its hoof. "I don't want the others to know about this. I know you're not looking forward to it and maybe it makes me selfish, but-"

The soft touch of Ishaan's lips against his cut him off, the words disappearing in a soft haze. Some of the tension holding him hostage melted away and he leaned into it, knowing they didn't have much time before someone came looking for them. He felt Ishaan's hand come to rest on his chest and smiled as a gentle warmth washed over him.

It was over too fast, but then again, it always felt that way when these little stolen moments slipped away. Neither of them pulled away much, their breaths mingling between them.

"When this is all over, I'm taking a vacation and we're going to take some time to just relax for once," he murmured. Their lips brushed as he spoke and he smiled, turning into a laugh when the horse butted its head between them to demand attention. After scratching its nose, he gave Ishaan a wry look. "Maybe a vacation close enough to walk to, so we'll finally stop being interrupted."

The grin his weak joke earned him from Ishaan somehow warmed him almost as much as that gentle kiss had. Gripping the reins with one hand, he held the other out to Ishaan. They'd have to separate eventually for the ride, but until it was time to leave, he planned to steal every last moment he could.

They were the last to join the group that had gathered just outside the stables, and he immediately wished they were back inside. The cold wind cut through his cloak like it was made of lace. It was pitch black outside, the sun still hours from rising, and the bite of winter was already in the air.

It may still be autumn in the south, but here in the northern mountains, it was already a fleeting memory.

"We were starting to worry you'd gotten lost." He saw Karsa trot past him to Ishaan just as Naema sidled up to him, leading her horse. The dog sat right on Ishaan's foot and stared up at him until he relented, releasing Theo's hand to squat down and pet her.

"You'd never know she's a highly trained military dog," he commented, sidestepping her teasing comment and nodding toward Karsa. She was leaning heavily against Ishaan, her bushy tail frantically thumping the frozen ground when he found that spot behind her ear that made her groan.

Naema shrugged. "She's off duty until we get moving. There's nothing wrong with letting her be a normal dog for a little longer and that was a terrible attempt at deflecting me."

"There's nothing to talk about. Mind your own business, Bhandari."

As expected, she just laughed at him. The best part of joining the reconnaissance team, for him, had been finding himself part of a tight-knit group that had quickly become his family. The downside of it was that they all treated each other like family and Naema took her role as 'older sister' to the group very seriously. She seemed to feel that it was her solemn duty to tease them all at every opportunity.

"I'll let it go for now, but only because we're about to spend the next several days in the mountains together, so we'll have plenty of time to talk."

"I can't wait," he deadpanned, earning another laugh from her. She kept her word, though, and let it go, instead focusing on Karsa and Ishaan. The dog had slowly melted down to the ground and was now on her back, her tongue lolling out the side of her mouth as Ishaan scratched her belly. He'd watched her rip a man's arm to shreds to protect Naema from an attacker, so it was always a little jarring to see her act like a pampered house pet when not working.

He was glad she'd taken to Ishaan, though. Everyone in the group would protect him, of course, but Karsa seemed to comfort him in a way most of the others couldn't. Maybe because it didn't matter as much if he didn't talk when he was around her?

"Oh, it looks like the captain is back. Time to go, I suppose." Naema tugged a knit cap out of her pocket and tucked it over her dark curls. "Sorry, Ishaan, but I'm going to have to steal her back."

Ishaan nodded and Theo held a hand out to help him up, ignoring the pointed look Naema gave him when neither of them let go once he was standing. He was positive he'd never hear the end of it until he confirmed what she already seemed to know, but for now, it was amusing to let them wonder a little while longer.

His amusement rapidly faded when he realized that the captain and Prince Kaelas were walking over to them, with a confused Alaric in tow. The look on the prince's face didn't give him much hope that the morning was going to run smoothly.

"I'm sure it's nothing," he murmured to Ishaan, gripping his hand. "Just stick close to me and everything will be fine."

"Alaric. Ishaan. Both of you will stay behind."

Those words hung in the air, silencing the entire group. The world itself seemed to go still and the air froze in Ishaan's lungs. He stared blankly at Captain Trieste, even though Prince Kaelas had been the one to speak. There was no way the captain hadn't had a hand in this decision.

Fingers brushed against his skin and didn't hesitate to take hold of Theo's hand, gripping it tightly. He couldn't even voice a protest, but he could tell just from the tension in Theo's body that he was about to, despite it going directly against his training as a soldier. He didn't get a chance to even open his mouth, though.

"Excuse me?" Alaric's voice was cold and sharp as ice, and the look on his face wasn't much better when he looked up at his cousin.

"You heard me. You and Ishaan will stay here in Yrasea," Kaelas repeated.

"Why? We decided last night that we would all go and, as one of the strongest mages here, it doesn't make sense for me not to go." Alaric sounded as though his teeth were clenched, barely holding back his anger. Prince Kaelas, however, seemed unfazed.

"I'm not arguing your strength. It's the reason you're staying. You know the situation and you're able to defend our home should anything go wrong."

"Like what? What could go wrong?" Alaric pressed. His fair skin was flushed with the same anger Ishaan felt thrumming through his veins. "The danger is up in the mountains, not in the city."

"This is not up for debate, Alaric," Kaelas ordered, voice hardening when Alaric opened his mouth to argue. "My decision is final. You will stay here and work with Hadiza to keep Yrasea safe."

Alaric stepped forward until there was almost no space between the two of them. "Is this how you're choosing to retaliate for disobeying you?" he hissed. Kaelas raised his hand and Ishaan flinched, waiting for a blow that never came. The prince merely put his hand on Alaric's chest and forced him back a step.

"I am not arguing about this any further. You will stay."

The air was brittle with tension, as though one wrong word would set everything aflame. Part of Ishaan almost wanted that. This wasn't *right*. Nothing good ever came from splitting the team apart.

But it's not splitting up the team, is it? he thought bitterly. *I'm not part of any team, and neither is Alaric.*

When Alaric finally spoke, his words were sharp and so formal they were almost an insult. "Yes, your Highness." He bowed low, far lower than someone of his status would have to, then turned on his heel and walked away from his cousin without another word. He kept his chin high and paused beside Ishaan.

"It would appear we have our orders," he spat, glaring over his shoulder at Kaelas.

"Wait just a moment." Theo took a step forward, his eyes on his captain. "What about Ishaan? Why is he staying? Isn't it safer to have him with us?"

Trieste's frown sent a shiver of fear down Ishaan's spine, and he just barely resisted the ingrained instinct to hide behind Theo. He refused to let the fear defeat him this time. Useless fury burned away within him, demanding answers.

"Remember your vows, soldier," Captain Trieste warned. "Ishaan is a civilian with no magic. This is a military operation. He will remain behind where it's safe. As Prince Kaelas said, this is not up for debate."

Theo's eyes went hard and Ishaan could see him readying a protest, but he could already tell that there would be no swaying either of them. Their decision was made and all that would come of this was Theo getting himself on the bad side of his captain right before a dangerous mission.

He tugged on Theo's hand until the man looked at him, then shook his head. It almost pained him to free his hands, but it was necessary.

"It's alright," he signed. He pressed his palms together so his hands were upright with his fingers spread, then lowered them until his fingertips pointed at Theo. It was a newer sign, another one they'd come up with together. "Be careful."

"I don't like this," Theo muttered, a statement Ishaan more than agreed with. He repeated the sign again until the soldier sighed and nodded.

"I'll stay with him, Theodric."

He'd forgotten that Alaric was still standing beside them. Aware of all the eyes on them, Ishaan reached up and lightly cupped Theo's cheek, lingering for as long as he dared.

"Both of you look out for each other," he warned. "You'll be safe in the city, but I'd rather you both be on your guard, anyway. We'll be back as quickly as possible."

Never in his life would Ishaan have believed he could feel such pain when stepping away from another person. Touch had been something to be feared for as long as he could remember. Finding comfort in another person was something for storybooks, not for someone like him. But now, it took an inhuman effort to let his hand fall and step to Alaric's side.

Theo closed his eyes for a moment, but, like Ishaan, he seemed to be aware that they were in front of an audience. He composed himself quickly and Ishaan watched the mask of a hardened soldier settle over him.

"We're losing time," Captain Trieste said, not unkindly, but the moment they'd stolen was over and it was time to get to work. The few who weren't already mounted climbed into their saddles and then they were gone, leaving Ishaan and Alaric standing alone in the dark with only one lingering backward glance from Theo.

Neither of them moved until the last rider faded into the shadows. Ishaan's stomach was in knots and his chest burned with a sensation he was coming to recognize. The dragon within him, though tiny and weak, was making itself known. Unlike Ishaan, though, it seemed almost happy at being left behind. It made sense, though, when he thought about it. Zex was still here.

"We should go find Hadiza and let them know about the change of plans," Alaric finally said, his voice unusually soft. Though it was hard to see, the darkness almost complete in the deep hours before dawn, there was no hiding the hurt on the young mage's face. It was a feeling Ishaan was all too familiar with and he felt a twinge of sympathy for the man.

A gentle nudge of his hand against Alaric's arm got his attention and Ishaan sighed heavily, dramatic enough to draw a faint smile from Alaric.

"I know exactly what you mean," he murmured. He took one more long look in the direction the riders had gone, then straightened, some of his usual confidence restored. "Let's head inside. We'll handle everything here until they get back, then I plan to have a very, very long talk with my cousin."

Ishaan almost wished he'd be able to witness that. He had a feeling Prince Kaelas would never hear the end of this.

Nodding, he emulated Alaric and found a little steel in his spine, straightening to his full height. The approving nod it got him gave him a tiny boost of confidence that he desperately needed right now.

He didn't know how long the others would be gone, but as he followed Alaric back toward the castle, he made himself a promise. He would use this time well and find a way to make himself useful. There was no telling what the future held, but there was one thing he was certain of: this would be the very last time he was left behind.

CHAPTER 27

Tension hung thick in the air even as the sun began to rise, burning away the lingering fog blanketing the mountains. As much as he knew he needed to put his personal feelings aside and deal with the mission, Theo couldn't help the lingering resentment clawing at him. It warred with the fear he couldn't suppress, both for Ishaan and for himself. He knew he'd come to rely too much on the other man, counting on him to pull him back when he lost track of time.

"You're going to get removed from the mission if you can't get yourself together."

Theo scowled at James, who rode beside him at the back of the group. They were still following the trail he'd found yesterday, moving as fast as they dared in the darkness. They didn't want to risk magelights giving away their position, not when they didn't know where their quarry was.

"I have a right to be frustrated," he snapped, though he kept his voice low. "They waited until the very last minute to tell us they were leaving two members of the team behind."

"I assume it's because they knew you'd react like this." He hated that James had a point. "I notice you're not upset that we left Vesa behind as well."

"That's different and you know it. Even with the Sarkhyrian healers working on her, she's still too injured to be on a horse for hours."

"It's not that different. Get that look off your face," James ordered when Theo shot him an annoyed glare. "Vesa is injured, but Ishaan and Alaric aren't part of the team."

The bolt of fury surprised him with its intensity, but he let it wash through him. It kept him in the moment and gave his mind a focus. "That's bullshit and you fucking know it," he hissed. His anger only grew when James shook his head.

"Theo, you need to get yourself under control," he shot back. "It's not an insult. I like him well enough and I know you have feelings for him, but at the end of the day, we're a military unit and he's a civilian. He's not even from Nevarre, remember? He's Gavarrian, as far as I can tell."

"That's not-"

"No." James slashed a hand through the air, cutting him off. "Just... no. This is a military operation. He would be a liability and you know it. You'd be so worried about protecting him if anything went wrong that you'd lose sight of the mission. Don't say you wouldn't, either, because it's happened before. The captain made the right choice. They'll be safe back in Yrasea. Isn't that what you want? For him to be safe?"

The truth burned almost as much as the anger. Deep down, he knew James was right. If this had been any other situation, Theo would have been the first one to agree with Captain Trieste's decision. Civilians had no place on a mission like this. But this wasn't just a civilian. This was *Ishaan*.

The silence grew. It was a technique James had learned from his mother and one that made it difficult to argue with the mage. He wouldn't let this go. He would wait and let the silence grow thick and uncomfortable, not relenting until he got an answer. Unfortunately for James, Theo was more than willing to wait him out. He'd known his friend too long to let a little awkward silence get to him.

In the end, James broke first. He sighed heavily, then nudged his horse over until his knees almost bumped Theo's. "What's this really about, Theo?" he asked quietly.

There was no one close enough to hear them, not over the sound of the horses. Still, Theo hesitated. James was his best friend and he'd trusted him with his very life more times than he could count, but this was different. This could see him removed from the team. Without them, what did he have left?

"I know something's been going on with you," James persisted when Theo didn't respond. "I didn't want to push because it seemed like you were handling it, but I'm pushing now. I need you to trust me so I can help however I can."

Theo let out a slow breath. "I do trust you," he finally said. "It's not about trust."

"Then what *is* it about? Just tell me and stop dragging it out. I can't do anything if you don't talk to me."

There were few things Theo wanted less than to have this conversation. It had been hard enough with Ishaan. Admitting the truth to another soldier, even his best friend, left him feeling weak in a way he never had before. In the end, though, he did trust James more than anyone and without Ishaan here, he was going to need someone who knew the truth in case something happened.

"I... fuck." He sucked in a breath through clenched teeth. "I've been losing time. It's not often or even every day, usually, but it does happen."

"What do you mean, 'losing time'?" James clearly hadn't been expecting that answer.

"I mean that sometimes, I'm doing something or even talking to someone and the next thing I know, nothing makes sense. It's usually just a few minutes, but once or twice it's as though I blink and it's suddenly a few hours later."

"Hours..?" James gaped at him, stunned. "W-what? How? Why?" He paused, a sudden fury in his eyes. "The blood magic. That's it, isn't it?"

"It's been happening since I was in that cabin with Zex. He used his magic and got inside my head. I don't know what he did, but..."

"Ishaan knows?" James guessed, and Theo nodded. "That's why he's been staying close to you. Well, closer than usual. He's been helping you when it happens. Theo... why didn't you tell me? I could have helped, too."

"I didn't want anyone to know. If the captain found out, he would have taken me off the mission and left me behind as well."

"Most likely. It's not weak to need time to heal. You know that. Do you think Vesa is weak? Or me?" James gestured to the healing wound across his face, remnants of the fight outside Esterdon. Even with the healers' help, it was going to leave a scar.

"You know I don't. Any other time, I'd be the first to admit that I should probably take some time. The captain's lessons tend to stick." He tried for a weak smile, but it fell flat. "This is different, though. It's personal. And before you say anything... I know it shouldn't be. One of the first things we're told is to never take it personally, but how can I not? I can't sit this one out, James."

James was quiet for an uncomfortably long time, the miles passing in silence. It wasn't an easy position Theo had left him in. As a soldier, his duty would be to report it to the captain and let him make the final decision. As a friend, he would want to support Theo, no matter what. He didn't like putting him in the middle, but he also didn't want to keep lying to him. James deserved better than that.

"I don't like it, Theo," he finally said. He kept his eyes on the ground in front of them, but even in the darkness, Theo could see his friend glancing over at him every few seconds. "It's idiotic at best and incredibly dangerous at worst. I get it, though," he sighed. "I'm not going to tell the captain. Not right now, at least."

"Thank you, James."

The mage scoffed. "Don't thank me. I still don't think this is a good idea and I have a feeling it's going to end badly, but I'm your friend. As such, if you have even the slightest slip and you don't tell me about it, I'm going to use that curse I told you about. Stick close to me and tell me if anything happens or I will report you so fast your head will spin. Is that clear?"

It was better than Theo deserved, really, so he nodded. "Clear. I promise I won't keep anything else from you."

"In that case, care to tell me why you and Ishaan took so long to get back to the room after the meeting last night?"

Memories of last night, of a secluded hallway and soft kisses, flashed through his mind and he felt his face heat. It shouldn't have been visible, but James chuckled anyway. Just like that, the tension between them melted away, as he was sure James had intended.

"We got lost."

"One of the best trackers in the Nevarrean military got lost on his way back from dinner? That's the story you're choosing?"

Theo shrugged. "It's a big castle. Lots of hallways."

"Not that big, but if you insist."

Theo risked a long glance at his friend, trusting his horse not to stumble on the rough ground. "Thank you, James. Seriously."

"You're seriously welcome. Now stop getting mushy on me and keep an eye on the ground. We're getting into unknown territory here and I'd hate for my best friend to embarrass me by losing the trail."

The early morning sunlight didn't make the trail in front of him any less confusing.

Theo reined his horse in and slid down from the saddle to get a better look at the ground in front of him. They'd been following the trail for hours now, delving ever deeper into the mountains. Whoever this mage was, he was clever enough to have covered his tracks well. It wasn't perfect, though, not enough to hide him from both Captain Trieste and himself. With the two of them combing the ground and the mages searching for traces of magic, they'd stayed on the tail of the killer.

The rocky terrain made it difficult to find many signs, but that was why he was on the team. He'd spent his childhood learning how to track, learning from a retired soldier who'd once been one of the best trackers in the history of Nevarre. Those skills had been what caught Captain Trieste's eye initially and earned him a spot on the highly exclusive reconnaissance team.

Now, though, the trail changed, becoming more obvious. It almost appeared their quarry was going out of his way to leave tracks. Every bit of half-frozen mud held a hint of a boot print and tiny stands of crushed mountain grass. It was a dramatic change from the barely there hints they'd been dealing with.

Cautious now, he held up his hand in the signal for 'wait'. The others were spread out behind him, with the mages near the back as an added layer of protection. Theo caught the captain's eyes and waved him over from where he was tracking. Unbidden, Prince Kaelas joined them.

"What's going on?" he demanded. "Why are we stopping? Did you lose the trail?"

Theo had to work to keep his expression even. The man was getting on his nerves. "I didn't lose the trail. I-"

"Then let's keep moving. We're wasting time!"

"What is it, Rhoan?" Captain Trieste asked, overriding the prince with his deep, calm voice. Prince Kaelas didn't bother to hide his displeasure.

"Something doesn't feel right," he reported, focusing on his captain. "Following the trail hasn't been easy, even with the mages helping, but look at this." He nodded toward the frozen mud at his feet, which clearly showed the heel of a boot. "Why is it so obvious now?"

"Whoever it is, he clearly thought he was safe now and didn't have to keep hiding his tracks. He's let his guard down, which is why we need to find him *quickly*."

Captain Trieste ignored the prince's demands, frowning down at the track. "It's suspicious," he conceded, then glanced at Kaelas. "Whoever this person is, he's clever enough to have evaded capture this long. He didn't do it by being careless."

"Then what do *you* think this is, then?"

Theo found himself missing Alaric. He might not be as fond of the young mage as Ishaan was, but he seemed to be the only one who knew how to rein in Prince Kaelas' temper, which was something they needed at the moment.

"Maybe he's trying to throw us off?" he suggested to the captain. "Laying a more obvious trail in the hope that we'll follow that and miss wherever he's really going?"

Trieste nodded. "It would make sense, especially if he wasn't aware there were specialists on his trail. To the untrained eye, the tracks aren't too much more obvious, just enough to draw attention to them."

"So what now? We wait for however long it takes to find a second trail that might not even exist?" Prince Kaelas prodded.

"Yes," Trieste said simply. "Rhoan and I will search the area for another trail. If we find nothing else, we'll continue after this one. I'd rather find out now if these tracks are false, rather than waste hours following a fake trail."

Kaelas clearly didn't agree, but to Theo's surprise, he gave a tight nod. "Fine. We'll stop for half an hour and let the horses rest. If neither of you find anything in that time, we're moving on and following the trail in front of us."

Captain Trieste nodded. "Very well. Viers, Bhandari." He motioned to the two and handed over his reins to Naema when she joined them. Theo did the same, handing his to Irric. "Water our horses, if you would. Rhoan and I are going to keep hunting."

"Yes, sir," they chorused. Word spread quickly and everyone dismounted to take a break. With this many people in the party, they had to spread out a little to make room.

"Let's get moving, soldier," Trieste ordered. "This trail goes almost straight to the east. I'll head south, you take north. Keep your eyes open."

They split up, and Theo trained his eyes on the ground, searching for any signs. Having something that required his full attention and focus seemed to help, and he hadn't experienced any time slips since they'd started following the trail. He could only hope it continued long enough to find what he was looking for.

Aware of the limited time frame, he moved as fast as he dared, scanning the area for even the tiniest disturbance. There was a chance he was wrong and there was no other trail, but his gut told him something was wrong. One of the first lessons he'd ever learned as a soldier was to trust his instincts and they didn't fail him this time, either.

It took nearly twenty minutes of hunting, but he found the sign he was looking for. The man was clever, Theo would give him that. It appeared he'd watched every step, being careful only to cross bare rock. The one slip-up he'd made was barely noticeable at all, and if it weren't for his years of training, Theo likely would have missed it.

There was a stretch of scrubby grass between two patches of rock, and it looked as though the man had attempted to jump over it. He'd made it, as there were no marks in the grass, but it appeared his foot had come down on a handful of loose rocks and he'd slipped, sending a scattering of pebbles into the grass behind him. Stepping carefully to avoid disturbing anything, Theo examined the second stretch of bare ground until he found what he was looking for.

There, barely visible against the dark stone, was a single drop of blood, smeared to almost nothing. His quarry had likely scraped his hand when falling. He probably hadn't even realized he was bleeding and wouldn't have thought to look for spots to clean up. The mage truly was very clever, but this one mistake was all it took to unravel his plan.

Theo's moment of triumph washed away when the implication of what he'd found finally set in, though. He stared at the tiny smear, then slowly lifted his head and really took in where that trail led. It would have made sense for the trail to continue east, deeper into the mountains where the killer could hide and recoup. That's what they'd expected, and that's why it had taken so long for him to realize that something was wrong.

Going north made no sense at all. Instead of fleeing toward safety, the mage was heading...

"Oh fuck," Theo breathed as the pieces of the puzzle finally clicked together in his head. The killer wasn't running away. He was going back to Yrasea, the city they'd left almost entirely undefended. The city he'd thought was the safest place to be.

The city where he'd left Ishaan.

CHAPTER 28

Breakfast was a quiet affair. Ishaan sat at a small table in Alaric's sitting room, just the two of them. Hadiza had ordered a breakfast platter for them after they'd reported back, but it sat mostly untouched. The coffee pot, on the other hand, was rapidly disappearing.

"I'm sure they'll be perfectly fine," Alaric murmured, breaking the silence. It was the third time he'd said it since they'd sat down and Ishaan wasn't sure he believed it anymore now than he had the first time. His journal sat beside his plate, also untouched. He opened it now, though, if only to distract himself from the growing anxiety buzzing within him.

"How long do you think they'll be gone?" he asked, sliding it across to Alaric to read the words.

"I wish I knew. We have no idea how far into the mountains the murderer went. It could be a few days or..." He trailed off and took a sip from his cup. The helplessness in his voice echoed the feeling lodged beneath Ishaan's skin, like a splinter he couldn't work out.

"At least you can yell at Prince Kaelas when they return. If I tried that with Captain Trieste, he would probably leave me here."

That got a faint smile from Alaric when he read it. "You're welcome to stay here as long as you'd like, you know. At the very least, we need you to stay until we can undo the spell that was done and remove the portion of the dragon that is within you."

The moment of levity flickered and died, a snuffed candle in the face of that truth. He could still feel the foreign presence within him, a little ember of warmth in his chest. It was weak enough that he could still control it, but that could change at any moment. It had taken him over more than once, after all, and he was sure it could happen again.

He pulled the journal back and flipped the page, writing quickly. "Will the process take long?"

"It could take a bit of time," Alaric said slowly. "This situation is unprecedented and a large portion of it depends on Zex cooperating. If he doesn't, we'll have to find another way."

Ishaan sighed, but he'd been expecting something like that. "Is it something we could start on now, while they're gone?" he finally asked. Alaric studied the page, clearly thinking about it.

"We probably could, actually," he said, a hint of excitement in his voice. "We could do research, at the very least, and try to find alternatives in case they're needed. It would be a good distraction, too."

A distraction they both desperately needed at the moment. "Let's do that after breakfast, unless there's something you need to attend to?"

Alaric shook his head. "Hadiza is acting in Kas' stead at the moment. They can handle things for now. The chancellors handle all the day-to-day needs of the kingdom, anyway, so barring an emergency of some sort, I doubt anyone outside the palace will even realize he's gone before they return."

Appetite restored now that he had a purpose, Ishaan tucked into breakfast, eating quickly. He couldn't recall a time he'd ever been excited by the idea of reading dusty old textbooks all day. If it allowed the mages to remove the thing inside him faster, though, he'd do everything he could to expedite the process.

He could admit that some of his urgency was grounded in fear. Not only did he worry he would lose control of himself, but there was also the fear of being left behind. How long would Captain Trieste and his team be willing to wait in Sarkhyr before losing patience and going back to Nevarre without him?

It was a question that had kept him awake long after midnight on more than one occasion already.

By mid afternoon, they'd settled in Alaric's study with a massive stack of books teetering on the table between them. Given the nature of the ritual and how few people actually knew that dragons still existed, it only made sense to do their research in private. The guest wing was too easily accessible, so Alaric's well-warded suite was the best choice.

The books varied wildly in subject, from modern theories of magic to ancient rituals to a study of Sarkhyr's history. That was the one Ishaan had elected to read. The books of magic reminded him too much of the endless hours spent in the basement laboratory of his childhood home, forced to help the twins study the spells that would often be used on him later.

It's different this time. For once, it will be a spell to help me. It's nothing like those other times, he reminded himself whenever he felt the familiar fear bubble up again.

So far, the book held nothing of value. Not that he could make out, anyway. There were mentions of dragons, but nothing substantial. Like the people of Sarkhyr believed, the book stated that there had once been real dragons that had gifted the use of magic to humans, but they'd disappeared hundreds of years ago. Now, they were nothing more than myths and legends.

Alaric cleared his throat, the sudden sound shattering the silence and making Ishaan jump.

"I didn't mean to startle you," he winced. "Have you had any luck yet? I certainly haven't."

Ishaan shook his head. They'd been sitting for hours and he was starting to feel stiff, so he marked his page and put the book down, getting up to stretch.

"Well, whether we like it or not, we have time. I would be surprised if we found any answers on our first try." Alaric followed his example, putting his book down to pace the room a few times. "We seem to have worked through lunch, but I'm sure we could find something in the kitchens to tide us over until supper?"

As if on cue, Ishaan's stomach rumbled, drawing a quiet laugh from Alaric.

"We'll take a break and come back to this with fresh eyes," he decided. "We can take the back hallways. With any luck, we'll avoid any chancellors or courtiers. They love to gossip almost as much as soldiers do."

Alaric lead him through a maze of narrow corridors, just as tall as the regular hallways, but much less opulent. At Ishaan's questioning look, he'd explained that palace staff typically used these back ways to allow them to go about their tasks without having to dodge around residents of the castle.

"A bored courtier is a needy courtier and the staff have enough to handle without catering to the whims of a spoiled countess or bored earl," Alaric explained with a little smile. The longer the two of them spent together, the more the other man seemed to relax and lower his guard. He smiled more frequently and his side comments about everyday life in Yrasea were dryly amusing. Ishaan was beginning to realize just how much Alaric kept hidden beneath that mask of his.

They finally stopped in front of a solid wood door. Like the others they'd passed, this one was unmarked, with nothing to set it apart from any of the others. "The kitchens are through here. It's going to be busy and probably a little chaotic, so just stay close to me."

Together, they eased through the door, directly into the organized chaos that was the palace kitchens. A wall of noise blasted him, shouted orders and the heavy metal of pots and pans banging. There seemed to be several head cooks, each overseeing a different part of the kitchens. It was easy to spot the one in charge, though. In a hurricane of noise and pandemonium, he was the eye of the storm. He clearly didn't miss a single thing that happened in his domain, and his eyes landed on them the moment the door opened.

"Supper isn't for a few more hours yet, my lord," he said, raising his voice a bit to be heard over the din.

Alaric gave Ishaan's arm a gentle tug, urging him to follow as they quickly wove through the workers. "I'm sorry to disturb you while you're busy, Dayne. My friend and I were working straight through lunch. I was hoping I could presume upon you for something to hold us over until evening?"

Ishaan kept close to Alaric, watching the man, Dayne, warily. Up close, he was massive. With thick, muscled arms, a barrel chest, and scarred hands nearly the size of Ishaan's head, he cut an intimidating figure. Despite the stern look on his face, he didn't come off as overly threatening. Still, he kept his guard up out of pure habit.

"I'll make an exception for you, sir, only because it *is* an exception." He strode away, apparently to personally prepare their food, leaving them standing near the far wall.

Confused, Ishaan nudged Alaric, giving him a questioning look when the other man turned to him.

"Sir Dayne has very strong feelings about schedules," he confided with a little smile. "Some chancellors and courtiers feel that, because they are allowed to live in the castle, they should be able to order the staff around as they please. The cooks got fed up with having to stop their work to prepare special orders from nobles too lazy or spoiled to come to the common meals. I had a word with Kas and he let everyone know they could eat with everyone else or find their own meal."

Ishaan wasn't sure what he'd been expecting, but it certainly wasn't this. So far, his impression of Prince Kaelas was of a temperamental, somewhat egotistical leader with a penchant for breaking the rules. It was a bit jarring to think of him going out of his way to make the lives of his staff easier by going against his own courtiers and chancellors.

"Exceptions are made for those who are ill, injured, or have a reason they can't eat in the main hall, of course," Alaric went on. "A few people still try to skirt the rules or bully younger staff members into doing what they want, but Dayne puts a stop to it. If anyone persists, Kas or I deal with them directly."

The silence that fell between them was companionable after that, both staying out of the way against the wall and watching the workers. Ishaan began to notice the little things he'd missed the longer he watched. The kitchens were loud and chaotic, yes, but within the noise, he could make out jokes and laughter. These people actually seemed to enjoy their work.

Everything he knew about castles and courtiers came from the story-books he'd stolen from Doran as a child, but within those pages, he'd been led to believe that those who worked in a place like this were servants, not staff. Overworked, underpaid, and usually forced into the position.

I suppose I shouldn't have believed it just because it was in a story, he thought.

Dayne returned only a few moments later, a covered plate in his hand. "It'll be enough to hold you both for a few hours." He handed it to Ishaan, surprising him so much that he almost dropped it, fumbling for a moment before steadying himself.

"Thank you, sir," Alaric said with a smooth bow. "We'll return the dishes shortly." Nodding his head for Ishaan to follow, the two of them slipped out of the kitchen through yet another door. This one took them to what appeared to be the main dining hall Alaric had mentioned, deserted at this hour.

They settled at the end of one of the massive tables with the plate between them. Ishaan's stomach rumbled when he lifted the lid and found two large sandwiches. Thick bread toasted golden brown with layers of cheese and meat between the slices, almost too big to handle easily.

"He comes off gruff, but Dayne is a good man," Alaric grinned. He took one sandwich and tucked in, his usually impeccable manners left by the wayside. Ishaan followed his lead, digging in eagerly.

There were only crumbs left by the time they finished and he felt almost uncomfortably full, but in the best way. He tapped lightly on the table to get Alaric's attention, then made the sign for 'thank you'.

"Thank you for keeping me company while we wait," Alaric countered. "The least I could do was feed you." He groaned softly, stretching. "I suppose we should get back to work, but I'm afraid all I want now is a nap."

He wasn't the only one. Given how early the party had risen, they'd already been up for half a day with few breaks. His chest throbbed and Ishaan rubbed his hand against it, right over the warm ember of the dragon that never left him.

"You can feel it?" Alaric's voice was quieter now and there was something close to awe there when he spoke. "The dragon?"

He nodded once, slowly, then pulled the journal from the pouch he never left behind.

"I didn't know what it was, at first. It saved my life, though," he wrote.

"May I ask what happened?"

Memories of fire and the smell of smoke made his stomach churn and he shuddered, suddenly wishing he hadn't eaten quite so much.

"You don't have to talk about it if it makes you uncomfortable," Alaric quickly assured him. The discomfort on his face must have been obvious.

All Ishaan wanted to do was forget that night. He wanted to lock it in the box in the back of his mind and bury it deep, never to see the light of day again. At the same time, though, he owed it to Alaric, didn't he? Alaric was the only one taking the time to help him undo whatever spell had been done that night.

"It'll take a few minutes to write it all out," he warned, but Alaric just nodded when he read the words, telling him to take his time.

Good. He was going to need it.

Ishaan's hand shook as he wrote, though not as bad as the first time he'd told his story. He kept to the basic facts, supplemented now by what he'd learned from Kaelas. He wrote about his parents disappearing for months, only to return with what he now knew was a dragon's egg. He skimmed over most of the ritual, only including how Doran and Dhanara had been the ones to anchor it.

As he wrote, flashes of that night kept appearing behind his eyes, no matter how hard he tried to repress it. Images of Dhanara on the ground, nothing more than a pile of charred bones. Of Doran on his knees, waiting for the fire to consume him, lost in the madness and grief of losing his twin. He hadn't seen what had become of his parents, but it was all too easy to imagine two more burnt bodies left to molder in the basement when the whole house collapsed in on itself.

He was cold and weary by the time he finished, the phantom smell of burning flesh haunting him as he slid the journal over to Alaric. The silence was heavy now with the weight of his memories. His chest felt tight, his breaths fast and shallow.

Think of Theo.

Ishaan closed his eyes, wishing the tracker was here with him, holding his hand and guiding him back from the edge of panic. Maybe it was weak to need someone else so much, but he did.

Thankfully Alaric was a quick reader, because he looked up from the pages before Ishaan could descend too far into the endless pit of his own mind.

"I'm so sorry you had to deal with that, Ishaan," he whispered. "I promise you I will do everything in my power to help undo this so you can finally live the life of your choosing."

When he held out his hand, Ishaan took it. He probably held on far too tight, needing the pressure to anchor him, but Alaric didn't protest. They sat together until he felt normal again, or as normal as possible for him.

Embarrassed, he tried to sign 'thank you' again, but Alaric brushed him off. "You don't have to thank me for anything. We're friends, aren't we? Friends help each other."

It seemed like Alaric was the one doing all the helping, but Ishaan nodded anyway. One of these days, he'd find a way to repay the mage for everything he'd done, but for now all he could do was squeeze Alaric's hand in his own in gratitude.

"Do you want to go back to my room and work some more?"

Alaric's suggestion was exactly what he needed; a project to keep his mind occupied and his memories buried. He nodded, grateful Alaric let the subject of his past drop for now.

"Let's get this plate back to Dayne before I accidentally drop it or something," Alaric laughed softly. "I would never hear the end of it if I did that."

They were quick in the kitchens, ducking in and passing the empty plate to Dayne, who nodded approvingly before pointing them toward the door.

"We'll take the main hallway this time," Alaric said, his reluctance clear. "I need to show my face to the chancellors so they know I'm still here. It will take some pressure off Hadiza if we're both dealing with problems as they arise."

Another unmarked door let them out into one of the decorated hallways Ishaan was used to, with tall columns, broad windows, and exquisite tapestries over shimmering walls. They were in the heart of the castle, the safest place in all of Yrasea.

The bloodcurdling scream that echoed through the hallways, bouncing off those beautifully painted walls, took them completely by surprise.

Ishaan and Alaric both froze, trying to figure out where the sound had come from. There was no one in the corridor with them, no one wandering by. They were alone.

There was a beat of silence and Ishaan tensed, his heart racing, ready to flee.

Another agonized scream turned his blood to ice, but he never got the chance to run. They'd barely taken a single step before a flash of light blinded them, followed by a blast of sound from the explosion that brought the walls toppling down on them in a rain of dust, stone, and mortar.

CHAPTER 29

Consciousness came in slow, painful flashes. The world was blurry and muffled, his head swimming. The first thing Ishaan became aware of was pain. Not the searing agony he'd felt after the fire, but a sharp, throbbing ache from head to toe. He felt battered, as though he'd been in a fight and lost.

Or as though the hallway collapsed on me.

The memories came rushing back and he struggled to think clearly. He'd been walking down the hallway with Alaric. Something had startled them, but he couldn't remember...

A scream. Someone had screamed, the sound one of absolute terror.

"Ishaan?"

He turned his head toward the sound, groaning in pain when the movement sent a sharp jolt of pain through his head. He was on his back, surrounded by rubble, in the remains of the corridor. Alaric was on his knees beside him, pale and shaken. His hair was a mess, matted with dust and blood from the deep cut just above his eye. It had barely missed blinding him.

"I know you're hurt, but I need you to move, alright?" The strain was thick in Alaric's voice, but it still took several seconds for him to understand why. He blinked, his mind hazy as he looked up. Directly above him was a mass of shattered stone, only inches from his face. He didn't even have room to sit up. It clicked then. Alaric was using his magic to hold it back.

"Slide over to me as best you can. I can't lift it any higher," the mage grunted. He was sweating and the stones shifted as his magic wavered.

Moving hurt, but at least pain was something Ishaan was used to. He squirmed and crawled on his back, pushing his feet against the floor for extra traction. It seemed to take years, but he finally made it to Alaric. The second Ishaan was clear, he let go and the rubble hit the ground hard. If he'd been under there, he wouldn't have stood a chance.

What the fuck was going on?

He looked up at Alaric, silently asking that same question.

"I don't know what happened," he said, his voice shaking with pain and fatigue. "It's not safe here, though. Can you stand?"

There was nothing he wanted less than to try, but what choice did he have?

Alaric stood and held out his hand, carefully helping Ishaan to his feet. He wavered, black dots swimming across his vision. Alaric had to help steady him, but thankfully, it only took a few seconds for his head to clear. He had to keep hold of Alaric to stay upright as he looked around, trying to make sense of what he was seeing.

The long hallway they'd been walking down was almost completely gone. The far end, furthest from the center of the castle, was intact, but only just. Nothing remained in the area where they stood now. The outer wall was nothing but a smoking pile of stone, and the interior wall wasn't much better. If Alaric hadn't been with him, he would be dead right now.

"We have to find out what happened and help anyone who's trapped. Can you make it?" Alaric asked. He honestly wasn't sure, but he nodded anyway because Alaric was right. "We're still close to the kitchens, but we'll have to climb over the rubble."

With the mage's help, Ishaan somehow managed. He was grateful Alaric had a general idea of where they were going, because nothing looked the same now. But unerringly, Alaric got them there. Portions of the wall remained standing in some areas, but none of the windows had held up. The rubble was strewn with shattered glass and debris, and every step had to be taken with caution.

"I think I hear someone." Alaric halted just outside the kitchens. Or what had once been the kitchens. The walls were blown in and from here, Ishaan could see the way the ceiling was listing to the side and sagging, ready to collapse under the weight of the floors above.

A sound caught his attention and he jerked, pointing toward a pile of debris near them. Silence, then it came again. A voice calling for help, muffled and weak. Without hesitation, the two of them scrambled over the remains of the walls, careful not to disturb anything.

"We're going to get you out!" Alaric called. "Ishaan, I'm going to use magic to lift as much of the stone as I can. I need you to help whoever's under there get free. Can you manage?"

Ishaan nodded, determination giving him a burst of strength. He was going to do this. He wouldn't fail.

Once he was in place, Alaric took a deep breath and got to work. To Ishaan, he was just standing still, but a moment later, the mess of stone lifted, revealing the prone form of Dayne, the head cook. His face was dripping blood and Ishaan had to swallow back bile when he caught sight of the man's arm. It was bent at an unnatural angle and he saw a hint of bone before he quickly looked away.

"Dayne, Ishaan is going to help you," Alaric gasped out. His hands trembled at his sides from the strain and Ishaan knew he needed to hurry. He held out both hands to the injured man, taking his uninjured arm and gripping tight. Dayne struggled to help, but he was mostly dead weight. By the time he was free, they were both sweating and Alaric looked ready to collapse. Still, the mage held on until Dayne was free before letting the stone fall.

"What's happening, Lord Alaric?" Dayne asked. He cradled his shattered arm against his chest, leaning heavily on Ishaan for support.

Alaric shook his head. "I don't know, but I'm going to try to find more survivors. Do you know how many people were here with you when it happened?"

"Most of the staff. I'll help you find-"

Another explosion ripped through the castle and Ishaan lost his footing as the floor shook beneath them.

"Go!" Dayne grabbed Ishaan with his uninjured arm and dragged him back the way he and Alaric had just come, the mage right on their heels. He didn't understand, not at first. Not until the ceiling began to cave in above them, crushing everything beneath it.

The three of them barely made it out before it finally collapsed, but there was no time to catch their breath.

"The rest of it'll be coming down soon, too. We have to keep going," Dayne growled. He looked back at the kitchens and Ishaan saw the tears in his eyes. How many people had just died? Too many.

"Follow me," Alaric ordered suddenly, looking paler than usual. "Dayne, will you keep searching for any survivors you can find and get them out?"

"You can't stay here, sir," the man protested. "This entire section of the castle could collapse at any moment!"

"We'll be fine. Please, Dayne. Help get them out."

He wanted to protest more. Ishaan could see it in his eyes. But instead, he nodded once. "Stay safe, sir." Then he was gone.

Ishaan gave Alaric a questioning look, pointing after Dayne. They should leave, too.

"I know, but we have to get to the prison cells. Zex is trapped down there, remember? If he dies, we can't help you. We could lose Kas, too, from the breaking of the bond."

Fuck. As much as Ishaan wanted nothing more than to abandon the man who'd damaged Theo so deeply, he knew Alaric had a point. He reluctantly nodded, and the two of them picked their way through the smoldering debris. Every time the ceiling overhead groaned, fear ate away at Ishaan. He didn't want to be here, following Alaric deeper into danger. All of his instincts were screaming at him to run, to leave the other man to his madness and save himself.

He kept going.

They were nearly there when another explosion rocked the castle. It sounded further away this time, but that did nothing to ease his fear.

"This was deliberate," Alaric hissed, voicing the thoughts in Ishaan's head. "One could have been an accident, but this..." He looked back at Ishaan, a ferocity in his eyes that Ishaan had never seen there before. "Stay close to me. We're going to get Zex and get out of here. We are going to make it."

The door to the basement was gone.

They stood at the top of the stairs, looking down the damaged wooden steps. Dust choked the air, making it hard to breathe and even harder to see, but it was impossible to miss the gaping hole where the door had once been.

Ishaan was no tracker, but it was obvious even to him that this wasn't like the explosions. The walls here were still standing solid, save for this doorway. Someone had deliberately destroyed this door to get to what lay behind it.

"We have to get down there," Alaric hissed, but Ishaan grabbed his arm, shaking his head frantically. There was no time to struggle with the journal still secured at his waist.

"Trap?" he mouthed the word as best he was able, over and over, until Alaric caught on.

"I don't think so. No one knew we were here except Hadiza and the kitchen staff, remember? Either way, though, we have to get down there before they kill him."

Ishaan was more worried that they would *free* the man, honestly, but he followed Alaric's orders and stayed behind him, close on his heels as they made their way down the staircase.

"No guards," Alaric whispered when they reached the bottom, and Ishaan peered around him. There were two chairs at a small table, leading him to think there should have been two guards here, but there was no sign of them. The door they were to have been guarding had suffered the same fate as the previous one, laying in shattered bits on the floor, revealing another, shorter staircase.

Alaric made to hurry down it, but Ishaan stopped him again, cocking his head. When Alaric glanced at him, he cupped his free hand around his ear. He could hear something. It sounded like voices. Several voices.

His stomach churned, a sick feeling welling up until he tasted bile. His instincts were screaming at him, telling him to *run, run, run* and never look back. To get away from this place as fast as he could. The dragon within him stirred in response to the terror coursing through him, an ember of warmth in the sudden icy chill coating him.

"Ishaan? I have to get down there. Stay with me. I'll protect you." Alaric's voice came from the end of a long tunnel, muffled and distorted. He shook his head, a tiny whimper escaping. He didn't understand this sudden, paralyzing fear, but he just knew something horrific waited for him at the bottom of those stairs.

"Ishaan?" Alaric's hands cupped his face, forcing him to look up until their eyes met. "You can stay here. I understand. I have to go down there, but you can wait for me here."

The understanding in his friend's eyes managed to stop the panic from escalating, giving him a moment to *think*. He wanted to run, wanted it more than anything, but looking up at Alaric, he knew he wouldn't. Not this time. He would not abandon him.

He dragged in a shuddering breath, his head clearing a little more. He grasped Alaric's wrists, giving them a quick squeeze to show his gratitude, then stepped back, forcing himself to stand up straight and take a step toward the stairs. Thankfully, the other man understood and joined him, the two of them carefully making their way down into the depths of the castle.

The voices became clearer, but the dust was still heavy down here. Ishaan spotted the guards first. One of them, a woman, lay facedown on the floor, her eyes wide and sightless. A small pool of blood spread out beneath her. Above her stood the other guard, a man. He looked vaguely familiar, but Ishaan couldn't remember his name. His immediate attention went to the bloody knife in the man's hand. Whoever he was, he'd clearly killed his partner.

"Grayan?" Alaric sounded gutted, stumbling over the final step. The guard spun, raising the knife, his eyes going wide with shock when he saw them.

"Lord Alaric? What are you doing here? You left with Prince Kaelas this morning!" He sounded almost accusatory, and Ishaan noticed he hadn't lowered the knife.

"We came back," Alaric said faintly. "Grayan, what did you do?"

"Oh, we have guests?" A woman's voice cut through whatever Grayan was about to say and a moment later, Chancellor Jaserra appeared out of the swirling dust. "Lord Alaric. Well... this is unfortunate."

"What's going on?" A new voice called. A man.

I know that voice…

Deep, visceral terror cut through Ishaan, slicing through the sliver of courage he'd managed to hold on to. He couldn't move, couldn't breathe, couldn't *think* through the fear choking him.

This isn't possible. He's dead. He's not real. He's dead!

A shadow appeared in the dust clouds, moving closer. Tall and slender, he moved with a casual grace that Ishaan had always tried to emulate but never managed. An errant wisp of air scattered the thick dust and he appeared, his dark eyes finding Ishaan's instantly.

There was a flicker of shock, there and gone, before something so much darker settled in. A horrifying satisfaction, the twisted pleasure of a predator spotting new prey, but even that didn't hold a candle to the raw hatred in those sickeningly familiar eyes.

"Now this is a surprise," he purred, closing the distance between them and Ishaan wanted to run, to flee, hide, but his body refused to move, frozen in shock and fear.

The hand that came up to grip his face was cruel, almost as cruel as the smile that appeared a moment later.

"It is so very good to see you again, little brother."

PEOPLE AND PLACES

This list contains spoilers up to the end of book two. Please be aware before proceeding.

Characters

Nevarre

The Reconnaissance Team: One of four active specialist teams for the Nevarrean military. This team specializes in intelligence-gathering and covert missions. Specialists are essentially legalized mercenaries. They operate within the bounds of the military and answer to the ruler of their country, but are never officially acknowledged. Unofficially, they're given more leeway to operate outside their own borders, so long as they're quick and covert.

Captain Garrett Trieste: The leader of the eight-person recon team and their main tracker. Trieste is tough but fair and always expects his soldiers to give their very best. He's fiercely protective of all of them, though he doesn't like to admit it out loud.

Lieutenant Kellan Sol: Second-in-command, Kellan is also one of the most knowledgeable mages in the world. He's the mother hen of the group and his favorite thing to do is talk about his young daughter, Mellie and wife, Syra.

Irric Viers: He's been on the team longer than any of the others and loves what he does. One of the strongest fighters on the team, he's also the only one they can trust to cook a decent meal. Despite being the quietest member of the group, he's closest to Kya.

Theodric Rhoan: Hand-picked by Trieste to follow in his footsteps, Theo loves being a soldier. He's been learning to track since he was a child, training under Arden Isaacs (a retired soldier). Despite a troubled past, he faces the future with sunny optimism, though his light has dimmed recently.

James Delphine: The third and youngest child of Queen Isadore Delphine of Nevarre, James is also an extremely talented mage. He's fascinated by all aspects of magic and uses his time in the military to broaden his horizons and learn new spells and techniques. His best friend is Theo.

Naema Bhandari: With her canine partner, Karsa, she is another tracker, following trails not visible to the human eye. She specializes in infiltration and is also a talented archer. She's the big sister of the group and lives to tease the others, but she'd protect them with her life.

Vesa C'Van: The strongest fighter the team possesses. Vesa chooses her words carefully and doesn't say anything she doesn't mean. She may come off as unassuming, but she is absolutely deadly. Half Canjiri, she's learned to ignore the callous words of anyone who isn't important to her.

Kya Saleed: The youngest and newest member of the team, with only a year of experience under her belt. She's endlessly upbeat and always looking for her next adventure. On her first day as part of the team, she took one look at the stoic Irric and declared them best friends. They've been inseparable ever since.

Ishaan Khatre: Not officially part of the team, but he's found himself adopted by them. The youngest child of two ruthless mages, he ended up with the power of a dragon living within him as a result of their spell. His parents, Rasacon and Allesha, as well as his siblings, twins Doran and Dhanara, perished and he lost his voice in the resulting fire. Since then, he has struggled with learning new ways to communicate. He's still searching for his place in the world, but he knows it will be wherever Theo is.

Lord Coras Wyrenian: The Nevarrean ambassador to Sarkhyr. Well-respected by the courts of every country for his honesty and generosity. He believes in the good in everyone, even after years as a politician.

Sir Embry Falloran: Lord Wyrenian's apprentice. As a young man from Canjir, becoming a Nevarrean politician seems to be an unexpected life choice, but he's determined. Calm and methodical, he keeps his emotions locked down tight, believing them to be a weakness. He's kind in his own ways, though.

Yann Dulara: A Nevarrean soldier, tasked with guarding the ambassadors to Sarkhyr. He's rarely met a person he didn't want to befriend and he has a strong protective streak of those he cares about.

Jayakatong Ny: A Nevarrean soldier, tasked with guarding the ambassadors to Sarkhyr. Jaya, as his team calls him, is a fierce protector but a gentle soul. He has trouble speaking sometimes, but it doesn't interfere with his job. The others learned basic sign language to communicate with him when his words get stuck.

Rhea Mennez: A Nevarrean soldier, tasked with guarding the ambassadors to Sarkhyr. Rhea is a mage specializing in battle magic and wards. She's the most level-headed of the three and knows how to keep calm in any emergency. She takes awhile to warm up to someone but once she does, there isn't a better friend to have than Rhea.

Arden Isaacs: A former Nevarrean specialist, dishonorably discharged for interfering in the Gavarrian Civil War. Privately, the royal family of Nevarre thanked him for his work saving civilians. He's something of a folk hero in Nevarre and Gavarria. He retired to a small village in the mountains, where he stumbled across young Theodric Rhoan. He saw the potential in the boy and taught him everything he knew about tracking, the military, and how to be a good man. He's more of a father to Theo than his actual father ever was.

Sarkhyr

Prince Kaelas: The ruler of Sarkhyr. Traditionally, the country has always been ruled by a pair, but he's been alone since his co-ruler fled justice. He holds the gold dragon within him. As his bond with his other half frays, Kaelas has begun to lose control of the dragon and of his own temper. He knows it's only a matter of time before he snaps.

Alaric Cevira: Prince Kaelas' most trusted adviser, as well as his cousin. Alaric spent most of his life training for a role in the government, but when Zex ran, his role was shifted and he was sent to Yrasea to aid Kaelas. He hides his true self behind the mask of a calm, even-tempered noble. Very few get to see the true Alaric, but he's found a good friend in Ishaan.

Zex: Formerly the second prince of Sarkhyr, now a fugitive from justice. Holding the power of the silver dragon, Zex is the strongest magic-user in the world, which makes him incredibly dangerous. He wields forbidden blood magic in his search for what was stolen from him and he doesn't care who gets in his way. Sarcastic and uncaring of nearly everyone. There are depths to him that few bother to see, though.

Hadiza Adeyemi: The only person Kaelas trusts as much as Alaric, Hadiza is more than an adviser. They helped mentor young Kaelas and Zex when they were children. When Kaelas isn't in Yrasea, Hadiza steps in and keeps things running smoothly. Even those most critical of Prince Kaelas can find little fault in Hadiza.

Yiruma Mendalesi: Head of staff at the castle, she runs everything and misses very little. She's wary of strangers but will not let that impact the hospitality shown them.

Jaserra Baravish: A chancellor, one of eight on the council in Sarkhyr, tasked with handling the day to day matters of the country, leaving Prince Kaelas free to deal with major issues. The council has grown in power since Kaelas and Zex took the throne, though. Jaserra, in particular, fought for Zex's execution for his crimes. She is the most vocally critical of Prince Kaelas.

Grayan: A Sarkhyrian guard who has developed an unhealthy fascination with a certain adviser. He is found holding a bloody knife, standing over the body of his partner, at the end of 'Ash to Ember'

Ereyan: Grayan's nephew. A young mage, new to the ranks of the guards, he's eager to prove himself.

Lady Heraldra: A Sarkhyrian noblewoman, found murdered outside Yrasea.

Elias: A Sarkhyrian soldier who defected to join Zex. He lost his whole family to the plague seven years ago and has become disillusioned with the way things are in Sarkhyr. While trying to gather information in Yrasea, he stumbled across Lady Heraldra and her murderer. He was brutally attacked and lost his eye.

Places

Nevarre: A country spanning the western half of the continent, down to the southern coast. Traditionally a matriarchy, ruled from the capital city of Traelum. With the Adelaar Ocean to the west, the Morehan Forest to the east, and miles of fertile farmland in between, Nevarre is a highly prosperous country. Their position to the west is their only disadvantage, making it difficult to trade across the sea to Caranyvik, but their many trade agreements and peace treaties make up for it. They are the unofficial peacekeepers of the continent, with ambassadors in every country.

Sarkhyr: The northernmost country on the continent, cut off from the others by the Darsheen Mountains. Traditionally, they've been ruled by a pair. Unbeknownst to most people, even their own, those two rulers have been the living embodiment of dragons. The capital city of Yrasea was once the center of trade for the country, situated only miles from the end of the only official safe pass through the mountains. However, the country abruptly closed their borders a hundred years ago and their people haven't been seen south of the mountains in nearly that long. Seven years before the start of the story, the country was ravaged by a plague. Thousands lost their lives before it could be isolated and finally overcome. Overcome by desperation, anger, and grief, they turned all of it on Zex when his crimes came to light, with many believing his use of blood magic was the cause of the plague. The country is slowly recovering, but it's been a struggle.

Gavarria: The country spanning the eastern half of the continent. Gavarria is currently recovering from a twenty year long civil war. Formerly ruled by King Kelstavar, a selfish ruler who cared little for his people and decimated the economy. When he fell ill, he refused to name a successor, so when he finally died, the country fell to chaos, with different factions vying for control. Legally, the other countries could not interfere, but covertly, all of them did. The youngest son of Kelstavar, a man named Astavar, was able to build enough support to claim the throne and end the war. The complete opposite of his father, he has ushered in an era of tentative hope as he rebuilds his country. The vast Morehan Forest stretches across the western half of the country and into Nevarre.

Vaetreas: The southernmost country on the continent, ruled by Queen Delia Vardor. Being on the coast, the country is the biggest importer and exporter of all manner of goods. They are separated from Canjir by the Karjul Straits, a treacherous span of water that few can navigate safely.

The Canjiri have learned the secret, though, and frequently raid the coastal towns of Vaetreas for supplies. In retaliation, the merchants of Vaetreas are known to overcharge any Canjiri attempting to legally purchase goods.

Canjir: An island nation to the south of the continent (capital: Maizar). Once a lush paradise, a massive volcanic eruption hundreds of years ago turned Canjir into a desert. Unwilling to give up their homeland, the Canjiri people were forced to find new ways to survive. They tend to be excellent sailors and fishermen. After years of dealing with merchants overcharging them and import taxes taking what little profit they could make, many turned to raiding and piracy simply to survive. When the new king, King Viyeri, took the throne (the previous queen died under mysterious circumstances), he encouraged a level of violence in raiding that has never been present before. The various powerful families do what they can to keep him in check, but to little avail. Tensions are reaching a boiling point.

Caranyvik: A massive empire to the east, across the Barenden Sea (capital: Tostevya). Ruled by Emperor Rekhavarian, who is currently preparing his son Kivenari to take over in a few years. A peaceful nation, they have the best schools of magic in the world. All mages eventually tend to travel to Caranyvik at some point in their lives. Caranish, an ancient form of their current language, is the base of all spells used by mages.

Kargha: Another island nation, but unlike Canjir, they are a flourishing tropical island. East of Gavarria, out of reach of any but the most desperate and determined raiders. Their navy is nothing to scoff at and is the second most powerful in the area, behind Canjir. They have a tentative peace with the other kingdoms, but it's shaky. Being situated between the two main continents, they're a prime location for ships traveling back and forth and serves as a layover for nearly every ship traveling across the sea. Gavarria and Caranyvik have both, at various points in history, tried to annex the island nation and failed.

Osirith: A Nevarrean garrison city, on the border between Nevarre and Gavarria. Originally where Captain Trieste wanted to leave Ishaan, but two of Zex's soldiers attacked Theo, James, Vesa, and Ishaan on their way to the city. Knowing Ishaan would be vulnerable there, they fled to join the rest of the team in Esterdon.

Esterdon: A large city near the base of the Darsheen Mountains. Esterdon is a hub of trade for Gavarria, helping to rejuvenate the country after the war. The reconnaissance team were to meet there to regroup before heading into the mountains. Theo, James, Vesa, and Ishaan were ambushed just outside the city limits by Zex and his fighters. Rather than allow them all to be taken and likely killed, Theo held the fighters back to allow the other three to escape. He was badly injured and captured by Zex.

Althaea: A small city on the northern coast of Sarkhyr. The birthplace of Alaric.

Menearia: A little mountain town in Nevarre, near the mountains. Theo's birthplace.

ACKNOWLEDGEMENTS

So many people have helped me get to where I am today and I know it's almost impossible to thank you all! Special mentions go to my sisters, Nikki and Courtney, for their never-ending support. I can't count how many times I blew up our chat when my Imposter Syndrome latched on and I needed someone to remind me that I can do this.

I was lucky enough to befriend so many fabulous authors along the way, but two in particular encouraged me to take a chance and write long before I believed I could do it. Thank you to Alexa Land and Sheena Jolie for all the advice and encouragement as I figured out this whole writing thing!

To my readers, I can't begin to thank you enough for taking a chance on this story and sticking with me for the ride. It's been the absolute best time of my life and I can't wait to see where we go next!

About the Author

Lyra Haven has been telling stories all their life, ever since they were old enough to daydream. When their third-grade teacher published their book about a little lost elf in the school library, the spark was lit. However, life had other plans, and dreams of sharing their stories went on the back burner.

An avid reader, once they discovered the world of queer romance, there was no going back. Finding such an amazing community was finally what prompted them to take a leap of faith and share the stories in their head with the rest of the world.

After a decade full of travel and living in three different states and two countries, they finally came back to their Midwestern hometown. They now live in Indiana in a drafty old house with their two cats and crazy husky (who has more Instagram followers than they do).

Keep Up With Lyra

Scan the QR code for my LinkTree to find me on social media!